Academy Mystery Novellas

Volume 3
LOCKED ROOM
PUZZLES

Academy Mystery Novellas

Volume 3
LOCKED ROOM PUZZLES

Edited by
Martin H. Greenberg & Bill Pronzini

Published by The Reader's Digest Association, Inc.,
1991, through special arrangement with Academy
Chicago Publishers.

Library of Congress Cataloging-in-Publication Data
Locked room puzzles.
    (Academy mystery novellas; v.3)
    Contents: Day of the wizard / by Edward D. Hoch—
Booktaker / by Bill Pronzini—From another world /
by Clayton Rawson—[etc.]
    1. Detective and mystery stories, American.
I. Greenberg, Martin Harry. II. Pronzini, Bill.
III. Hoch, Edward D., 1930—   . IV. Series.
PS648.D4L63 1986 813'.0872'08 86-22319
ISBN 0-89733-225-3 (pbk.)

Academy Mystery Novellas are collections of long stories chosen on the basis of two criteria—(1) their excellence as mystery/suspense fiction and (2) their relative obscurity. This second criterion is due solely to the special limitations of the short novel/novella length—too short to be published alone as a novel, but too long to be easily anthologized or collected since they tend to take up too much space in a typical volume.

The series features long fiction by some of the best-known names in the crime fiction field, including such masters as Cornell Woolrich, Ed McBain, Georges Simenon, Donald E. Westlake, and many others. Each volume is organized around a type of crime story (locked room, police procedural) or theme (type of detective, humor).

We are proud to bring these excellent works of fiction to your attention, and hope that you will enjoy reading them as much as we enjoyed the process of selecting them for you.

Martin H. Greenberg
Bill Pronzini

Contents

The Third Bullet
   John Dickson Carr 1

Booktaker
   Bill Pronzini 109

From Another World
   Clayton Rawson 157

Day of the Wizard
   Edward D. Hoch 193

THE THIRD BULLET
by John Dickson Carr

John Dickson Carr (1906–1977), the acknowledged master of the locked room–impossible crime story, was born in Uniontown, Pennsylvania, although he lived in England for many years and his work has a strong English flavor. The Mystery Writers of America honored him with its Edgar award in 1949, when he was serving as President of the organization, and conferred its coveted Grand Master Award on him in 1962. He reviewed books for Ellery Queen's Mystery Magazine *from 1969 until his death.*

Carr has left us with superb series detectives: Dr Gideon Fell appears in more than twenty books written between 1933 and 1967, including Hag's Nook, The Man Who Could Not Shudder, In Spite of Thunder, The Problem of the Wire Cage *and* Dark of the Moon; *Henri Bencolin, a Parisian detective, is featured in four novels, the best of which is* Castle Skull *(1931); and Sir Henry Merrivale solves crimes in some twenty-two novels written under the pseudonym of Carter Dickson.*

Carr also wrote short stories. The Third Bullet and Other Stories *(1957) and* The Men Who Explained Miracles *(1963) are two outstanding collections.*

On the edge of the Assistant Commissioner's desk a folded newspaper lay so as to expose a part of a headline: *Mr. Justice Mortlake Murdered. . . .* On top of it was an official report sheet covered with Inspector Page's trim handwriting. And on top of the report sheet, trigger guard to trigger guard, lay two pistols. One was an Ivor-Johnson .38 revolver. The other was a Browning .32 automatic.

Though it was not yet eleven in the morning, a raw and rainy day looked in at the windows over the Embankment, and the green-shaded lamp was burning above the desk. Colonel Marquis, the Assistant Commissioner of Metropolitan Police, leaned back at ease and smoked a cigarette with an air of doing so cynically. Colonel Marquis was a long, stringy man whose thick and wrinkled eyelids gave him a sardonic look not altogether deserved. Though he was not bald, his white hair had begun to recede from the skull, as though in sympathy with the close cropping of the gray mustache. His bony face was as unmistakably of the Army as it was now unmistakably out of it; and the reason became plain whenever he got up—he limped. But he had a bright little eye, which was amused.

"Yes?" he said.

Inspector Page, though young and not particularly ambitious, was as gloomy as the day outside.

"The Superintendent said he'd warn you, sir," John Page answered. "I'm here with two purposes. First, to offer you my resignation—"

Colonel Marquis snorted.

"—and second," said Page, looking at him, "to ask for it back again."

"Ah, that's better," said the Assistant Commissioner, "why the double offer?"

"Because of this Mortlake case, sir. It doesn't make sense. As you can see by my report. . . ."

"I have not read your report," said the Assistant Commissioner. "God willing, I do not intend to read your report. Inspector Page, I am bored; bloody bored; bored stiff and green. And this Mortlake case does not appear to offer anything very startling. It's unfortunate, of course," he added rather hurriedly. "Yes, yes. But correct me if I am wrong. Mr. Justice Mortlake, recently retired, was a judge of the King's Bench Division, officiating at the Central Criminal Court. He was what they call the 'red judge,' and sat in Courtroom Number 1 on serious offenses like murder or manslaughter. Some time ago he sentenced a man called White to fifteen strokes of the cat and eighteen months' hard labor for robbery with violence. White made threats against the judge. Which is nothing new; all the old lags do it. The only difference here is that, when White got out of jail, he really did keep his threat. He came back and killed the judge." Colonel Marquis scowled. "Well? Any doubt about that?"

Page shook his head. "No, sir, apparently not," he admitted. "*I* can testify to that. Mortlake was shot through the chest yesterday afternoon at half-past five. Sergeant Borden and I practically saw the thing done. Mortlake was alone—with White—in a sort of pavilion on the grounds of his house. It is absolutely impossible for anyone else to have reached him, let alone shoot him. So, if White didn't kill him, the case is a monstrosity. But that's just the trouble. For if White did kill him—well, it's still a monstrosity."

Colonel Marquis's rather speckled face was alight with new pleasure. "Go on," he said.

"First of all, to give you the background," said Page. He now uncovered the newspaper, on the front page of which was a large photograph of the dead judge in his robes. It showed a little man dwarfed by a great flowing wig. Out of the wig peered a face with a parrot-like curiosity in it, but with a mildness approaching meekness. "I don't know whether you knew him?"

"No. I've heard he was active in the Bar Mess."

"He retired at seventy-two, which is early for a judge. Apparently he was as sharp-witted as ever. But the most important point about him was his leniency on the bench—his extreme leniency. It is known, from a speech I looked up, that he disapproved of using the cat-o'-nine-tails even in extreme cases."

"Yet he sentenced this fellow White to fifteen of the best?"

"Yes sir. That's the other side of the picture, the side nobody can understand." Page hesitated. "Now, take this fellow Gabriel White. He's not an old lag; it was his first offense, mind you. He's young, and handsome as a film actor, and a cursed sight too artistic to suit me. Also, he's well educated and it seems certain that 'Gabriel White' isn't his real name—though we didn't bother with that beyond making sure he wasn't in the files.

"The robbery-with-violence charge was a pretty ugly business, *if* White was guilty. It was done on an old woman who kept a tobacconist's shop in Poplar, and was reputed to be a very wealthy miser: the old stuff. Well, someone came into her shop on a foggy evening, under pretense of buying cigarettes—bashed up her face pretty badly even after she was unconscious—and got away with only two pound notes and some loose silver out of the till. Gabriel White was caught running away from the place. In his pocket was found one of the stolen notes, identified by a number; and an unopened packet of cigarettes, although it was shown he did not smoke. His story was that, as he was walking along, somebody cannoned into him in the fog, stuck a hand into his pocket, and ran. He thought he was the victim of a running pickpocket. He automatically started to run after the man, until he felt in his pocket and found something had been *put* there. This was just before a constable stopped him."

Again Page hesitated.

"You see, sir, there were several weak points in the prosecution. For one thing, the old woman couldn't identify him beyond doubt as the right man. If he'd had competent counsel, and if it hadn't been for the judge, I don't think there's much doubt that he'd have been acquitted. But, instead of taking any one of the good men the court was willing to appoint to defend him, the fool insisted on defending himself. Also, his manner in court wasn't liked. And the judge turned dead against him. Old Mortlake made out a devilish case against him in his charge to the jury, and practically directed them to find him guilty. When he was asked whether he had anything to say why sentence should not be passed against him, he said just this: '*You are a fool, and I will see you presently.*' I suppose that could be taken as a threat. All the same, he nearly fainted when Mortlake calmly gave him fifteen strokes of the cat."

The Assistant Commissioner said: "Look here, Page, I don't like this. Weren't there grounds for an appeal?"

"White didn't appeal. He said nothing more, though they tell me he didn't stand the flogging at all well. But the trouble is, sir, that all opinions about White are conflicting. People are either dead in his favor, or dead against him. They think he's a thoroughly wronged man, or else a thorough wrong 'un. He served his time at Wormwood Scrubs. Now, the governor of the prison and the prison doctor both think he's a fine type, and would back him anywhere. But the chaplain of the prison, and Sergeant Borden (the officer who arrested him) both think he's a complete rotter. Anyway, he was a model prisoner. He got the customary one-sixth of his sentence remitted for good behavior, and he was released six weeks ago—on September twenty-fourth."

"Still threatening?"

Page was positive on this. "No, sir. Of course, he was on ticket of leave and we kept an eye on him. But everything seemed to be going well until yesterday afternoon. At just four o'clock we got a phone message from a pawnbroker that Gabriel White had just bought a gun in his place. This gun."

Across the table Page pushed the Ivor-Johnson .38 revolver. With a glance of curiosity at the little automatic beside it, Colonel Marquis picked up the revolver. One shot had been fired from an otherwise fully loaded magazine.

"So," Page went on, "we sent out orders to pick him up — just in case. But that was no sooner done than we got another message by phone. It was from a woman, and it was pretty hysterical. It said that Gabriel White was going to kill old Mortlake, and couldn't we do anything about it? It was from Miss Ida Mortlake, the judge's daughter."

"H'm. I do not wish," observed the other, with a sour and sardonic inflection, "to jump to conclusions. But are you going to tell me that Miss Ida Mortlake is young and charming; that our Adonis with the painful name, Gabriel White, is well acquainted with her; and that the judge knew it when he issued that whacking sentence?"

"Yes, sir. But I'll come to that in a moment. As soon as that message came in, the Superintendent thought I had better get out to Hampstead at once — that's where the Mortlakes live. I took along Sergeant Borden because he had handled White before. We hopped into a police car and got out there in double time.

"Now, the lay of the land is important. The house has fairly extensive grounds around it. But the suburbs round Hampstead Heath have grown in such a way that houses and villas crowd right up against the grounds; and there's a stone wall, all of fifteen feet high, round the judge's property.

"And there are only two entrances: a main carriage drive, and a tradesman's entrance. The first is presided over by an old retainer, named Robinson, who lives at a lodge just inside. He opened the gates for us. It was nearly half-past five when we got there, and almost dark. Also, it was raining and blowing in full November style.

"Robinson, the caretaker, told us where the judge was. He was in a pavilion, a kind of glorified outbuilding, in a clump of trees about two hundred yards from the house. It's a small place; there are only two rooms, with a hallway dividing them. The judge used one of the rooms as a study. Robinson was sure he was there. It seems that the judge was expecting an old crony of his to tea; and so, about half-past three, he had phoned Robinson at the lodge gates. He said that he was going from the house across to the pavilion; and when the crony showed up, Robinson was to direct the visitor straight across to the pavilion.

"Borden and I went up a path to the left. We could see the pavilion straight ahead. Though there were trees round it, none of the trees came within a dozen feet of the pavilion, and we had a good view of the place. There was a door in the middle, with a fanlight up over it; and on each side of the door there were two windows. The two windows to the right of the door were dark. The two windows of the room to the left, though they had heavy curtains drawn over them, showed chinks of light. Also, there was a light in the hall; you could see it in that glass pane up over the top of the door. And that was how we saw a tall man duck out of the belt of trees toward the right, and run straight for the front door.

"But it wasn't all. The rain was blowing straight down the back of our necks, and there was a good deal of thunder. The lightning came just before that man got his hand on the front door. It was a real blaze, too. For a couple of seconds the whole place was as dead-bright as a photographer's studio. As soon as we had seen the man duck out from the trees, Borden let out a bellow. The man heard us, and he turned round.

"It was Gabriel White, right enough; the lightning made no doubt of that. And when he saw us, he took that revolver out of his pocket. But he didn't go for us. He opened the door of the pavilion, and now we could see him fully. From where we were standing (or running, now) we could see straight down the little hall inside; he was making for the door to the judge's study on the left.

"We started running—Borden was well ahead of me—and Borden let out another bellow as loud as doomsday.

"That was what brought the judge to the window. In the room on the left-hand side Mr. Justice Mortlake drew back the curtains of the window nearest the front door and looked out. I want to emphasize this to show there had been no funny business or hocus-pocus. It was old Mortlake: I've seen him too many times in court, and at this time he was alive and well. He pushed up the window a little way and looked out; I saw his bald head shine. He called out, 'Who's there?' Then something else took his attention away from the window. He turned back into the room.

"What took his attention was the fact that Gabriel White had opened the hall door to his study, had run into the study, and had turned the key in the lock as he went through. Sergeant Borden was on White's tail, but a few seconds too late to get him before he locked the door. I saw that *my* quickest way into the study, if I wanted to head off anything, would be through that window—now partly open. Then I heard the first shot.

"Yes, sir: I said the *first* shot. I heard it when I was about twenty running paces away from the window. Then, when I was ten paces from the window, I heard the second shot. The black curtains were only partly drawn and I couldn't see inside until I had drawn level with the window.

"Inside, a little way out and to my left, old Mortlake was lying forward on his face across a flat-topped desk. In the middle of the room Gabriel White stood holding the Ivor-Johnson revolver out stiffly in front of him, and looking stupid. He wasn't savage, or defiant, or even weepy; he'd only got a silly sort of look on his face. Well, sir, the only thing for me to do was to climb through the window. There wasn't much danger in it. White paid no attention to me and I doubt if he even saw me. The first thing I did was to go over and take the gun out of White's hand. He didn't resist. The next thing I did was to unlock the door leading into the hallway — Borden was still hammering at it outside — so that Borden could get in.

"Then I went to the body of Mr. Justice Mortlake.

"He was lying on his face across a big writing table. From the ceiling over the desk hung a big brass lamp shaped like a Chinese dragon, with a powerful electric bulb inside. It poured down a flood of light on the writing desk, and it was the only light in the room. At the judge's left hand was a standing dictaphone, with its rubber cover off. And the judge was dead, right enough. He had been shot through the heart at fairly close range, and death had been almost instantaneous. There had been two shots. One of the bullets had killed him. The other bullet had smashed the glass mouth of the speaking tube hung on the dictaphone, and was embedded in the wall behind him. I dug it out later.

"If you look at the plan I've drawn, you will get a good general idea of the room. It was a large, square room, furnished chiefly with bookcases and leather chairs. There was no fireplace, but in the north wall a

PLAN OF STUDY IN PAVILION

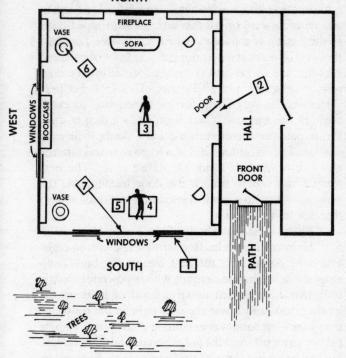

1. Window by which Inspector Page entered.
2. Door outside which Sergeant Borden stood.
3. Where White was standing when police entered.
4. Position of body across writing table.
5. Dictaphone.
6. Vase in which Browning .32 automatic was found.
7. Arrow shows position in wall where bullet from Ivor-Johnson .38 revolver lodged.

two-bar electric fire (turned on) had been let into the wall. In the west wall there were two windows. (But both of these windows were locked on the inside; and in addition, their heavy wooden shutters were also locked on the inside.) In the south wall there were two windows. (But this was the side by which I had entered myself. One of these windows was locked and shuttered; the other, through which I climbed, I had kept under observation the whole time.) There was only one other exit from the room—the door to the hall. (But this door had been under the observation of Sergeant Borden from the moment White ran inside and locked it.)

"Of course, sir, all this was routine. We knew the answer. We had White in a closed circle with his victim. Nobody else could have escaped from that room. Nobody was hiding there when we entered; as a matter of routine, we searched that room thoroughly. Gabriel White had fired two bullets, one of which had killed the old man, and the other had missed him and stuck in the wall. It was all smooth, easy sailing—until it occurred to me, purely as routine, to break open the Ivor-Johnson revolver and look at the cylinder."

"Well?" inquired Colonel Marquis.

"Well," Inspector Page said grimly, *"only one bullet had been fired from White's gun."*

That his chief was enjoying this, Page had no doubt. Colonel Marquis had sat up straighter; and his speckled shiny face had grown less sardonic.

"Admirable," he said, lighting another cigarette. "What I like, Inspector, is your informal style of making a report."

Page was never certain how to take the man, but he went at it with a grin.

"Frankly, sir, we couldn't believe our eyes. The gun was just as you see it now: fully loaded except for one exploded cartridge case. Theoretically, of course, he *might* have walked into that room and fired one bullet; then he might have carefully opened the cylinder, extracted the spent cartridge case, put another bullet in its place, and fired that—leaving the cylinder as we found it."

"Rubbish," said Colonel Marquis.

"Yes, sir. Why should anybody have done such a crazy trick as that, when the cylinder was full to begin with? Besides, he couldn't have done it. In that case, there'd have been an extra shell to account for—the cartridge case of the first bullet—and it wasn't anywhere in the room or on his person. We made sure of that."

"What did the accused say?"

Page took a notebook out of his pocket and got the right place.

"I'll read you his testimony verbatim," Page said, "although he was in pretty bad shape and what he said wasn't any more coherent than the rest of this business. First, I warned him that anything he said would be taken down and might be used in evidence. And here it is:

Q. So you shot him after all?
A. I don't know.
Q. What do you mean, you don't know? You don't deny you shot him?
A. I shot *at* him. Then things went all queer. I don't know.
Q. And you shot at him twice?
A. No, I didn't. So help me God, I didn't. I only shot at him once. I don't know whether I hit him; but he didn't fall or anything.
Q. Are you trying to tell me there was only one shot?

A. No, no, there were two shots right enough. I heard them.

Q. Which one of them did you fire?

A. The first one. I shot at the old swine as soon as I got in here. He was just turning round from that window and he put out his hands toward me and I shot at him.

Q. Do you mean that there was somebody in here who fired a second shot?

A. I don't know.

Q. Well, did you see anybody else in here?

A. No. There isn't any light except that one directly over the desk, and I couldn't see.

Q. Do you mean to say that if somebody let off a gun in this room right under your nose, you wouldn't see the man or the gun or anything else?

A. I don't know. I'm just telling you. I shot at the old swine and he didn't fall. He started to run over to the other window to get away from me, and shouted at me. Then I heard another shot. He stopped, and put his hands up to his chest, and took a couple of steps forward again, and fell over, on his face across that table.

Q. What direction did this shot come from?

A. I don't know.

"I had just asked him this question when Sergeant Borden made a discovery. Borden had been prowling over along the west wall, near those two enormous yellow porcelain vases. They were standing in the two corners of the room along that wall (*see the plan*). Borden bent over beside one of them, in the northwest angle of the wall. And he picked up a spent cartridge case.

"At first, of course, Borden thought it was the shell we were looking for out of the Ivor-Johnson revolver. But as soon as I glanced at it I saw it wasn't. It was a shell ejected from a .32 automatic. And then we looked inside that vase and we found this."

Again grinning wryly, Page pushed across the table the Browning .32 automatic.

"This pistol was lying at the bottom of the vase, where somebody had dropped it. The vase was too high to reach down inside with an arm. But the judge had brought an umbrella to the pavilion; we found it leaning up against the wall in the hall, so we reached down and fished out the gun with the crook of the umbrella.

"By the smell of the barrel I could tell that the Browning .32 had been fired within the last few minutes. One bullet was missing from the clip. The cartridge case from that bullet (our firearms expert swears to this) was the one we found lying beside the vase. The cartridge case, when I touched it, was still very faintly warm: in other words, sir, it had been fired within the last few seconds."

Page tapped one finger on the edge of the desk.

"Consequently, sir," he said, "there is absolutely no doubt that a second shot was fired from that Browning automatic; that it was fired by somebody *inside the room*; and that afterward somebody dropped the gun into that vase."

"Which bullet killed him?"

"That's the point, sir; we don't know."

"You don't know?" repeated the other sharply. "I should think it would be fairly easy. There were two bullets, a .38 revolver and a .32 automatic. One of them was, to put it in an undignified way, in the judge; the other was in the wall. You tell me you dug out the one in the wall. Which was it?"

From his pocket Page took a labeled envelope and shook out of it a lead pellet which had been flattened and partly chipped.

"This was in the wall," he said. "It's a brick wall and the bullet's been splintered a little. So we can't go entirely by weight — that is, not beyond any doubt. I'm almost certain this is the .38 bullet from White's revolver. But it can't be put into the record until I get the post-mortem report from Dr. Blaine and get my claws on the one in the judge's body. Dr. Blaine is doing the post-mortem this morning."

Colonel Marquis's expression became a broad grin, changing to extreme gravity.

"You are thorough, Inspector," he said. "All the same, where do you think we stand? If that bullet turns out to be from the .38 revolver, then Gabriel White fired and missed. So far, so good. But what happened afterward? Not more than a few seconds afterward, according to your story, someone blazed away with the Browning automatic and killed Mr. Justice Mortlake. By the way, were there fingerprints on the Browning?"

"No, sir. But then White was wearing gloves."

Colonel Marquis raised his eyebrows. "I see. You think White may have fired both shots after all?"

"I think it's a possibility. He may have come to the pavilion equipped with two guns and done all that funny business as a deliberate blind, to make us think that the second shot which really killed the judge was fired by someone else. And yet —"

"It's a very large 'and yet,' " grunted the other. "I agree. If he has indulged in any such elaborate hocus-pocus as that, he would have taken good care to see that the room wasn't sealed up like a box; he wouldn't have taken such precautions to prove that nobody else *could* have fired the shot. His actions, in blazing away directly under the noses of the police, sound more like a deliberate bid for martyrdom. That's reasonable enough; there are plenty of cranks. But the use of two pistols, under such circumstances, would be rank insanity. Whether Gabriel White is a crank or whether he isn't, I presume you don't think he is three times madder than a March hare."

Page was disturbed. "I know, sir. Also, they talk about 'acting,' but I would be willing to swear that the expression on White's face—when I looked through that window—was absolutely genuine. There isn't an actor alive who could have managed it. The man was staggered with surprise—half out of his wits at what he saw. But there it is! What else can we believe? The room was, as you say, sealed up like a box. So White must have fired both shots. Nobody else could have done it."

"You don't see any alternative?"

"Yes, sir," said Page. "I do."

"Ah, I hoped you would," said Colonel Marquis. "Well?"

"There's the possibility that White might be shielding somebody. For instance, suppose somebody else had been in that room, armed with the Browning. White fires, and misses. X, the unknown, fires and rings the bell. Whereupon—the police being at the door—X hops out one of the windows in the west wall, and White locks the windows and the shutters after X has gone."

He raised his eyes and the other nodded.

"Yes. Let's suppose, just for the sake of argument," said Colonel Marquis, "that White didn't kill the judge after all. Let's have a little personal information. Was anyone else interested in killing him? What about his household or his friends?"

"His household is small. He's a widower; he married rather late in life and his wife died about five years ago. He leaves two daughters—Carolyn, the elder (twenty-eight), and Ida, the younger (twenty-five). Aside from servants, the only other member of the household is an old man by the name of Penney: he's been the judge's legal clerk for years, and was taken into the house after the judge's retirement to help Mortlake on his book about *Fifty Years at Bench and Bar*, or some such thing—"

"Inevitable, of course," said the colonel. "What about friends?"

"He's got only one close friend. You remember my telling you, sir, that a crony of the judge was expected to come to tea yesterday afternoon and the judge sent word that he should come over to the pavilion as soon as he arrived? That's the man. He's a good deal younger than Mortlake. You may be interested to know that he's Sir Andrew Travers—the greatest criminal lawyer of 'em all. He's upset more than one of our best-prepared cases."

The Assistant Commissioner stared.

"I *am* interested," he said. "Travers. Yes. I don't know him personally, but I know a good deal about him. So Travers was invited to tea yesterday. Did he get there?"

"No. He was delayed; he phoned afterward, I understand."

Colonel Marquis reflected. "What about this household? I don't suppose you've had a chance to interview all of them; but one lead stands and shines. You say that the younger daughter, Ida, got in touch with you and told you Gabriel White was going to kill her father; you also think she knew White personally?"

"Yes, sir. I've seen Miss Ida Mortlake. She's the only one of the household I have seen, because both Miss Carolyn Mortlake and Penney, the clerk, were out yesterday afternoon. You want my honest opinion of her? Well, she's grand," said Page, dropping into humanity with such violence that Marquis blinked.

"Do you mean," asked the other, "that she has the grand manner, or merely what I think you mean?"

"Grand manner? Far from it. I mean I'd back her

against any field," replied Page. He could admit how much he had been impressed. He remembered the big house, a sort of larger and more ornate version of the pavilion itself; and Ida Mortlake, white-faced, coming down the stairs to meet him. "Whatever happened at the pavilion," he went on, "it's certain she had nothing to do with it. There's nothing hard-boiled or modern about her. She's fine."

"I see. Anyhow, I take it you questioned her? You asked her about her association with White, if there was any association?"

"The fact is, sir, I didn't question her too closely. She was rather upset, as you can imagine, and she promised to tell me the whole story today. She admitted that she knew White, but she knows him only slightly and acknowledges that she doesn't particularly like him. I gather that he'd been attentive. She met him at a studio party in Chelsea. Studio parties seem to be a craze of the elder daughter, who appears to be along the hard-boiled line. On this occasion Ida Mortlake went along and met—"

Whenever there appeared on Colonel Marquis's face a wolfish grin, as happened now, it seemed to crackle the face like the skin of a roast pig. He remained sitting bolt upright, studying Page with a bleak eye.

"Inspector," he said, "your record has been good and I will refrain from comment. I say nothing against this young lady. All I should like to know is, why are you so certain she couldn't have had anything to do with this? You yourself admitted the possibility that White might be shielding somebody. You yourself admitted that there might have been somebody else in the room who got out of a window after the shot was fired, and that White might have locked the window afterward?"

"Did I?" said Page, glad to hit back at the old so-and-so. "I don't think I said that, Colonel. I considered it. I also found, later, that it wouldn't work."

"Why?"

"Before and after the shots I had the two south windows under my eye. Nobody came out of either window at any time. Borden was watching the door. The only remaining way out would be one of the west windows. But we learned from Robinson, the gatekeeper, that neither of the west windows had been touched for over a year. It seems that those two windows were loose in the frame and let in bad drafts. The judge used that pavilion, as a rule, only in the evening; and he was afraid of drafts. So the windows were always locked and the shutters always bolted into place outside them. You see, when Borden and I came to examine them, the locks were so rusted that it took our combined strength to budge them. The shutters outside the windows had their bolts so rusted from exposure that we couldn't move them at all. So that's definitely o-u-t."

Colonel Marquis used an unofficial word. "So we come directly round in a circle again?"

"I'm afraid so, sir. It really does seal the room up. Out of four sides of a square, one was a blank wall, one was impregnable with rusted bolts, and the other two were watched. We have got to believe Gabriel White fired both those shots — or go crazy."

The telephone on the Assistant Commissioner's desk rang sharply. Colonel Marquis, evidently about to hold forth on his refusal to go crazy, answered it with some annoyance; but his expression changed. He put a hand over the mouthpiece of the phone.

"Where is White now? You're holding him, naturally?"

"Naturally, sir. He's downstairs now. I thought you might like to have a talk with him."

"Send them both in," Marquis said to the telephone, and hung up in some satisfaction. "I think," he went on to Page, "it will be a good idea, presently, to confront everybody with everybody else. And I am very curious to form my own opinion of this saint-martyr, or rotter-murderer, Mr. Gabriel White. But at the moment we have visitors. No, don't get up. Miss Ida Mortlake and Sir Andrew Travers are on their way in."

Though Page was afraid he might have pitched it too strongly in his description of Ida Mortlake, her appearance reassured him. Seen now for the second time, she was a slender girl with a coolness and delicacy like Dresden china. Though she was rather tall, she did not seem tall. Her skin was very fair, her hair clear yellow under a black close-fitting hat with a short veil, her eyes blue; and she had a smile capable of loosening Page's judgment. She wore a mink coat which Page — who had been out after fur thieves in the West India Dock Road the week before — valued at fifteen hundred guineas.

This depressed him. For the first time it occurred to him that, with the old judge out of the way, Ida Mortlake would be a very rich woman.

"Colonel Marquis?" she said, her color rising. "I thought —"

A clearing of the throat behind her interrupted the speech, for someone towered there. Page had never seen Andrew Travers without his barrister's wig and gown; yet he had the same mannerisms in private life as in a courtroom. They had become, evidently, a part of him. Sir Andrew Travers had a massive head, a massive chest, a blue jowl, and an inscrutable eye. His wiry black hair was so thick that you expected it to be long, but it was cropped off just above the ears. He was formidable, but he was also affable. He wore a dark overcoat, through which showed a gray cravat; and he formally carried top hat and gloves. His full, rich voice compassed the room.

"In such a shocking affair, Colonel Marquis," he said, "you will readily understand Miss Mortlake's feelings. As a personal friend of poor Mortlake's, I asked the liberty of accompanying her here —"

Page had got up hastily to stand at attention against the wall, while Marquis indicated chairs. Ida recognized him and gave him a smile. As Sir Andrew Travers lowered himself into a chair, Page seemed to see a manservant at work brushing him to give him that gloss. Sir Andrew assumed his most winning air.

"Frankly, Colonel Marquis, we are here to ask for information —"

"Oh, *no*," said Ida. She flushed again and her eyes were bright. "It isn't that. But I do want to tell you that I can't believe Gabriel White killed Father."

Travers looked slightly annoyed and Colonel Marquis was very bland. He addressed himself to Travers.

"You are familiar with the details?" he asked.

"Only, I regret to say, what I have read here," said Travers. He reached out and touched the newspaper. "You can understand," Travers went on, "that I am in a position of some delicacy. I am a barrister, not a solicitor. At the moment I am here only as a friend of Miss Mortlake. Frankly, is there some doubt of this unfortunate man's guilt?"

The Assistant Commissioner considered. "There is," he said, "what I can only call — an *un*reasonable doubt. And therefore," Colonel Marquis went on, "would Miss Mortlake mind answering a few questions?"

"Of course not," the girl replied promptly. "That's why I'm here, although Andrew advised me not to. I tell you, I *know* Gabriel White couldn't have done it."

"Forgive the question, but are you interested in him?"

Her face became still more pink and she spoke with eagerness. "No! No, honestly I'm not; not in the way you mean, that is. In the way you mean, I think I rather dislike him, though he's been very nice to me."

"Yet you know that he was sentenced to flogging and imprisonment for a particularly brutal case of robbery with violence?"

"Yes, I knew it," she said calmly. "I know all about that. He told me. He was innocent, of course. You see, it's not in Gabriel's nature; he's too much of an idealist; a thing like that is directly opposed to all he believes in most strongly. He hates war and he hates violence of all kinds. He's a member of all kinds of societies opposed to war and violence and capital punishment. There's one political society, called the Utopians—he says it's the political science of the future—and he's the leading member of that. You remember when he was tried, the prosecution asked what a respectable citizen was *doing* in a slum district like Poplar on the night that poor old woman was robbed? And he refused to answer. And they made quite a lot of that." She was speaking in a somewhat breathless rush. "Actually, he was going to a meeting of the Utopians. But most of their members are very poor, and a lot of them are foreigners. Gabriel said that, if he had answered, the jury would merely have thought they were a lot of anarchists. And it would only have prejudiced the case still more against him."

"H'm," said Colonel Marquis, after a pause. "How long have you known him, Miss Mortlake?"

"Oh, nearly three years, I should think. I mean, I knew him about a year before he—before they put him in prison."

"What do you know about him?"

"He's an artist."

"There is just one thing," pursued Colonel Marquis, examining his hands, "which does not seem to square with this. You are willing to swear, Miss Mortlake, that White could not have killed your father. And yet, if I understand correctly, you were the one who rang up here yesterday afternoon at four-thirty o'clock and begged for men to protect your father because White had threatened to kill him. Is that true?"

"I know I said so," answered the girl, with a sort of astounding simplicity which never turned a hair; "but, of course, I never thought he would really. I was panicky, horribly panicky. The more I thought of it, the worse it seemed—you see, I met Gabriel yesterday afternoon between three-thirty and four o'clock, I think it was. If you remember, it started to rain about four or a little past. I wasn't very far down North End Road when I saw Gabriel. He was walking along with his head down, looking like thunder. I stopped the car. At first he didn't want to speak to me. But the car was right outside a Lyons', and he said in that curt way of his, 'Oh, come in and have some tea.' We did. At first he wouldn't talk much, but at last he broke out raving against my father. He said he was going to kill him—"

"And you weren't impressed?"

"Gabriel always talks like that," she answered. She made a slight, sharp gesture of her gloved hand. "But I didn't want a row in a public place like that. At last I said, 'Well, if you can't behave any better than this, perhaps I'd better go.' I left him sitting there with his elbows stuck out on the table. By that time it had begun to rain and lightning, and I'm frightened of storms. So I drove straight back home as soon as I'd got a book from the lending library."

"Yes?" he prompted, as she hesitated.

"Well, I warned Robinson—the gatekeeper—not to let anybody in, anybody at all, even by the tradesman's entrance. There's a big wall all around, with jagged glass on the top. As a matter of fact, I still don't see how Gabriel got in. I went up to the house. I suppose it was the fact that there was nobody in the house, and there was a storm outside that made me get panicky and still more panicky. At last I simply grabbed the phone, and—" She sat back, breathing hard. "I lost my silly head, that was all."

"Did your father know White, Miss Mortlake?" asked Marquis.

She was troubled. "Yes, I'm pretty sure he did. At least, he knew I had been—seeing Gabriel."

"And he didn't approve?"

"No; I'm sure I don't know why. He certainly never saw Gabriel in my presence."

"So you think there might have been a personal reason why he ordered a flogging? I am aware," Marquis snapped quickly, as Travers opened his mouth, "that you don't have to answer that, Miss Mortlake. Sir Andrew was going to advise you not to answer. But it strikes me that the defense will need all the help it can get. In spite of your gallant words in White's favor he admits firing one of the shots. You knew that?"

The girl's blue eyes widened and the color went out of her face, leaving it soft-looking and (for a second) curiously ineffectual. She glanced at Page. "No, I didn't," she said. "But this is horrible! If he really admits doing it after all—"

"No, he doesn't admit firing the shot that actually killed your father. That's the trouble." Colonel Marquis very rapidly gave a summary of the case. "So, you see, it seems we shall have to prosecute White or, as the

Inspector says, go crazy. Do you know of anyone else who might have wished to kill your father?"

"Nobody else in the world," she admitted. "Quite to the contrary, everybody in public life loved him. You've heard how lenient he was. He never had any animosity from any of the people he sentenced."

"And in private life?"

This evidently surprised her. "Private life? What on earth? Certainly not! Of course," she hesitated, "sometimes — there's no harm in my saying it, is there? — sometimes he was difficult. I mean, he had splendid humanitarian principles and he was always trying to make the world better; but I did wish sometimes he would be less gentle in court and at banquets and a little more humanitarian at home. Please don't misunderstand me! He was a wonderful man and I don't think he ever spoke an unkind word to us in his life. But he loved to lecture: on and on in that smooth, easy voice of his. I — I suppose it was for our own good, though."

For the first time, and with a sort of shock, it occurred to Page that the liberal and lenient Mr. Justice Charles Mortlake might have been a holy terror to live with. Colonel Marquis looked at Travers. "You agree with that, Sir Andrew?"

Travers clearly had to draw back his attention from other matters. He had picked up the little Browning automatic from the desk and was turning it over in his fingers.

"Agree? About Mortlake having any enemies? Oh, emphatically."

"You have nothing to add to that?"

"I have a great deal to add to it," said Travers with sharpness. He seemed to have developed a number of little wheezes in his throat. "So the second shot was fired from this? Well, it alters matters. I don't know whether or not White is guilty. But I know that now I can't undertake his defense . . . you see, *this Browning automatic belongs to me.*"

Ida Mortlake let out an exclamation. With great urbanity Travers reached into his breast pocket, drew out a wallet, and showed the card of a firearms license. "If you will compare the serial numbers," he said, "you will see that they agree."

"H'm," said Marquis, "are you going to confess to the murder, then?"

Travers's smile grew broader and more human. "God love us, I didn't kill him, if that's what you think. I liked him too well. But this is an unusual position for me, and I can't say it's a pleasant one. I thought I recognized this little weapon as soon as I came in here, although I thought it couldn't possibly be the same one. The last time I saw it, it was in my chambers at the Inner Temple. To be exact, it was in the lowest left-hand drawer of the desk in my study."

"Could White have stolen it from there?"

Travers shook his head.

"I don't think so. I should regard it as extremely unlikely. I don't know White; to my knowledge, I've never even seen him. And he's never been in my chambers, unless it was burglary."

"When did you last see the gun?"

"I'm afraid I can't answer that," said Travers. He was now at his ease, studying the matter as though in luxurious debate. But Page thought he was watchful. "The pistol was too much part of—the domestic furniture, so to speak. I think I can say I haven't taken it out of the drawer for over a year; I had no use for it. It may have been gone for a year. It may have been gone for no longer than a few days."

"Who could have stolen it?"

There was a heavy cloud on Travers's face. "I can hardly answer that, can I? Anyone with free access to my rooms might have done it."

"A member of Mr. Justice Mortlake's household, for instance?"

"Oh, yes, it's possible," replied Travers.

"Very well," said the Assistant Commissioner. "Would you mind, Sir Andrew, giving an account of your movements yesterday afternoon?"

The barrister reflected. "I was in court until about half-past three in the afternoon. Afterward I walked across the street to the Temple. Let me see. When I passed through the Fountain Court, I remember noticing by the sundial on the wall that it was twenty minutes to four. I had promised to be at Hampstead, for tea with Mortlake, by four-thirty at the latest. Unfortunately, my clerk told me that Gordon Bates had gone on the sick list and had insisted on turning the brief in the Lake case over to me. The Lake case comes up for trial today, and it's a rather complicated business. I knew that I should have to swot up on it all yesterday afternoon and probably all night, to be in shape to argue it today. Which killed any possibility of my going to Hampstead for tea. So I stayed in my chambers with the brief. It was twenty minutes to six when I suddenly realized I hadn't made any excuses over the phone. But by that time — well, poor Mortlake was dead. I understand he was shot about half-past five."

"And all this time you were in your chambers? Have you any confirmation of this?"

"I believe I have," the other affirmed with grave

attention. "My clerk should confirm it. He was in the outer room until nearly six o'clock. I was in the inner part of the chambers: my living quarters. There is only one way out of the chambers; and to leave them, I should have had to pass through the room where my clerk was. I believe he will give me an alibi."

Supporting himself on his cane, Colonel Marquis got up with great formality and nodded.

"Right," he said. "I have just one request. I wonder whether I can trespass on your time by asking you to wait in another room for about ten minutes? There is something I must do, and then I should like to speak with both of you again."

He pressed a buzzer on his desk. He swept them out of the room with such effortless smoothness that even Travers had scarcely time to protest.

"Remarkable! Excellent!" said Colonel Marquis, who was rubbing his hands with fiendish glee. Page felt that if his chief had not been lame, he would have danced. Marquis pointed a long forefinger at his subordinate. "You are shocked," he went on. "In the depths of your soul you are shocked at my lack of dignity. Wait until you are my age. Then you will realize that the greatest joy of passing sixty is being able to act as you jolly well please. Inspector, this case is a sizzler; it has possibilities; and doubtless you see them?"

Page considered. "As for the possibilities, sir, there seems to be something very fishy about that theft of Sir Andrew Travers's gun. If White couldn't have done it—"

"Ah, White. Yes. That's why I wanted our friends out of the room; I should like to have a little talk with White, alone."

He got on the telephone again and gave orders for White to be brought up.

There was little change in the young man's appearance since last night, Page noticed, except that he was now dry and brushed. Two constables brought him in: a tall, rather lanky figure still wearing his shabby topcoat. His darkish fair hair was worn rather long, brushed back from the forehead, and he smoothed at it nervously. His face was strong, with a delicate nose but a strong jaw; and he had good gray eyes under pinched brows. His face was slightly hollow, his movements jerky. At the moment he seemed half-belligerent, half-despairing.

"Why don't you tell us what really happened at that pavilion?" Marquis began.

"I wish you'd tell *me,*" the other said simply. "Do you think I've been pounding my head about anything else since they nabbed me? Whatever happens, I'm due for a long stretch at the Moor, because I really did take a crack at the old swine. But, believe it or not, I —*did— not—kill—him.*"

"Well, that's what we're here to discover," Marquis said comfortably. "You are an artist, I've heard?"

"I am a painter," said White, still shortly. "Whether or not I am an artist remains to be seen." The light of the fanatic came into his eyes. "By heaven, I wish Philistines would not persist in misusing terms they do not understand! I wish —"

"We are coming to that. I understand you've got some strong political views. What do you believe in?"

"So you want to know what I believe in?" he demanded. "I believe in a new world, an enlightened world, a world free from the muddle we have made of this. I want a world of light and progress, that a man can breathe decently in; a world without violence or war; a world, in that fine phrase of Wells's, 'waste, austere and wonderful.' That's all I want, and it's little enough."

"And how would you bring this about?"

"First," said White, "all capitalists would be taken out and hanged. Those who opposed us, of course, would merely be shot. But capitalists would be hanged, because they have brought about this muddle and made us their tools. I say it again: we are tools, tools, tools, TOOLS."

Page thought: The fellow's off his onion. But there was about Gabriel White such a complete and flaming earnestness that it carried conviction. White stopped, breathing so hard that it choked him.

"And you think Mr. Justice White deserved death?"

"He was a swine," answered White calmly. "You don't need political science to tell you that."

"Did you know him personally?"

"No," said White, after a hesitation.

"But you know Miss Ida Mortlake?"

"I know her slightly." He was still inscrutable. "Not that it matters. There is no need to drag her into this; she knows nothing of it."

"Naturally not. Well, suppose you tell us exactly what happened yesterday afternoon. To begin with, how did you get inside the grounds?"

White looked dogged. "I'd better tell you about that, yes, because it's the one thing I'm ashamed of. You see, I met Ida yesterday afternoon. We were at a Lyons' in Hampstead. Naturally I didn't want to meet her just then; but I felt bound to warn her I was going to kill the old man if I could." There was a dull flush under his cheekbones. His fine, rather large-knuckled hands were fidgeting on his knees. "The fact is, I hid in the back of her car. She didn't know it. After she'd left the teashop, she was going to a lending library just down the road. I knew that. So I followed. While she was in the library, I nipped into the back of the car and got down under a rug. It was a very dark day and raining hard, so I knew she wouldn't notice me. Otherwise I couldn't have got inside the grounds at all. The gatekeeper keeps a sharp lookout.

"She drove through the gates and up to the house. When she put the car in the garage, I sneaked out. The trouble was I didn't know *where* the old swine was. How was I to know he was at the pavilion? I thought I should find him in the house.

"I wasted nearly an hour trying to get into that house. There seemed to be servants all over the place. Finally I did get in—through a side window. And I nearly walked into the butler. He was just going into a front room, drawing room or the like, where Ida Mortlake was sitting. He said it was getting very late, and asked whether she wanted tea served? She said yes; she said to go ahead and serve it, because her father was at the pavilion and probably wouldn't be up for tea. That was how I knew, you see. So I hopped out the side window again."

"What time was this?"

"God knows; I wasn't paying any attention to that. Stop a bit, though." White reflected. "You can easily enough find out. I ran straight down to the pavilion, as hard as I could pelt. There I ran into your police officers—I supposed they were police officers—and by that time I was determined to kill the old devil if it was the last thing I ever did."

The breath whistled out of his nostrils. Colonel Marquis asked: "We can put it, then, at half-past five? Good. Go on. Everything!"

"I've gone over it a hundred times since then," said White. He shut his eyes, and spoke slowly. "I ran to the door of the study. I ran inside and locked the door. Mortlake had been standing at the window, shouting something to the police officer outside. When he heard me come in, he turned round from the window . . ."

"Did he say anything?"

"Yes. He said, 'What is the meaning of this?' or 'What do you want here?' or something of that sort. I can't remember the exact words. Then he put his hand up in front of him, as though I were going to hit him, when he saw the gun in my hand. Then I fired. With that pistol," said White, touching the Ivor-Johnson .38.

"H'm, yes. D'you hit him?"

"Sir, I'm practically certain I didn't," declared the other, bringing down his fist on the edge of the desk. "Look here: there was a very bright light up over the desk. It was in a brass holder of some kind, and it left most of the room pretty dark because it was concentrated. But it lit up the desk and space between the windows. Just as I pulled the trigger, I saw the bullet hole jump up black in the wall behind him. And he was still moving and running. Besides . . ."

"Well?"

"It isn't as easy," said White, suddenly looking like an old man, "to kill a man as you might think. It's all right until your hand is actually on the trigger. Then something seems to wash all out of you. It seems as though you can't, physically you can't, do it. It's like hitting a man when he's down. And it's a queer thing — just at that second, I almost pitied the old beggar. He looked so *scared*, flapping away from my gun like a bat trying to get out."

"Just a moment," interposed Marquis. "Are you accustomed to using firearms?"

White was puzzled. "No, I don't suppose I've ever handled anything more deadly than an air rifle when I was a boy. But I thought, shut up in a room, I couldn't very well miss. Then — I did miss. Do you want me to go on? He started to run away from me, along the back wall. He was alive then, all right. I want you to understand that the whole thing was such a brief matter of seconds, all compressed, that it's a bit confused. At this time he was facing, slightly sideways, the wall behind me on my right . . ."

"Facing, then, the corner where the yellow vase stood? The vase where the automatic was later found?"

"Yes. It seemed as though he'd turned round to swing out into the room. Then I heard another shot. It seemed to come from behind me and to my right. I felt — a kind of wind, if you know what I mean.

"After this he put his hands up to his chest. He turned round and took a few steps back the way he'd come, and swung a little back again, and then fell head-first across the desk. Just as he fell, your police officer" — White nodded toward Page — "came in through the window. And that's the best I can do."

"Did you see anybody else in the room, either before or after this shot?"

"No."

The Assistant Commissioner's somber eyes wandered over to Page. "A question for you, Inspector. Would it be possible for there to have been any mechanical device in that room, hidden somewhere, which could have fired a shot and concealed the pistol without anyone else being there?"

Page was prompt. He and Borden had searched that room too well.

"It's absolutely impossible, sir," he answered. "We nearly took the pavilion to pieces. Also," he smiled a little, "you can rule out any idea of a secret passage or a trap door. There wasn't so much as a mousehole . . . Besides, there's the gun in the yellow vase, which really was fired inside that room."

Colonel Marquis nodded dully. He said:

"Yes, I think we have got to acknowledge that the second shot was fired by somebody inside the room. Look here, White: how far were you away from the judge when you shot at him?"

"About fifteen feet, I should think."

"H'm, yes. Very well. We assume somebody dropped that pistol into the vase. You say the vase was much too high for anybody's arm to reach down inside and deposit the gun there. So it must have made some noise when it fell." He looked at White. "Did you hear any noise?"

White was troubled. "I don't know. I honestly don't know. I can't remember—"

"You realize," said Marquis, with sudden harshness, "that you are telling us an absolutely impossible thing? You are saying that somebody must have escaped from a room which was locked and guarded on all sides? How? . . . Yes, yes, what is it?"

He broke off as his secretary came into the room and spoke in a low tone. Colonel Marquis nodded, becoming affable again.

"It's the police surgeon," he said to Page. "He's performed the postmortem. And the results seem to be so interesting that he wants to see me directly. Most unusual. Send him in."

There was a silence. White sat quietly in his chair; but he had braced his elbows against the back of the chair and his heavy handsome face had a blankness of waiting. Page knew what goblins had come into the room to surround the prisoner. If the bullet in the judge's body turned out to be a .38 after all, it meant the end of him. Dr. Gallatin, the police surgeon, a worried bustling man, came into the room with a briefcase in his hand.

"Good morning, doctor," said Colonel Marquis. "We were waiting for you. We can't go any further until we know. What's the verdict?" He pushed the two pistols across the desk. "Public opinion is divided. One branch thinks Mr. Justice Mortlake was killed by a bullet from an Ivor-Johnson .38 revolver, fired from a distance of about fifteen feet. The other branch denies this and says he was killed by a bullet from a Browning .32 automatic, fired from a distance of about twenty-five feet. Which side is right?"

"Neither," said the doctor.

Colonel Marquis sat up very slowly. "What the devil do you mean, neither?"

"I said neither," replied the doctor, "because both sides are wrong, sir. As a matter of fact, he was killed by a bullet from an Erckmann air pistol, roughly corresponding to a .22 caliber fired from a distance of about ten feet."

Although Marquis did not bat an eyelid, Page felt that the old so-and-so had seldom in his life received so unexpected an announcement. He remained sitting bolt upright, looking coldly at the doctor.

"I trust, Dr. Gallatin," he said, "that you are sober?"

"Quite sober, worse luck," agreed the doctor.

"And you are seriously trying to tell me that there was still a *third* shot fired in that room?"

"I don't know anything about the case, sir. All I know is that he was plugged at fairly short range"— Gallatin opened the little cardboard box and took out a flattish lump of lead —"by this bullet from an Erckmann air pistol. As a rule you see the Erckmann army pistol, which is a lot heavier than this. But this one is a dangerous job, because it's got much more power than an ordinary firearm, and it's almost noiseless."

Colonel Marquis turned to White. "What have *you* got to say to this?"

White was evidently so strung up that he had forgotten his role as light bringer and social reformer; he spoke like a schoolboy, with sullen petulance. "Here, I say! Fair play! I don't know any more about it than you do."

"Did you hear or see *another* shot fired in that room?"

"No, I did not."

"Inspector Page: you searched the room immediately after you went in. Did you find any air pistol?"

"No, sir," said Page firmly. "If there had been one, I'm certain we should have found it."

"And you also searched the prisoner. Did he have any such pistol on him, or could he have disposed of it?"

"He did not and he could not," replied Page. "Besides, three pistols carried by one man would be coming it a little too strong. In a case like that, I should think it would have been simpler to have used a machine gun." He saw the Colonel's eye grow dangerous, and added: "May I ask a question? Doctor, would it have been possible for that air-pistol bullet to have been fired either from a Browning .32 or an Ivor-Johnson .38? A sort of fraud to make us think a third gun had been used?"

Dr. Gallatin grinned. "You don't know much about ballistics, do you?" he asked. "It's not only impossible, it's mad. Ask your firearms man. This little pellet had to be fired, and was fired, from an Erckmann air pistol."

Now that the reaction had set in, White was deadly pale. He looked from one to the other of them.

"Excuse me," he said, with the first trace of humanity he had shown, "but does this mean I'm cleared of the actual — murder?"

"Yes," said Colonel Marquis. "Brace up, man! Here, pull yourself together. I'm sending you downstairs for a while. This alters matters considerably."

He pressed the buzzer on his desk. White was escorted out, talking volubly but incomprehensibly about nothing at all. The Assistant Commissioner remained staring after him with sombre concentration, and knocking his knuckles against his desk.

Page and the doctor watched him.

"This is insanity," he went on. "Let us see where we stand: There is now no doubt that three shots were fired: from the Ivor-Johnson, *and* the Browning, *and* the missing Erckmann. The trouble is that we lack a bullet, for only two of the three bullets have been found. By the way, Inspector, pass me over that pellet you found stuck in the wall." Page gave it to him and Colonel Marquis weighed it in his hand. "You say this is from the Ivor-Johnson .38. I agree, decidedly. We'll get a third opinion; what's your guess, doctor?"

Gallatin took the bullet and studied it.

"It's a .38, all right," he agreed. "No doubt of it. I've handled too many of them. This has been chipped a bit, that's all."

"Right, then. This is the one White admits having fired at the judge, as soon as he walked into the judge's study. So far, so good. But what about afterwards? What sort of witchcraft or hocus-pocus happened in the next two or three seconds? — By the way, Doctor, you said an Erckmann air pistol is almost noiseless. *How* noiseless?"

Gallatin was cautious. "That's out of my department, you know. But I think I can give you an idea. It isn't a great deal louder than the noise you make when you press the catch of an electric-light switch."

"Then, sir," interposed Page slowly, "you mean the

Erckmann might have been fired in that room almost under White's nose, and (especially with a storm going on outside) he mightn't have heard it at all?"

Marquis nodded. "But take it in order," he said. "After White fires his revolver, the judge starts to run away. Then someone else—standing behind and to the right of White, over in the corner by the yellow vase— fires a shot with the Browning automatic. This shot is heard by Inspector Page, who is within ten steps of the window. But the *bullet* from the Browning disappears. If it didn't kill the judge, where did it go? Where did it lodge? Where is it now?

"Finally, someone cuts loose with an Erckmann air pistol and fires the shot which really does kill Mortlake. But this time the *gun* disappears. Whoosh!" said Colonel Marquis, with an imaginative flourish. "Just as Mortlake falls forward dead across the writing table, Inspector Page arrives at the window, in time to find the room sealed up impregnably from every side—the only point being that the *murderer* has disappeared."

He paused, letting them picture the scene for themselves.

"Gentlemen, I don't believe it. But there it is. Have you any suggestions?"

"Only questions," Page said gloomily. "I take it we agree, sir, that White can't be the murderer?"

"Yes, we can safely say that."

Page took out his notebook and wrote: "Three questions seem to be indicated, all tied up with each other. (1) Did the same person who fired the Browning automatic also fire the Erckmann air pistol? And, if not, were there two people in the room besides White? (2) Was the fatal shot fired immediately before, or immediately after, the shot from the Browning? (3) In either case, where was the actual murderer standing?"

He looked up from his notebook, and Marquis nodded.

"Yes, I see the point. Number three is the hardest question of the lot," the Assistant Commissioner said. "According to the doctor here, Mortlake was shot through the heart at a distance of about ten feet. White, by his own confession, was standing fifteen feet away from Mortlake. How the devil does it happen, then, that White didn't see the murderer? Gentlemen, there is something so infernally fishy about this case."

"You mean," Page volunteered, "you mean the old idea that White might be shielding somebody?"

"But that's the trouble. Even if White is shielding anybody, how did anybody get out of the room? There was certainly one other person in there, and possibly two. Suppose one, or two, or six people took a shot at the judge: where did the whole procession vanish to — in the course of about eight or ten seconds?" He shook his head. "I say, Doctor, is there anything in the medical evidence that would help us?"

"Not about the vanishing, certainly," said Gallatin. "And not much about anything. Death was almost instantaneous. He might have taken a step or two afterward, or made a movement; but not much more."

"In that case," said the colonel, "*I* am going to find out. Let's have a car round here, Page, and run out to Hampstead. This interests me."

He limped across after his hat and coat. In his dark blue overcoat and soft gray hat, Colonel Marquis presented a figure of great sartorial elegance, except for the fact that he jammed on the hat so malevolently as to give it a high crown like Guy Fawkes's. First, Page had to issue instructions: a man must be sent to verify Travers's alibi, and the files of the firearms department ransacked to find any record of who might own an Erckmann air pistol. Then Colonel Marquis went limping out, towering over nearly everyone in the office. When Page protested that Ida Mortlake and Sir Andrew Travers were still waiting, he grunted.

"Let 'em wait," he said impolitely. "The case has taken such a turn that they will only confuse matters. Between ourselves, Inspector, I don't care to have Travers about when I examine the scene. Travers is a trifle too shrewd." He said little more while the police car moved through wet and gusty streets toward Hampstead. Page prompted him.

"It seems," the Inspector said, "that we've now got a very restricted circle."

"Restricted circle?"

"Like this, sir. There seems no reason why Travers should have killed the judge; and, on top of it, he's got a sound alibi. Next, Ida Mortlake has an alibi—an unintentional alibi—"

"Ah, you noticed that," observed Colonel Marquis, looking at him.

"Provided, unintentionally, by White himself. You remember what White said. He got through a window into the judge's house, not knowing the judge was at the pavilion. And he didn't learn the truth until he heard the butler asking Ida whether tea should be served. As soon as he heard this, he nipped out of the window and ran straight to the pavilion. This was at five-thirty, for he met Borden and myself on the way. Consequently, Ida must still have been at the house; and we can probably get the butler's corroboration. That's a sound alibi."

"Quite. Anything else?"

"If," answered Page thoughtfully, "if, as seems likely, no outsider could have got into the grounds—well, it looks as though he must have been killed either by one of the servants or by Miss Carolyn Mortlake or by old Penney, the clerk."

Colonel Marquis grunted out something which might have been assent or disagreement and pointed out that they would soon know. The car had swung into the broad suburban thoroughfare along one side of which ran the high wall of the judge's house. It was a busy street, where a tram line and a bus route crossed. Along one side were several shops, contrasting with the lonely stone wall across the street, beyond which elms showed tattered against a drizzling sky. They stopped before iron-grilled gates; and old Robinson, recognizing the police car, hastened to open.

"Anything new?" Page asked.

Robinson, the gatekeeper, a little man with a veined forehead and a dogged eye, thrust his head into the back of the car.

"Nossir," he said. "Except your sergeant is still dead set trying to find out whether anybody could have sneaked in here yesterday afternoon without my knowing—"

"And could anybody have done that?" asked Colonel Marquis.

Robinson studied him, wondering. "Well, sir, they told me to keep people out—or Miss Ida did, yesterday—and I *did* keep people out. That's my job. You just take a look at them walls. Anybody'd need a ladder to get over 'em, and there's no side of the walls where you could prop up a ladder without being seen by half the people in Hampstead. There's a main road in front and there's people's back gardens coming up against the walls on every other side." He cleared his throat, like a man about to spit, and grew more dogged. "There's only two gates, as you can see for yourself, and I was sitting right by one of them."

"What about the other gate—the tradesmen's entrance?"

"Locked," said Robinson promptly. "When Miss Ida come back from her drive yesterday, about four-twenty, no more, she told me to lock it and I did. There's only one other key besides mine, and Miss Ida's got that."

"You said that both Miss Carolyn Mortlake and Mr. Penney weren't here yesterday afternoon?"

"I don't remember whether I said so to you. But it's true."

"What time did they go?"

"Miss Carolyn—'bout quarter to four. Yes. Becos she'd wanted the car. And Miss Ida had already taken the car and gone out a quarter of an hour before that. Miss Carolyn, she was pretty mad; she was going to a cocktail party (people name o' Fischer at Golder's Green); and she wanted that car. As for Alfred Eric Penney, don't ask me when *he* went out. About ten minutes past four, I think."

Colonel Marquis was bland. "For the sake of clearness, we had better make this a timetable. The judge went from his house across to the pavilion—when?"

"Half past three," answered Robinson firmly. "That's certain."

"Good. Ida Mortlake leaves here in the car about the same time. Correct? Good. Carolyn Mortlake leaves for a cocktail party at fifteen minutes to four. At ten minutes past four, Penney also leaves. At twenty minutes past four, the rain having then begun, Ida Mortlake returns in the car. They all seem to have missed each other most conveniently; but that, I take it, is the timetable."

"I suppose it is; yes, sir," Robinson admitted.

"Drive on," said Colonel Marquis.

The car sped up a gravel drive between doleful elms. Page indicated where a branch of this path turned toward the pavilion, but the pavilion was some distance away, hidden in an ornamental clump of trees, and Marquis could not see it. The house itself would not have pleased an architect. It was of three stories, stuccoed, and built in that bastard style of Gothic architecture first seen at Strawberry Hill, but revived with gusto by designers during the middle of the nineteenth century. Its discolored pinnacles huddled together under the rain. Most of the long windows were shuttered, but smoke dropped down from all the chimneys. Though it was a landmark of solid Victorian respectability and prosperity there was about it something close-lipped and definitely evil.

The height of respectability also was the grizzled, heavy-headed manservant who admitted them. He fitted; you would have expected him. Page had seen him yesterday, although he had taken no statement. They now learned his name, which was Davies.

"If you don't mind, sir," he said, "I'll call Miss Carolyn. As a matter of fact, Miss Carolyn was just about to set out to see you. She —"

"And if *you* don't mind," said a new voice, "I should prefer to handle this myself, please."

The hall was shadowed by a window of red glass at the back. A woman came out between the bead curtains (which still exist) of an archway to the right. Carolyn Mortlake was one of those startling family contrasts (which, also, still exist). Where Ida was rather tall and soft, Carolyn was short, stocky and hard. Where Ida was fair, Carolyn was dark. She had a square, very good-looking but very hard face; with black eyes of a snapping luminousness and a mouth painted dark red. They could see her jaw muscles. She came forward at a free stride, wearing a tilted hat and a plain dark coat with a fur collar. But Page noticed, curiously enough, that her eyelids were puffy and reddish. She appraised them coolly, a heavy handbag under her arm.

"You are — ?" she said.

Colonel Marquis made the introductions, and in his politeness the girl seemed to find something suspicious.

"We are honored," she told him, "to have the Assistant Commissioner visit us in person. Perhaps I had better give you this."

With a decisive snap she opened the catch of her handbag, and took out a nickeled pistol with a rather long and top-heavy barrel.

"It is an Erckmann air pistol," she said.

"So it is, Miss Mortlake. Where did you get it?"

"From the bottom drawer of the bureau in my bedroom," replied Carolyn Mortlake, and lifted her head to stare at him defiantly.

"Perhaps," she said after a pause, "you had better come this way." In spite of her defiance, it was clear that she was shaking with some strong inner strain. But she was as cool as ever when she led them through the bead curtains into a thick-cluttered drawing room.

"I don't know quite what the game is," she went on. "I can't see why anybody should want to do it, because obviously my father wasn't killed with that gun . . . But I think I know what I was intended to do when I found it. I was supposed to become panicky, and hide the gun away again in case I should be suspected of something, and generally behave like a silly ass. Well, you jolly well won't find *me* doing things like that; I'm not such a fool." She smiled, without humor, and reached for a cigarette box. "There's the gun and you may take it or leave it."

Colonel Marquis turned the pistol over in his fingers. "You think, then," he said, "that somebody deliberately hid this in your room? You have probably observed that one bullet has been fired from it."

"I am not going to pretend to misunderstand when I understand perfectly well what you mean. Or what I think you mean. Yes. I thought of that too. But it's absolutely impossible. There were only two guns, a .32 and a .38; and this isn't either."

"Well... waiving that for a moment; you don't happen to know who owns this gun? You've never seen it before?"

"Of course I've seen it before—dozens of times. It belonged to father."

Page stared at this extraordinary witness who spoke with such contempt in amazement. But the Assistant Commissioner only nodded, with an appreciative smile.

"Ah, yes. Where did your father keep it?"

"In the drawer of his writing table at the pavilion."

"And when did you see it last, if you can remember?"

"I saw it yesterday afternoon, in the writing table drawer as usual."

"You will perceive, by the haste with which Inspector Page goes after his notebook," Marquis told her suavely, "that these discoveries are coming fast. Suppose, Miss Mortlake, we keep from going too fast, and get these things in order? First of all, naturally, I should like to convey my sympathies in the death of your father . . ."

"Thank you," she said.

"Can you give any reason, Miss Mortlake, why your father seems to have been disliked in his own house? Neither you nor your sister seems to show any great grief at his death."

"Whether I felt any grief or whether I didn't," said

Carolyn dispassionately, "I should not be inclined to discuss it with someone I had just met. But didn't you know? He is not our father, really. We were very young when he married our mother; but our real father is dead. I do not see that it matters, but you had better have the facts straight."

This was news both to Page and Marquis, who looked at each other. The Assistant Commissioner ignored the justifiable thrust in reply to his question.

"I have no intention, Miss Mortlake, of trying to trap you or hide things from you. Your father—we'll call him that—really was shot with the air pistol." He gave a very terse but very clever account of the affair, up to the point they had reached. "That," he added, "is why I need your help."

She had been staring at him, her face dark and rather terrible. But she spoke calmly enough. "So someone really was trying to throw suspicion on me?"

"It would seem so. Again, while it's *possible* that an outsider could have committed the crime, still you'll agree with me that it's very improbable. It would appear to be somebody in this house. Is there anybody here who has a grudge against you?"

"No, certainly not!"

"Tell me frankly, then: how did you get on with your father?"

"As well as people do in most families, I dare say." For the first time she looked troubled.

"You and your sister, I take it, are your father's heirs?"

She tried to force a hard smile. "The old problem of the will, eh?" she inquired, with a mocking ghastliness of waggery. "Yes, so far as I know we are. He made no secret of that. There are small legacies for the servants and a substantial one for Penney, but Ida and I inherit jointly. That's how it used to be, anyhow. He made a will when my mother died. Of course, he may have changed it since, but I don't think so."

Colonel Marquis nodded, and held up the air pistol. "This pistol, Miss Mortlake . . . you say your father kept it constantly by him?"

"Good Lord, no! I didn't say that. No; or he wouldn't have kept it at the pavilion. He kept it as a kind of curio. You see, a friend of his was in the Secret Service during the war, and made him a present of it; I believe those air guns are a rarity."

"Yes. What I meant was, he didn't keep the gun by him because he feared an attack?"

"No, I'm positive he didn't."

"What about the threats made by Gabriel White?"

"Oh, Gabriel—" she said. Her gestures seemed to sum up a great deal; then she considered. "Besides, until I saw Ida last night and read the newspapers this morning, I didn't know Gabriel *had* made any threats. Not that he would not have had reason to. My father knew Gabriel—or, at least he knew of him. I don't know how. He never spoke much about it. But he never troubled to conceal his belief that Gabriel was a swine."

"You liked White?"

"Yes. No. I don't know." She paused, and her square handsome face had an expression of cynicism so deep that it seemed to have been put there with a stamp. "My opinion! You flatter me, Colonel. I have been asked my opinion more times in the last ten minutes than I have been asked for it in the last ten months. I rather like Gabriel, to tell you the truth; and I think he's quite straight. But, my God, I hate lame ducks!"

"I see. Now, for the benefit of Inspector Page's notebook, how did you spend yesterday afternoon?"

"Ah, the alibi," murmured Carolyn, slightly showing

her teeth. "Well, let's see. The earlier part of the afternoon I spent interviewing a horde of prospective servants. Our maid—we boast only one—is leaving us next month to get married. Ah, romance! So we've got to replace her."

Inspector Page interposed.

"There seem to be a lot of things we haven't heard of, Miss Mortlake," he said. "You mean there were a number of outsiders here in the grounds yesterday afternoon?"

She studied him and at length decided to be civil. "You may set your mind and notebook at rest, Inspector," she informed him. "All of the lot were out of the house and out of the grounds at least two hours before my father was shot. Robinson at the gate can tell you that, if he overcomes his usual closed-mouth tactics. He let 'em in, and counted 'em, and let 'em out.

"The last of them left between half-past three and a quarter to four. I know that, because I was anxious to get out of the house myself. Then I discovered that Ida had gone out and taken the car. That was a bloody bore because I had been rather under the impression it was promised to me. But there it was. I could get a taxi, anyhow. First, however, I went down to the pavilion . . ."

"Why did you go to the pavilion, Miss Mortlake?"

She flushed a little. "I wanted some pocket money. Besides, I wanted to tell him, in a dutiful way, that I had engaged a new maid."

"Go on, please."

"He had only been at the pavilion five minutes or so when I got there; he went down about half-past three. You may be interested to know that I got the money. That, incidentally, is how I happen to know the air pistol was in the drawer of his writing table at that time. He opened the drawer to get his check book. It was too late for the bank, but I knew where I could get the check cashed. When he opened the drawer I saw the gun."

"Was the drawer locked or unlocked?"

She reflected, her hand shading her eyes. "It was locked. I remember: he got a bunch of keys out of his pocket and opened it."

"Did he lock it afterwards?"

"I'm not sure. I didn't notice—after I'd got the check. But I rather think he did. His precious manuscript was there."

"I see. Did he do or say anything notable that you remember?"

"Notable is good. No, not that I remember. He was a little short, because he doesn't like being interrupted when he's down there reciting chapters of his book to that dictaphone. He wrote down the name of the maid I was going to engage: he wanted to check her credentials before she came here next month. . .Oh, yes; and he mentioned that Sir Andrew Travers was coming there to tea. They were going to have tea at the pavilion. In the other room at the pavilion—the one across the hall from the study—he has an electric kettle and all the doings. I suggested that he'd better switch on the electric fire in the room across the hall or it would be freezing cold when Andrew got there."

"And did he switch it on?"

She was puzzled. "Yes. Or, rather, I did it for him."

"Inspector, when you and Sergeant Borden searched the pavilion, I suppose you looked into this other room across the hall? Was the electric fire burning in that room?"

Page saw an angry flush come into Carolyn Mortlake's face, but he checked her outburst.

"Yes, sir, the fire was on."

"Thank you," snapped Carolyn Mortlake.

"I don't think you quite understand the meaning of the last question," the Colonel told her calmly. "Now, will you go on with your story, please?"

"I left the pavilion, and the grounds; that was about a quarter to four."

"Yes; and afterward?"

She folded her hands in her lap with great nicety. Taking a deep breath, she lifted her head and looked him in the eye. Something had blazed and hardened, like the effect of a fire.

"I'm sorry," she said; "but that's where the story stops. That's all I have to say."

"I don't understand this," said Colonel Marquis sharply. "You mean you won't tell us what you did after you left the house?"

"Yes."

"But that's absurd. Don't be a young fool! Your gatekeeper himself told us you were going to a cocktail party at Golder's Green."

"He had no right to tell you any such thing," she flared. "You'll only waste your time inquiring after me at the Fischers'. I didn't go. I intended to go, but an hour or so before I left the house I got a telephone message which made me change my mind. That's all I can tell you."

"But why shouldn't you tell us?"

"In the first place, because you wouldn't believe me. In the second place, because I can't prove where I was during the afternoon, so it's no good as an alibi. In the third place—well, that's what I prefer to keep to myself. It's no good coming the high official over me. I've said I won't tell you, and I mean it."

"You realize, Miss Mortlake, that this puts you under suspicion for murder?"

"Yes."

Page felt that she was about to add something else; but at that moment all emotion, protest, or explanation was washed out of her. She became again a person of shuttered defiance. For someone had come into the room—they heard hesitant footsteps, and the faint clicking of the bead curtains at the door.

The newcomer was a little, deprecating man with a stoop and a nervously complaisant manner. They felt that it must be Alfred Penney, the clerk. Penney's feet were enormous and his hands seemed all knuckles. He had a few strands of iron-gray hair brushed across his skull like the skeleton of a fish, and something suspiciously like side whiskers. But he had a faithful eye, blinking at them while he dabbed his hand at it.

"I beg your pardon," he said, wheeling round quickly.

Carolyn Mortlake rose. "Alfred, this is Colonel Marquis, the Assistant Commissioner of Police, and Inspector Page. Tell them what you can. For the moment, I think they will excuse *me*."

While Penney blinked at them, his mouth a little open, she strode past out of the room. Then his face assumed his legal manner. "I really beg your pardon," he repeated. "I should not have intruded, but I saw Davies, the butler, in the hall intently listening to what was going on in here, and—no matter. You are the police? Yes; of course."

"Sit down, Mr. Penney," said Colonel Marquis.

"This is a terrible thing, gentlemen. Terrible," said Penney, balancing himself gingerly on the edge of a chair. "You cannot realize what a shock it has been to me. I have been associated with him for thirty years. Twenty-nine and a half, to be exact." His voice grew even more mild. "I trust you will not think me vindictive, gentlemen, if I ask you whether you have taken any steps with regard to this young hound who killed him?"

"Gabriel White?"

"If you prefer to call him that."

"So?" prompted Marquis, with a gleam of interest. He lifted his eyebrows. "It has been suggested, Mr. Penney, that 'Gabriel White' is nct the man's real name. The judge knew him?"

The little man nodded. "I am not ashamed to tell you," he replied, tilting up his chin, "that he did. If he condemned him, he dealt out moral justice; and moral justice was always Charles Mortlake's aim. Charles Mortlake knew the young man's father very well and has been acquainted with the young man since he was a boy. 'Gabriel White' is really Lord Edward Whiteford, a son of the Earl of Cray."

There was a pause, while Penney stared sideways at the fire. "Fortunately," he went on, knitting the baggy skin of his forehead, "the Earl of Cray does not know where his son is, or how he has sunk; and Charles Mortlake was not so inhumane as to enlighten him. . . . Gabriel White, since he prefers to call himself that, started in the world with every advantage. At Oxford he had a distinguished career. He was a leading member of the Union and great things were predicted for him. Also, he was a popular athlete. I believe he holds the university record for the broad jump; and he was also an expert swordsman and pistol shot. But, like so many who start with advantages —"

"Hold on," interrupted Marquis in a voice so sharp and official that Penney jumped a little. "I want to get this straight. You say he was an expert pistol shot? In my office this morning he told us that he had never handled a gun in his life."

"I am afraid he lied, then," Penney said without rancor. "Lying is a habit of his."

Marquis took the air pistol from the chair and held it up.

"Ever see this before?"

"Yes, sir. Often," said Penney, taken aback. "It belonged to Charles Mortlake. May I ask why—"

"When did you last see it?"

"A few days ago, I think; but I am afraid I cannot swear to the exact time. He kept it in the drawer of his writing table at the pavilion."

"Were you at the pavilion yesterday afternoon?"

"Yes, I was at the pavilion yesterday afternoon— for a very brief time. Five minutes, perhaps. Yesterday afternoon I was going to the Guildhall Library to verify a series of references for the book he was writing. I left the house at shortly after four o'clock—it had begun to rain, I may remark—and on my way down to the gate it occurred to me that I had better go to the pavilion and inquire whether there were any additional material he wished me to consult.

"I found him alone at the pavilion, speaking to the dictaphone." The clerk paused and something like the edge of a tear appeared in the corner of each eye. "He said there was nothing further he wished me to do at the library. So I left the grounds about ten minutes past four. It was the last time I ever saw him alive. But . . ."

"But?"

"I should have been warned," said Penney, fixing his questioner with grave attention. "There was somebody prowling round the pavilion even then. While we were speaking together, I distinctly heard footsteps approaching the windows."

"Which windows?"

"The west windows, sir. The windows whose locks and shutters are so rusted it is impossible to open them."

"Go on."

"Immediately after that, I was under the impression that I heard a sound of someone softly pulling or rattling at one of the west windows, as though trying to open it. But the rain was making some noise then, and I am not certain of this."

"The judge heard it as well?"

"Yes. I am afraid he regarded it as imagination. But only a few seconds afterward something struck the outer shutter of one of the *other* windows. I am under the impression that it was a pebble, or light stone of some kind, which had been thrown. This window was one of those in the south wall. . . . Judging from accounts I have heard," he turned mildly to Page, "it was the window through which you, Inspector, were obliged to climb nearly an hour and a half afterward. When Charles Mortlake heard this noise, he pushed back the curtains, pushed up the window, unlocked the shutters, and looked out. There was nothing to be seen."

"What did he do then?"

"He closed and relocked the window, although he did not relock the shutters. He left them open against the wall. He was . . . I fear he was somewhat annoyed. He accused me of entertaining fancies. There is a tree some dozen or so feet away from the window; and he declared that a twig or the like had probably come loose in the storm, and had blown against the shutter. It is true that there was a strong wind, but I could not credit this explanation."

"Do you know whether this air pistol was then in the table drawer?"

"I don't know; I should suppose so. He had no occasion to open the drawer. But my thoughts did not

go—well, quite to the edge of violence in that line."
His eyes did not fall before Marquis's steady stare; and
presently he went on: "You will wish to know what I
did afterward. I went from here, by Underground, to
Mansion House station, and thence to the Guildhall
Library on foot. I arrived there at four-thirty-five, since
I happened to notice the clock. I left the library at just
five o'clock. In coming home I experienced some delay
and did not arrive here until five-forty, when Charles
Mortlake was dead. I am afraid that is all I have to
say. . . . And now may I ask why are you concerned with
that air pistol?"

Again Colonel Marquis told the familiar story. As
he did so, Penney did not look startled; he only looked
witless. He remained sitting by the fire, a gnome with
veined hands, and he hardly seemed to breathe. Marquis
concluded:

"You see, we are compelled to accept White's innocence. Even if you argue that the air pistol was in the
table drawer and White might have used it himself, still
he would not have had the time to fire *three* shots. Next,
though he was seized by police officers instantly, the air
pistol had completely vanished; and he could not have
concealed it. Finally, he was at once taken to the police
station; so that he could not have conveyed the air pistol
to this house. But it was actually found here this
morning."

Penney said, "Good heaven!—" and somehow the
expletive seemed as weak and ineffectual as himself.
"But this is surely the most preposterous thing I have
heard of," he stammered. "I cannot imagine you are
serious. You are? But there is no reason in it! Life works
by reason and system. You cannot believe that there
were three prospective murderers shut up in that
room?"

At this point Penney had the impression that Marquis was playing with his witness; that he was juggling facts for his own amusement, or to show his skill; and that the colonel had an excellent idea of what really happened in the locked room. Marquis remained urbane.

"Will you argue theories, Mr. Penney? Not necessarily *three,* but certainly two. Has it occurred to you, for example, that the same person who fired the Browning may also have fired the Erckmann air pistol?"

"I do not know what has occurred to me," Penney retorted simply. He lifted up his arms and dropped them with an oddly flapping gesture. "I only know that, however my poor friend was killed, Lord Edward Whiteford—or Gabriel White, if you prefer—killed him. Sir, you do not know that young man. I do. It sounds exactly like him. He would, and he could, deceive the devil himself! I cannot tell you how strongly I feel about this, or how clever that young hound is. With him it is always the twisted way, the ingenious way."

"Still, you don't maintain he can perform miracles?"

"Apparent miracles, yes," Penney replied quite seriously. "You don't know his cleverness, I repeat; and you won't know it until he somehow hoodwinks and humiliates you as well. For instance, how did he get into the grounds at all?"

"He has already answered that himself. While Miss Ida Mortlake was getting a book at a lending library, he got into her car and crouched down under a rug in the tonneau. When she drove up to the garage, he waited until she had gone and then got out. The day was too dark for her to notice him."

At the doorway someone coughed. It was hardly a cough at all, so modest and self-effacing was the sound. They looked up to see the grizzled and heavy-faced Davies, the butler.

"May I say a word, sir?" he inquired.

"Eh?" said Colonel Marquis irritably. "All right: what is it?"

"Well, sir, under the circumstances I'll make no bones about saying I overheard what was being said. I mean about the man White, sir, and how he got in by hiding under the rug in Miss Ida's car. However he got into the grounds, it certainly wasn't that way. *He wasn't hiding in the back of the car* — and I can prove it!"

As Davies came into the room, his hands folded in front of him, Penney gave a mutter of petulant protest which changed to interest as soon as he appeared to understand what Davies was talking about. Beyond any doubt Davies looked competent; he was bulbous-nosed and bulbous-eyed, but he had a strong jaw.

"Yes, sir, I admit I listened," he said. "But I look at it like this. We're all shut up in here. Like a ship, as it were. It's to our advantage, servants most of all, to show we didn't have anything to do with killing the poor judge. If you see what I mean, sir. We've got to do it. Besides, it isn't as though I was a proper *butler*. I'm not even allowed to engage a maid, as a proper butler would. Fact is, sir, I was a court crier down on my luck (the drink did it, in Leeds) when the judge picked me up and gave me this job to make good. And I think I did make good, though all I ever knew about being a butler I got from the judge and out of a book. Now that he's dead, my lady friend and I are going to marry and settle down. But, just because he is dead, it doesn't mean we don't care who killed him and that we don't appreciate what he's done for us. So — I listened."

Penney almost sputtered. He acted as though a picture on the wall had suddenly made a face at him.

"You never acted like this before. You never talked like this before —"

"No, sir," said Davies. "But I never had occasion to talk like this before. The judge would've sacked me." He looked at Marquis steadily. "But I think I can do a bit of good."

Colonel Marquis was interested. "A court crier turned butler, eh?" he said, turning the idea over in his mind. "Been with the judge long?"

"Eleven years, sir."

"Benefit under the judge's will?"

"Yes, sir : five hundred pounds. He showed me the will. And I've got a bit saved as well."

"All right. Let's hear about this business of White, or Lord Edward Whiteford; and how he didn't get in here by hiding in Miss Mortlake's car, and how you knew about it."

Davies nodded, not relaxing his butleresque stance. "The thing is, sir, she went out in the car yesterday afternoon. It started to rain, and I knew she hadn't an umbrella with her. Now, the garage is twenty yards or so from the house. At near on half-past four—maybe twenty or twenty-five past—I saw her drive back. I was in the kitchen, looking out of the window, when I saw the car swing round the drive. So I got an umbrella and went out to the garage and held it over her coming back to the house so she shouldn't get wet."

"Yes; go on."

"Now, I was out to the garage before she'd even got out of the car. I did what you naturally do; as soon as Miss Ida got out, I opened the door of the back and looked to see whether she'd brought any parcels. There was nobody in the back of that car. And nobody could have nipped out before I looked in, because there was nowhere to go."

"Would it have been possible," Page asked, "for him to have slipped out of the car as it came through the gates, or somewhere on the drive before Miss Mortlake reached the garage?"

"I can't tell you that, sir. You'd better ask Robinson or Miss Ida. But if he *said* he didn't slip out until the car came to the garage —?"

Colonel Marquis did not comment. For a brief time he stared across the room. "Anything else?" he prompted.

"Yes, sir. A bit of exoneration," replied Davies promptly. "Even though I'm not a proper butler, still I feel responsible for the other servants. If you see what I mean. Now, sir, there's only three of us, excluding Robinson, of course, but then he rarely comes to the house. There used to be four, when the judge kept a chauffeur; but he let the chauffeur go and pensioned him handsome. At present, then, there's the cook, the maid, and me. Can I take it for granted that the judge was killed between, say, twenty minutes past five and twenty minutes to six?"

"You can," Colonel Marquis agreed, and glanced at Page. "Did you note, Inspector, the exact time to the minute or second when all the shots were being fired?"

Page nodded. "I looked at my watch as soon as I got into the pavilion and took the gun out of White's hand. It was half-past five, almost to the second."

"Thank you, sir," said Davies, with heartiness and almost with a smile. "Because all three of us, cook, maid and me, happened to be in the kitchen at that time. We were together until a quarter to six, as a matter of fact. I know that, because it's the time the evening post arrives, and I went to the door to see whether there were any letters. So we can produce a corporate alibi, if you see what I mean."

Marquis spoke musingly, his fingertips together and his cane propped against his leg. "By the way, we might check up on another part of White's story and see whether it tallies. He admits that he came here in order to kill the judge —"

"Ah," said Penney softly.

" — and thinking the judge was here in the house, he prowled round until he got through a side window. He says that at close to half-past five he was here in hiding, and heard you ask Miss Ida Mortlake whether tea should be served at last. Is that true?"

"So that's why the window was unfastened," muttered Davies, and pulled himself up. "Yes, sir: quite true. It was at twenty minutes past five. Just after I asked her that, I went out to the kitchen; that's how I know all the servants were together. She also told me she had telephoned the police about this man White — or whoever he is — and the cook was in a considerable flutter."

"There's something on your mind," Marquis said quietly. "Better speak up. What is it?"

For the first time Davies was showing signs of discomfort. He started to glance over his shoulder; but, evidently thinking that would be unbecoming, he assumed a stolid expression.

"Yes, sir, I know I've got to speak up. It's about Miss Carolyn. I think I can tell you where she went yesterday.

"As you heard, sir, the maid is leaving next month to get married. Yesterday Miss Carolyn was interviewing a lot of applicants. Now, it happens that the maid's got a cousin — a nice girl — and she was anxious for her cousin to get the place. But Miss Carolyn said sentiment has no business in a thing like that. Well, Millie Reilly (that's the maid) wasn't afraid of her cousin being beat out of it by casual applicants who might come here, but she was afraid the Agency might dig up somebody with references a yard long. And the Agency has been phoning here several times. So the long and short of it is,"

Davies squirmed a little but spoke in his best court voice, "that Millie's got into the habit of listening in to all the phone conversations, in case it should be the Agency. There's a phone extension upstairs."

Colonel Marquis leaned forward.

"Good," he said. "I was hoping we should come across something like that. Don't apologize for the delinquencies. Miss Mortlake told us that she intended to go to a cocktail party, but that she received a phone message which caused her to change her mind. Did Millie hear that message?"

"Yes, sir." Davies's discomfort had grown acute, and he fiddled with his cuffs; he spoke almost violently: "She listened. A man's voice said, 'If you want to know something that vitally concerns you and Ralph Stratfield, go to the stationer's shop at 66 Hastings Street, W.C.1, and ask for a letter written to you under the name of Carolyn Baer. Don't fail, or it may be the worse for you.'"

Colonel Marquis sat up and Page almost whistled. Unless there was a coincidence of names, here was again a crossing of the ways with the C.I.D. The Ralph Stratfield he knew was well known to Scotland Yard, although they had never been able to obtain a conviction and Stratfield swanked it in the West End with his thumb to his nose. Ralph Stratfield was a supergigolo who lived off women. Several times he had skirted the line of blackmail and once he had been brought to court for it. But he had been ably defended—by Sir Andrew Travers, Page now remembered—and had come off scot-free. Also, Page realized why Carolyn Mortlake might have been so determined to keep her mouth shut, even under bad risks.

The bead curtains were swept aside. Carolyn Mortlake came into the room with short, quick steps. Her face was sallow with rage and the eyes so dead that they looked like currants in dough. She stood trying to control her voice, but behind this shaking there was an inner emotion; and that inner emotion was shame.

"You may go, Davies," she said, calmly enough. "I will speak to you later. But I should advise you to begin packing at once. You will have to accept a month's wages in place of notice."

"Stay here, Davies," said Colonel Marquis.

He hoisted himself to his feet, supporting himself on his cane. He towered over her in the firelight.

"I'm afraid the police have first claim, Miss Mortlake," he went on, after an explosive pause. "You can't order the witnesses about like that, you know, when they have something to tell us. You are at liberty to discharge him, naturally; but I should be sorry to see you do it. He was only trying to protect you."

"You —," said the girl. It was an ugly word, and it had even more startling a quality in this sheltered Victorian room.

"Ralph Stratfield is poor company, Miss Mortlake."

"I think," she said with sudden politeness, "it is none of your damned business with whom I choose to go, or whom I see. Or is it?"

"Under the circumstances, yes. Look here, you know how you're feeling as well as I do. Now that it's said and done, there's no reason why it should not come out. All we care about is where you happened to be yesterday afternoon. Will it do any great harm to tell us whether you really went there?"

She had herself well in hand now. "I'm sure I don't know. I'm sure it won't do any particular good. You needn't preach about Ralph Stratfield: Ralph had nothing to do with that message. It was a fake. In other words, Mr. Clever, I was got out of the way by one of the oldest, most bewhiskered tricks ever used in shilling shockers. There is no such address as 66 Hastings Street. There is only one stationer's in the street and that wasn't the place. It took me quite a time to tumble to it, unfortunately, and it succeeded. For, you see, I can't prove where I was yesterday and I'm in exactly the same situation I was before. Why anyone should —"

She stopped, and for a moment Page had an uncomfortable feeling that this hardheaded, savage young lady was going to collapse in tears. She almost ran out of the room. Penney, muttering inarticulately, followed her. When they had gone the force of her emotion surcharged the room still. Davies made a feint of mopping his forehead.

"It's a good thing I've got a bit of money saved," he said.

"It would appear," mused Colonel Marquis, "that neither of Mr. Justice Mortlake's daughters selected the company he would have chosen for them. By the way, did you ever see Gabriel White?"

"No, sir. He never came here. The only time I ever saw him was yesterday afternoon, between two police officers. Mr. Penney says he's a lord?"

Marquis smiled with tight-lipped amusement. "No, my lad. No: you're not supposed to question me. I'm supposed to question you. And I dare say you've kept your ears and eyes open. Who do you think killed the judge?"

"The only thing I've got, I admit, is a germ of an idea, and it may not be worth much. But if I were you, sir, I should keep a sharp eye out for Sir Andrew Travers."

"So? You think he's the murderer?"

"N-no, no, I don't mean that, exactly." Davies seemed a trifle hurried, and he was certainly not anxious to commit himself. "I only said, keep a sharp eye out. From what I heard it struck me that there's one thing that doesn't seem to fit anywhere. It's this: it's one of them shots, *and* Sir Andrew's gun. That's what's throwing you all skew-wiff. It's that one shot, from the Browning automatic, which won't fit in anywhere no matter how you explain the case. It's a kind of excrescence, if I've got the right word. Incidentally, sir, everybody seems all hot and bothered about one thing which seems fairly simple to me."

"I'm glad to hear it. What is that?"

"Well, you're wondering what happened to the bullet out of the Browning. Everything seems to have vanished, and that bullet vanished with it. But common sense must tell you where it went."

"Yes?"

"It went out the window," returned Davies promptly. "You didn't find it in the room and it can't have melted or anything. After the judge had opened the window, he turned back to see White, and White shot at him, and then everybody started firing all over the room. But the window was up a little way — with the Inspector here running toward it."

Colonel Marquis seemed genuinely delighted. He rubbed his hands, he jabbed the ferrule of his cane against the floor; and at length he consulted Page.

"What do you think of that suggestion, Inspector? Is it possible?"

Page felt a retrospective shiver. "*If* it happened," he said, "all I've got to say is, it's a wonder I'm not a dead man now. I don't see how it could have missed me. And as I told you, when I heard that shot I wasn't ten steps away from the window. Of course, it may have gone in a diagonal line. It probably did, being fired from the corner where the vase stands. But it's odd that I didn't hear it, or any sound to indicate it, if it came so close to me as that. I didn't notice anything."

Somewhere in the depths of the house a doorbell began to ring. It was a discreet, muffled doorbell, like the house and like the judge. When he heard it, Davies's big body stiffened back into its official posture, as though by an effect of magic or plaster of Paris. Though he had been about to speak, he went gravely to answer the bell. And then Sergeant Borden burst into the room.

"Robinson told me you were here, sir," he said. "I wish you would come down to the pavilion. I've found something that changes the whole case."

"Well?"

"First, there's some footprints. Pretty good footprints. But that's not the main thing. I've found a bullet fired from a .32 automatic, and probably the Browning."

"Where did you find it, Sergeant?" asked Colonel Marquis.

"Stuck in a tree some distance away from the window where you"—he nodded toward Page—"climbed through, sir." After a pause (while Davies, in the background, grinned broadly) Borden continued: "But some of the footprints don't make sense either, sir. It looks as though the murderer must have got in and out through one of the west windows—the ones that are so locked and rusted that you can't open them even now."

They walked down to the pavilion, taking a branch of the gravel path which led them to the back of it. Though the rain had cleared, the sky was still gray and heavy-looking, and what wet foliage still remained clinging to the trees hung down dispirited.

Rounding the side of the pavilion, they came on Robinson, in a cap and a big sou'wester, morosely regarding the ground. Under the west window nearest the northern end—just inside was the vase in which the Browning had been found—a few wooden boxes had been upended in a line to protect the exhibits from rain. Borden lifted the boxes almost reverently. Along the side of the wall ran what in summer must have been a flower bed, terminating in a brick border below the window. The flower bed was a big one, running out ten feet from the window. Five footprints were visible in the uneven soil, though they were so churned and blurred by the rain that they could be distinguished as little more than outlines of feet. But the toes were all pointing away from the pavilion, and all were made by the same pair of shoes.

Borden snapped on a flashlight, following the ragged line across the ten-foot expanse of flower bed, and Colonel Marquis studied it.

"Were those tracks here yesterday afternoon, sergeant?"

The sergeant hesitated and looked at Page, who undertook the responsibility. "I don't know, sir," Page answered. "I imagine they must have been, but we didn't go outside the pavilion once we found it was locked up from the inside. It's another oversight, but there it is. Anyhow, it seems to corroborate one thing Penney said, if you remember. He said that when he was talking to the judge yesterday a few minutes past four, he heard somebody prowling round the house; also, that he thought he heard the prowler testing the shutters on one of the west windows." Then Page stopped and looked at the tracks. "Hold on, though! That won't do. Because—"

"Exactly," said Marquis, with dry politeness. "Every one of these tracks comes *away* from the window, as though somebody got out the window and slogged back. Well, how did the prowler get *to* the window?"

He turned round almost savagely. "Let's understand things. Inspector, are you certain beyond any doubt that those windows haven't been tampered with?"

"Beyond any doubt," said Page, and Borden agreed with him.

"Robinson, do you agree with that?"

"I do," said the man. He pondered. "Here! Point o' fact, there was trouble about those same windows only a few days ago. Miss Ida, she wanted the judge to get new frames put in 'em, because the old ones are bad and that's why the shutters have to be kept up. She said it was sense, because then the judge could have light instead of being in the half-dark all the time. I was going to do it, but the judge wouldn't hear of it."

In the gloom Page could see that a slight transformation had gone over the Assistant Commissioner's face: an expression as though he were blinking, or making a face—or seeing light. He turned away, poking at the ground with his cane. When he turned back again, he was calm and almost brisk.

"Put your light on those tracks again," he ordered. "What do you make of them, Inspector?"

"It's a big shoe," said Page. "A number ten at the smallest. The trouble is that you can't make any clear estimate about the weight of the man who wore it, because the tracks are flooded and there's no indication of what their depth was."

"Does anyone we know wear a number ten?"

"White doesn't: I can tell you that. He's tall, but he doesn't wear more than a number seven or eight."

"Very well. For the moment . . . what other exhibits have you to show us, sergeant?"

"Round to the front, sir," said Borden. "There's that bullet in the tree; and to round it off, there's more footprints. And a woman's this time."

Colonel Marquis did not seem so surprised as Page would have expected. "Ah, I rather thought we should come to that," he remarked, with almost a comfortable air.

The front of the pavilion was unchanged, except that now the shutters on both windows of the study were folded back against the wall. Page tried to visualize the scene as it had been yesterday. But he was astonished at the tree to which Borden led them. This was a thick-waisted elm some fifteen feet away from the window in a direct line. Page remembered the tree well enough. When he had been running for the window, he had passed that tree so closely as to brush it; and retracing every step in his mind, he realized that he had been passing the tree at just about the time the second shot had been fired.

Sergeant Borden pointed with a pardonable air of triumph and directed the beam of his flashlight at the bole of the tree. "Now look sharp, sir — some little distance up. If you reach up you can touch it. That makes about the right height if it came out through the window. That's a bullet hole, and it's pretty sure to be a .32 Browning bullet embedded in there."

Colonel Marquis studied the crumbled and sodden little hole, and then looked back towards the window. "Dig it out," he said.

When Borden's penknife had produced another lead pellet, not quite so flattened by the soft wood in which it had been buried, it was passed from hand to hand and weighed. Page now had no doubt. "Subject to examination," he said cautiously, "I'd say that's certainly the .32 Browning bullet. But," he added with some explosiveness, "how in the name of God —?"

"You have doubts? H'm, yes," grinned the Colonel. "But wait until we have finished. Borden, as soon as you've shown us the footprints, get on the phone to the Yard and have the photographer out here. I want photographs and measurements of that bullet hole. You see the queer thing about it? The bullet went in an almost direct line."

"Photographer's coming, sir," Borden told him. "And here are the other footprints." Moving his companions back a little, Borden threw his light to indicate a spot some distance behind and to the right of the tree as you faced the pavilion. The grass under the tree was soft and sparse, well protected by the branches above. Impressed in the soil was the clear print of a woman's shoe, narrow, pointed, and high-heeled. It was the right shoe, a smudged toe print of the left one being about six inches away from it. It looked as though someone had been hiding behind the tree and peering round it. But — the moment Page saw that print — his skepticism increased to complete unbelief.

"We'd better go easy, sir," he said calmly. "This thing's fake."

Sergeant Borden made a protesting noise, but Marquis regarded him with bright and steady eyes of interest.

"Exactly what do you mean by that, Inspector?"

"I mean that somebody's been manufacturing evidence since yesterday afternoon. I'll take my oath there was nobody standing behind that tree. I know, because I passed within a couple of inches of it, and I should have seen anybody in that whole vicinity." He knelt beside the two prints and studied them. "Besides, take a look at the marks. (Got a tape measure, Borden?) They're much too deep. If a woman made that right-hand one, the woman must have been an Amazon or a fat lady out of a circus; whoever made those prints weighed twelve or thirteen stone. Or else — "

Marquis, who had been beating his hands together softly and peering round him, nodded. "Yes; I don't think there's much doubt of that. The person who made the marks was either a man, or else a woman who stamped violently on the ground with the right foot in order to leave a sharp, unmistakable impression. . . . It's manufactured evidence, right enough. So, I am inclined to think, are those other number-ten footprints on the far side of the pavilion. We were intended to find both sets of prints. But there's one thing which doesn't seem to fit in. What about the .32 bullet in the tree? Is that manufactured evidence too? — and if so, why?"

Page contemplated Old Man River, wondering whether this was a catechism or whether Old Man River really did not know the answer.

"I'll admit it, sir," he said, "that Davies's deductions seem to have been right. He said we'd find a bullet outside somewhere and here it is. But it's very fishy all the same. I was passing that tree when the shot was fired. How is it I didn't hear anything: the vibration of it or the sound of the bullet hitting the tree? It *might* have been done without my knowing it. It's possible. But there's one thing that's not possible at all. . . ."

"The line of the bullet?"

"The line of the bullet. As you say, it's gone into the tree on a dead straight line from that window. Well, the Browning was fired from the far corner of the room. As we stand here facing the pavilion, that corner is on our left. In order to get into the tree in this position, that bullet must have curved in the air like a boomerang — a kind of parabola, or whatever they call it. Which is nonsense."

"Yes," said Colonel Marquis. "Into the pavilion, now."

They tramped in during a gloomy silence. Page

switched up the lights in the little central hall, and opened the door of the study on the left. Nothing had been altered. The big room smelt close and stuffy. When Page touched another switch, a flood of light poured down from the dragon lamp hanging above the judge's writing table. It was true that little could be seen beyond the immediate neighborhood of the table; the opaque sides of the lamp gave it the effect of a spotlight, and the room became a masked shadow of bookshelves from which the big yellow vases gleamed faintly.

First Colonel Marquis went across to the west windows and satisfied himself that these were impregnable. "Yes," he growled. "Unless the murderer made himself as thin as a picture postcard, he didn't go out there. Also, this room is genuinely dark. We'll try a little experiment. I was careful to bring this along." With sour suavity he produced Sir Andrew Travers's Browning from his coat pocket. "But before we do . . ."

He juggled the pistol in one hand, his eye measuring distances. He then walked slowly round the room, examining each window. At the writing table he paused, and the other two followed him there.

The drawer of the writing table was unlocked. He pulled it out, exposing neat sheets of typewritten manuscript. On top of them lay a memorandum pad and a check book on the Whitehall Bank. On the memorandum pad were a few lines of small, precise handwriting :

Sara Samuels
36d, Hare Road, Putney

Refs.: Lady Emma Markleton, "Flowerdene," 18, Sheffield Terrace, Kensington, W. 8. (Have Penney write).
ox

"The new maid and her references," said Colonel Marquis. "Not much there. As a last hope let's try our reconstruction."

He limped across the room to the corner by the yellow vase in the far corner, and again he juggled Sir Andrew Travers's Browning.

"I am going to stand here and fire a shot in the general direction of where the judge was standing. Afterward I will drop the pistol into the vase. Inspector, you will represent White. Stand where White was standing, about the middle of the room. When you hear the shot, whirl around—and tell me whether you can see me."

Page took up his position. He had expected the shot immediately, but no shot came. Colonel Marquis was playing for time so as to take him off guard; so much he realized while he waited.

The shot was so loud that it seemed to make the room shake like a cabin at sea. Startled in spite of himself, he swung round against the vibrations. He had been looking at the brilliant beam of light from the dragon lamp, and he was a quarter blind when he stared into the corner. He could see absolutely nothing, for the darkness appeared to have speckles in it; but he heard a faint noise as of someone putting an umbrella into a porcelain umbrella stand.

"Well, can you see me?" rumbled a drawling voice out of the darkness.

Page's eyes were growing accustomed to the dark. "No, sir," he answered. "By this time I can only see a kind of shadow along the vase."

Colonel Marquis limped forward, twirling the pistol with his finger through the trigger guard. He put out a long arm and pointed. "You observe, Inspector, that the bullet did not go out of the window."

A much-annoyed Sergeant Borden was already examining the fresh scar. In the yellow-papered wall between the south windows there were now two bullet holes. The bullet fired by Colonel Marquis was close to the left-hand window, it is true; but it had come within a foot of going out the open space.

"Yes, but if it didn't go there," insisted Borden doggedly, "now, I ask you, sir, where did the other one go? I'm fair sick of bullets. It's raining bullets. And there's no sense in any of 'em."

At half-past five that afternoon Inspector Page emerged from the Underground at Westminster Station and tramped wearily up the Embankment to New Scotland Yard. He had made undeniable progress; his notebook contained evidence of both acquittal and accusation. But he had got no lunch and no beer.

Not more than a popgun's shot away from Scotland Yard there is a public house, tucked away in such fashion that it is not generally noticed; and, in fact, there is a pretense that it does not exist at all. But it is much patronized by members of the Force. Pushing up through the chilly dampness which was bringing fog off the river, Page found that the pub had just opened its doors. He did not go into the public bar. Moving on to a private room, where a bright fire burned, he was surprised to find it occupied. A figure sat with its long legs stretched out to the fire, showing a head with sparse white hair over the back of the chair, a pint tankard in a speckled hand, and a cloud of cigarette smoke over all. Then the figure craned round, revealing the grinning face of Colonel Marquis.

Now this was unheard-of. If Assistant Commissioners go into pubs, they do not go into pubs patronized by their subordinates; and it would cause surprise to see them drinking with anybody less than a chief inspector. But Colonel Marquis enjoyed above all things to break rules.

"Ah, Inspector," he said. "Come in. Yes, it is the old man in the flesh; don't stare. I had been rather expecting you." He took charge of matters. "Beer," he went on. "And take a long pull before you start to talk." When the beer was brought, he smoked thoughtfully while Page attacked it. "Now then. What luck?"

"Aaah," said Page, relaxing. "I don't know about luck, but there have certainly been plenty of developments. The case has gone pfft."

"What the devil do you mean, 'pfft'?" inquired Marquis with austerity. "Kindly stop making strange noises and answer my question. It is a regrettable thing if an inspector of Metropolitan Police —"

"Sorry, sir. I mean that two of our calculations have been upset. The person who looked most suspicious, and didn't have an alibi, is pretty well exonerated entirely. The person we regarded as being more or less above suspicion is — well, not above suspicion now."

Marquis opened his eyes. "H'm. I'm not surprised. Who is exonerated?"

"Carolyn Mortlake," Page answered wearily. "I wish she hadn't given us all that trouble. Maybe she doesn't know it herself, but she's got a cast-iron alibi. . . . She really did go to Hastings Street. I went there myself this afternoon to see whether I could pick up any trace of her. I was equipped with a photograph. There's no stationer's at Number 66, but there is a news agent's at Number 32: which is the closest anybody could find to it. And she tried that as a last resort. The woman who keeps the shop had noticed a woman prowling up and down the street, looking at numbers and acting queerly. Finally this stranger made a dash, came into the news agent's, and asked for a letter in the name of Carolyn Baer. I got out my photograph. There's no doubt of it; the proprietress of the shop identifies her as Carolyn Mortlake.... There was no letter, of course. The thing was a trumped-up job. But she was in that shop at twenty minutes past five yesterday, a shop in Bloomsbury. Not even if she had flown or used seven-leagued boots could she have got to Hampstead by five-thirty. And she's out of it."

Colonel Marquis drew a deep breath. For a brief time he remained staring at the fire, and then he nodded. "It clears the air, anyhow," he said. "What's next? If one person is exonerated, who's the one to go back under suspicion?"

"Sir Andrew Travers."

"Good God!" said Marquis.

He had clearly not expected this. He got up out of his chair and limped up and down the room with angry bumps of his cane.

"I see, sir," remarked Page, with a broad smile. "I'll lay you a small bet. I'll bet you thought I was going to say Miss Ida Mortlake."

"Shrewd lad," said Marquis, looking at him. "You're not a fool, then?"

"Not altogether," said Page, considering this. "I know you've been thinking that I've rather too pointedly overlooked her. You'll adduce evidence — of contradictory times. White says she was in the house, talking to the butler, at close on five-thirty; just before White himself rushed down to the pavilion. Result: alibi. Davies says she was talking to him at twenty minutes past five, and after that Davies left her. Result: no alibi."

"Yes, I'd thought of it," agreed the other shortly. "Waiter! More beer!"

"You could even say that there seems to be a woman's touch about this crime. And it's certain there was a strong effort to throw suspicion on Carolyn Mortlake. But my early opinion of Ida holds. And I'll tell you something more," continued Page with fierce earnestness, and tapped the table. "The brain behind this business is a man's."

"I agree, yes. But go on about Travers. Why is he back under suspicion?"

"Maybe that's too strong a statement. Sir Andrew stated that he was in his chambers all yesterday afternoon; and that there is no way out of the chambers except through the clerk's room. . . . Well, sir, that's a plain, flat, thundering lie. There is another way out. There's a fire escape at the back of the building and it runs past the window of Travers's study. Sir Andrew Travers could have gone down that. I don't say he *did,* you understand."

"H'm," said Marquis. He sat down again and eyed the overmantel dreamily. "There is a hive of offices thereabouts," he added. "Somehow, I can't help feeling that the spectacle of a portly and dignified barrister in a top hat climbing down a fire escape in the middle of the afternoon would be bound to excite some comment, not to say mirth. Damn it, Page, the picture is all wrong. In this case Sir Andrew Travers is like Sir Andrew Travers's own pistol: he's an excrescence. How does he fit in? Where is his motive for murdering his friend? How could he have got inside the grounds of the house under Robinson's watchful eye? No, I don't see that stately top hat involved in any such business as this."

"I thought you had some idea of the truth, sir?" Page suggested. He was not quite without malice in saying it, and he stung Marquis.

"You are quite right, young man. I know the murderer and I know how the crime was committed. But I need facts and I need proof; in addition to which, I have sufficient humility to think I may be wrong, though the possibility is so slight that it needn't bother us. H'm. Let's have facts. Did you dig up anything more today?"

"No more that concerns alibis. For instance, there's Davies." He looked sharply at the other, but Colonel Marquis was very bland. "His alibi—the story that he was in the kitchen with the cook and the maid between twenty minutes past five and a quarter to six—is more or less substantiated. I say 'more or less' because the cook says he was down in the cellar, fetching beer, for some three minutes round about five-thirty. The question is whether he would have had time to nip down to the pavilion, vanish and nip back again.

"There's only one other person associated with the case—old Alfred Penney. He hasn't got an alibi, in the sense that it's impossible to check it. He says he left the Guildhall Library at five o'clock and came home by Underground; but due to missing trains at a couple of changes and being held up generally, he didn't arrive home until five-forty. The last man in the world whose movements you can ever prove is someone traveling by Underground. Personally, I think he's telling the truth."

Page closed his notebook with a snap. "And that's the lot, sir," he concluded. "That's *everybody* connected with the case. It's got to be one of those. I have two pieces of evidence which round out my report, and I'll repeat them if you like; but they only go to show how narrow the circle has become."

"We'd better have everything."

"Yes, sir. I tried to find out who had faked those number ten shoeprints and also the woman's tracks. I had no difficulty getting permission to go through any wardrobe in the house I liked. That print of a woman's right slipper was a number four. Both Ida and Carolyn wear number fours. But there was no sign of mud on any of the shoes in the house, aside from the ordinary rain splashes you'd get walking about in the street. That's point number one. Point number two concerns the men's shoes. Only one person in that house wears number tens—"

"Who's that?" demanded Colonel Marquis sharply.

"Penney."

From the other's expression, Page could not tell whether he was stimulated or disappointed; but there was undoubtedly a reaction of some kind. He sat forward in the firelight, snapping his long fingers, and his eyes were shining. But since he did not comment, Page went on:

"Penney owns two pairs of shoes; no more. That's established. There's a brown pair and a black pair. The black pair he wore yesterday, and were wet. But neither pair had any mudstains; and mud is devilish difficult to clear off completely so that you leave *no* traces."

He stopped, because he noticed that the waiter who had served them was now poking his head cautiously round the door of the room and looking mysterious. The waiter approached.

"Excuse me," he said, "but are you Colonel Marquis? Yes. I think," he added in the manner of one making a decision, "you're wanted on the telephone."

The Assistant Commissioner got up sharply and Page observed that for the first time he looked uneasy. "All right," he said, and added to Page: "Look here, this is bad. Only my secretary knows where I am. I told him he wasn't to get in touch with me unless. . .you'd better come along, Inspector."

The telephone was in a narrow hallway, smelling of

old wood and beer, at the back of the house. A crooked light hung over it; Page could see the expression on his superior's face and the same uneasiness began to pluck at his own nerves. A heavy voice popped out of the telephone receiver, speaking so loudly and squeakily that Colonel Marquis had to hold the receiver away from his ear. Page heard every word. It was a man's voice and the man was badly rattled.

"Is that you?" said the voice. "Andrew Travers speaking." It cleared its throat, wavered, and became loud again. "I'm at Mortlake's place," the voice added.

"Anything wrong?"

"Yes. Do you know anything about a girl—named Sara Samuels, I think—who's just been engaged as a maid here, and who was to come next month to replace Millie Reilly? You do. Well, you know she was in the grounds here yesterday afternoon and was the last of the maid contingent to leave. She phoned here about an hour ago. She asked to speak to Carolyn; she said she had something vitally important to tell her, and was afraid to tell it to anybody else; Carolyn engaged her, you see, and she doesn't seem to trust anybody else. But Carolyn's out, seeing to the funeral arrangements. I said I was the—legal representative. I asked whether she couldn't tell me. She hemm'd and haw'd, but finally she said she would come round to the house as soon as she could."

"Well?"

Now Page could imagine Sir Andrew Travers's large white face, its chin showing more blue against the pallor, almost shouting to the telephone. "She never got to the house, Marquis," he said. "She's lying out in the driveway here, dead, with the knife out of a carving set run through her back."

Very slowly Colonel Marquis replaced the receiver,

contemplated the telephone, and turned away. "I might have expected that," he said. "My God, Inspector, I might have foreseen it. But I never saw the explanation of one thing until just that second when Travers spoke. . . . Evidently someone at Mortlake's was listening in on that telephone extension again."

"You mean she was killed to shut her mouth about something?" Page rubbed his forehead. "But I don't understand what it was she could have seen or heard. Even if she stayed a bit behind the others and went out after them, she must have gone before four o'clock. At that time the judge was alive and well."

His companion did not seem to hear him. Colonel Marquis had almost reached a point of biting his nails. "But that's not what is bothering me, Inspector. I might have assumed the murderer would have killed Sara Samuels. But in that way? No, no. That was a bad blunder, a fatal blunder. You can see that I've got my evidence now; one more thing to do and I can make an arrest. Yes, I can't understand why the murderer killed her in that particular way, and inside the grounds of the place; unless it was blind panic, of course, or unless —"

He swept his worry aside; he became brisk.

"You are in charge, Inspector. Hop into a squad car and get out there as fast as you can. Carry the usual routine until I get there. I'll follow in a very short time. I am going to bring two people along with me when I follow you. Both are very important witnesses. One is — you will see. But the other is Gabriel White."

Page stared at him. "I suppose you know what you're doing, sir. Do you think Gabriel White was guilty after all?"

"No. White didn't kill the judge. And it isn't likely he killed the Samuels girl while he was sitting under our eye at Scotland Yard. But he will be very useful in the reconstruction," said Colonel Marquis, with slow and terrifying pleasantry, "when I demonstrate, in about an hour's time, *how the murderer got out of the locked room!*"

The lights of the Scotland Yard car were turned almost diagonally across the drive in the darkness. Ahead the broad gravel driveway curved up a slight incline towards the house; there were elm trees on either side, and due to the ornamental curves of the drive, this point was visible neither from the house nor from the lodge gates. Outlines were still more blurred by a smoky white vapor, not light enough to be called mist or thick enough to be called fog, which clung to the ground like a facecloth and moved in gentle billows.

In the front of the police car Page stood up and looked over the windshield. The headlights played directly across on a body lying some two or three feet off the drive to the left, near the base of an elm. It was that of a woman, lying partly on her back and partly on her right side.

Page got out of the car, taking his flashlight. There were other figures, shrinking or motionless, drawn some distance away from the body. Sir Andrew Travers was there; hatless, and with the collar of his blue overcoat drawn up, he looked somewhat less impressive. Ida Mortlake was there, looking round the edge of a tree. Finally, Robinson the gatekeeper stood guard like a gnome in a sou'wester, holding a lantern.

The dead woman lay on a carpet of fallen leaves which, Page realized, would make it impossible to trace any footprints. By the condition of the leaves it was clear that she had been struck down in the driveway and then had been dragged over to where she lay. Without moving the body, he could see by stooping down the handle of the knife protruding from her back just under the left shoulder blade. His light showed that it was an ordinary carving knife, such as may be seen on any dinner table, with a black bone handle of fluted design. There was a good deal of blood.

She was a woman in the late twenties, short, rather plump, and quietly dressed. No good idea could be gained of the face under the tipsy hat, for the face was grimy with mud and cut with gravel. When the murderer took her from behind, she had evidently been flung forward on her face in the drive; and afterward she had been turned on her back and dragged to where she lay.

Page's light roamed round the spot, in and out of the trees, and across in the direction of the pavilion. "Damn," he said; and focused the beam. Some three or four feet away from the body there lay in the leaves a heavy hammer.

"Right," said Page, straightening up toward the police car. "Crosby, photographs first. Laine, fingerprints. The rest of you over here a little way, please. Who found the body?"

Robinson, defiantly, held up the lantern so as to illumine his swollen-veined face and telescopic neck.

"Me," he said. " 'Bout half an hour ago. Maybe. I dunno. Sir Andrew," he nodded, "phoned down and said to expect a woman name of Samuels, and to let her in. She got here and I did. When she went up the drive, I stuck my head out the door of the lodge and looked up after her. I couldn't see her, becos the drive turns so much. Like it is here. I was going to shut the door, but I heard a queer sort of noise."

"What sort of noise? A cry? A scream?"

Robinson jumped a little. "I dunno. More like a gurgle. Only loud. I didn't like it, but there wasn't nothing else to do. I got my lantern and started running up the drive. Just as I turned round the corner—right here—I see something like someone dropping something and running away. I didn't see much. Kind of a rustle, like, and something like a coat. It run away in the trees. It dropped something. If you want to know what I think it dropped, it was that." He pointed unsteadily towards the hammer lying among the leaves. "I'd got a bit of an idea that someone turned the poor damn woman over on her back and was going to bash in 'er face with that hammer. Only I got here too quick. Then I hopped it up to the house and told Sir Andrew."

At this point Page became conscious that the group was growing; that other people were silently drawn to the magnet of a dead body and the dull lights. A rich, husky, old-port voice, the voice of Davies, spoke up.

"If you'll let me get a better look, sir," said Davies grimly, "I think I can identify both the knife and the hammer. I think that's the carving knife out of the ordinary set in our dining room. The hammer looks like one that's kept at a workbench in the cellar."

"Sir Andrew Travers—?" said Page.

Travers, though a trifle hoarse, was master of himself again, as his courtroom manner showed. "At your service, Inspector," he intoned, in a vein of attentive irony.

"Were you here at the house all afternoon, Sir Andrew?" Page asked.

"All afternoon, since about three o'clock. I believe I reached here just as you, Inspector, were leaving. When Robinson brought the news to the house, I was playing backgammon with Miss Mortlake here. We have been in each other's company all afternoon. That's true, isn't it, Ida?"

Ida Mortlake opened her mouth and shut it again. "Yes, of course," she answered. "Why, certainly it's true.

They don't think any differently, do they, Andrew? Oh this is *horrible!* Mr. Page —?"

"Just a moment, miss," said Page, and swung round as he heard a step on gravel. "Who's there?"

Out of the dimness of flickering lights swam the white, square pale face of Carolyn Mortlake; and it had a startled expression which vanished instantly. What caused that startled expression Page could not see, but it became again the old cynical mockery which could not quite keep back fear. She cradled her arms in her sleeves and jeered.

"It's only the black sheep," she said. "Only the poor so-and-so, I mean, who runs around with blackmailers, turning up again like a bad pen —" She stopped. "I say, that reminds me. Where is Penney?"

"Mr. Penney's at the pavilion," Ida replied. "He went there an hour or so ago to straighten up some of father's papers."

Page interposed, "You say Mr. Penney is still at the pavilion? Hasn't anyone told him?"

"I'm afraid not," said Ida. "I-I'm afraid I never thought of it. And he probably hadn't heard anything."

"Look out!" cried Carolyn Mortlake suddenly.

With a roar, a flourish and a glare of headlamps, another police car had swung through the lodge gates a little way down the slope, and it came bucketing round the curve toward them in a way that made Page jump back. When it was almost on the group, the driver jammed on his brakes as though at a signal. The black bulk ground to a dead stop. Then, behind a faintly luminous windshield in the front seat, a tall figure rose with great politeness and lifted its hat.

"Good evening, ladies and gentlemen," said Colonel Marquis, like a B.B.C. announcer.

There was a silence. Page was well enough acquainted with his chief to be aware of the latter's deplorable fondness for flourish and gesture. Yet, as Colonel Marquis leaned his elbows on the windshield and peered out over the group with an air of refreshed interest, there was a curious grimness of certainty about him. In the rear of the car Page could see that three persons were sitting, but he could not tell who they were.

"Most of you are here, I notice," Colonel Marquis went on. "Good! I should be obliged if you would all come over to the pavilion with me. Yes, all of you. I have one other guest to increase our number. He calls himself Gabriel White, though some of you know him under another name." He made a gesture. One of the dark figures in the back of the car stirred and climbed out. In the group before the headlights there was silence; Page could read no expressions. But Gabriel White himself seemed drawn and nervous.

They walked in a sort of Indian file to the pavilion, choosing the path so they might not interfere with any traces round the body. All of them were aware that this was the end, although few of them knew what end.

The pavilion was illuminated in all its rooms, the curtains drawn across the windows. When that tramping procession went down to the study a somewhat frightened Mr. Alfred Penney — with a pair of spectacles down his nose — started up from behind the judge's desk.

"Join the group, Mr. Penney," said Colonel Marquis. "You will be interested in this."

Again from various pockets he produced his arsenal of three pistols and arranged them in a line on the writing table, from which Penney had moved back. Page noticed the positions of the various people. Ida Mortlake stood very far back from the table, in shadow, with Travers beside her. Carolyn Mortlake, her arms folded with a swaggering gesture, leaned against the east wall. Davies, imperturbable, but clearly enjoying this, was at Colonel Marquis's elbow as though to anticipate any want. Penney hovered in the background. The defiant Robinson (still refusing to remove his cap) was by the window. Gabriel White—who suddenly seemed on the verge of crumbling to pieces—stood in the middle of the room with his hands in his pockets.

And Colonel Marquis took up a position behind the table under the lamp, smiling at them, with the three pistols ranged before him. "At this moment, ladies and gentlemen, Sergeant Borden is showing the body of Sara Samuels to someone who may make a strange identification. But in the meantime, in order to round out my evidence, I should like to ask two questions . . . of Miss Ida Mortlake."

Ida took a step forward, more vigorous than Page had ever seen her. Her lovely face had little color; but it looked much less soft. "Whatever you wish to know," she said.

"Good! At the beginning of this investigation, Miss Mortlake, we heard that there were two keys to the tradesmen's entrance in the wall round these grounds. Robinson had one, you, in your nominal capacity as housekeeper, had the other. They were of value only yesterday afternoon. when you asked for that gate to be locked. Robinson locked the gate with his key. Where was, and is, yours?"

She looked at him calmly. "It was in the drawer of the butler's pantry, along with the other keys. And it's still there."

"But—a corollary to the first question—the key

could be taken out, a copy made, and put back again, without anyone being the wiser?"

"Well . . . yes, I should think so. It was never used. But why?"

"Good. My last question, then. Today our friend Robinson told us a significant thing. He said that a short time ago a great rumpus was being cut up about these west windows in here: the ones with the loose frames, on which the judge kept the shutters closed at all times. He said that you suggested getting new frames put into the windows, so that there could be more light in the room. I want you to think carefully before you answer. Was what Robinson said true?"

Her eyes widened. "Well . . . yes, in a way. That is, I was the one who actually *spoke* about it to Father. But he wouldn't hear of it; there was a most awful argument, and I let it drop. But it wasn't my idea, really."

"Then who suggested it to you? Can you remember?"

"Yes, of course. It—"

There was a clumping of feet outside in the hall and the door opened. Sergeant Borden appeared, saluting, his shining face well satisfied. "All set, sir," he reported. "It took a few minutes longer than we thought, because this Samuels girl's face was dirty and we had to wash it before the lady could be sure. But here she is and she's ready to testify any time you like."

He stood aside, to show a flustered, dumpy little woman, with a glassy eye and gray hair. She wore black; she took protection behind an umbrella; and at first glance Page thought he had never seen her before. Then he realized with a shock who she was. Colonel Marquis nodded to her. "That's settled, then," he said. "Your name, madam?"

"Clara McCann," replied the woman, getting her breath. "Mrs.", she added.

"What is your occupation, Mrs. McCann?"

"You know what it is, sir. I keep a news-agent's shop at Number 32 Hastings Street, Bloomsbury."

"You have just looked at the body of Sara Samuels, Mrs. McCann. Did you ever see her before?"

Mrs. McCann took a grip of her umbrella and spoke in a rush: "Yes, sir, I did. There's no mistake about it now, like there was when I only saw the photograph. She was the lady who came into my shop yesterday afternoon at twenty minutes past five and asked if I had a letter for her in the name of Carolyn Baer."

At the end of a dead silence, which sounded in Page's ears like a sort of roar, one face in the room shifted and changed. Colonel Marquis lifted his hand.

"Your warning, Inspector," he said. "It's not my duty to give it. But there's your prisoner."

Page said: "Carolyn Mortlake, I arrest you for the murder of Charles Mortlake and Sara Samuels. I have to warn you that anything you say will be taken down in writing and may be used as evidence."

For a space of time in which you might have counted five slowly, no one moved or spoke. Carolyn Mortlake remained leaning against the wall, her arms folded; the only change about her was that her eyes had acquired a steady, hard shine, and her dark-painted mouth stood out against her face.

"Don't—don't be an ass," she said harshly. "You can't prove that." Then she screamed one word at him, and was calm again.

"I can prove it, my young lady," said Colonel Marquis. "I'll show you just how far I can prove it by giving you time to think of an answer and a defense. I'll leave you alone with your thoughts for a few minutes, while I speak of somebody else."

He swung round abruptly, the light making harsh shadows on his face. There was a queer sucking sort of noise: the noise of Gabriel White trying to moisten his lips. White was not standing quite so erect. It was his face which had shifted and changed, not Carolyn Mortlake's.

"Yes, I mean you," said Colonel Marquis. "I mean Carolyn Mortlake's lover. I mean Gabriel White, or Lord Edward Whiteford, or whatever you care to call yourself. God's death, you're a pretty pair, you are!"

"You haven't got anything on me," said White. "*I* didn't kill him."

"I know you didn't," agreed the other. "But all the same, I can send you to the gallows as accessory before and after the fact."

White took a step forward. But Sergeant Borden put a hand on his shoulder. "Watch him, Borden," ordered Colonel Marquis. "I don't think he's got the nerve for anything now, but he's a dead shot — and he once beat a woman half to death in a tobacconist's shop merely because she had only a pound or two in the till when he needed a little spending money. The old judge was right. There seems to have been some doubt as to whether Friend White is a saint or a well-defined swine; but the old judge knew long before we did."

Marquis looked at the rest of them. "I owe some of you an explanation, I think," he went on; "and the shortest way will be to show you how I knew that White was lying from the very first — lying through and through — lying about even the things he *admitted* having done. That was (as he believed) the cleverness of his whole plan. Oh, yes; he was going to kill the judge. He would have killed the judge, if his sweetheart hadn't interfered. But he was never going to hang for it.

"Stand back, now, and look at certain bullet holes. There has been one basis in this case, one starting point for all investigation, one solid background which we all believed from the outset. We took it for granted. It concerns the two shots which were fired in here—the shots from the .38 Ivor-Johnson revolver and the .32 Browning automatic—the two shots which did *not* kill the judge. We accepted, on White's word, the statement that the first shot was from the .38 revolver and the second shot from the .32 automatic. We were meant to accept that statement. White's defense was based on it. And that statement was a lie.

"But even at first glance, if you look at the physical evidence, White's story seemed wildly improbable on the very points of guilt that he admitted. Look at this room. Look at your plan of it. What was his story? He said that he rushed into the room, flourishing the .38 revolver; that the judge was then at the open window; that the judge turned round, shouting something; and at this moment, while the judge was still in front of the window, he fired.

"Yes; but what happened to that .38 bullet? That bullet, which White said he fired as soon as he got in here, smashed the tube of the dictaphone and crashed into the wall *more than a full six feet away from the window where the judge was standing*. Now this is incredible. It cannot be believed that even the worst revolver shot, even one who did not know a pistol from a cabbage, could stand only fifteen feet away from the target and yet miss the target by six feet.

"And what follows? Outside the window—on a direct line with the window—there is a tree; and in this tree—also in a direct line with the window—we find embedded a bullet from the .32 Browning automatic. In other words, this Browning bullet is in precisely the position we should have expected if White, coming into the room had fired his first shot from the Browning .32. He missed the judge, though he came close; the bullet went through the open window and struck the tree.

"It is therefore plain that his first shot must have been fired from the Browning. As a clinching proof, we note that his story about the mysterious shot from the Browning—the second shot, fired from behind him and to the right, over in the corner by the yellow vase— is a manifest lie. The bullet could not have first described a curve, then gone out the window, and then entered the tree in a straight line. More! Not only was it a lie, but obviously he knew it was a lie.

"So the course of events was like this. He entered this room, he fired with the Browning .32, and he missed. (I will presently show you why he missed.) White then ran across the room, dropped the Browning into the vase, ran back, and *then* fired the second shot with the Ivor-Johnson .38. Do you care for proof? My own officers can supply it. This morning I conducted a little experiment here. I stood over there in the corner by the vase and I myself fired a shot. I was not aiming at anything in particular, except in the direction of the wall between the windows. It struck the wall between the windows, a foot to the right of the open one. Had I been farther out into the room, more on a line with the table, my bullet would have struck exactly the spot where the Ivor-Johnson .38 shot went into the wall. In other words, where White was standing when he pulled a trigger for the second time."

Sir Andrew Travers pushed to the forefront.

"Are you saying that White fired both shots after all? But that's insane! You said so yourself. Why did he do it in a room that was sealed up? What was the sense of it?"

"I will try to show you," said Colonel Marquis, "for it was one of the most ingenious tricks I know of. But it went wrong. . . .

"The next bit of evidence to claim our attention is a set of well-stamped footprints, made by a man's number-ten shoe, crossing a ten-foot flowerbed outside the west windows. All these tracks led away from the window. We were meant to believe that someone in a number-ten shoe (which was larger than White's) had got out of that window and run away. But it was impossible for anybody to have got out there, due to the condition of the window sashes. So the footprints were obviously faked. Yet, if they were faked, how did the person who made them get *across* that big stretch of flowerbed in order to make a line of tracks coming away from the window? It was even asked whether he flew. And the person must have done just that. In other words, he jumped. He jumped across, and walked back, thus faking his evidence an hour or so before the judge was actually killed. There is only one person in the case who is capable of making a leap like that: Gabriel White, who, as Mr. Penney told us this afternoon, holds an unbeaten record for the broadjump at Oxford. . . .

"And next? Next we hear from Robinson of a sudden and energetic plan, originating in the judge's household not long ago, to open up those windows so that they shall be like ordinary windows. All things — you begin to see — center round a phantom murderer who shall kill the judge and escape from that window, leaving his tracks and his gun behind.

"White's plan was just this. He meant to kill Mr. Justice Mortlake, but he is clever enough — kindly look at him now — to know that, no matter how the judge died, he is bound to be suspected. I do not need to review the case to convince you of that. He cannot possibly commit a murder where *no* suspicion will attach to him. If he tries some subtle trick to keep out of the limelight and the public eye, they will nail him. But he can commit a murder for which there will not be enough evidence to convict him, and of which most people will believe him innocent.

"He can — with the assistance of an accomplice in Mortlake's household — obtain possession of a Browning pistol belonging to some friend of the family. It does not really matter what pistol, so long as it can be shown that *White* could not have stolen it. Very well. He can make wild threats against the judge in the hearing of anyone. He can with blatant swagger and obviousness purchase a .38 calibre gun from a pawnbroker whom he knows to be a copper's nark — and who, he also knows quite well, will immediately report it. He can also procure, from any source you like, a pair of number-ten shoes which are nothing like his own shoes. He can get, from his accomplice, a duplicate key to the tradesmen's entrance which will enable him to enter the grounds when he likes. Finally, he can get his accomplice's word that the rusted windows and shutters are now in ordinary working order.

"Then he is ready. On any given afternoon, when the judge is alone in the pavilion, he can get into the grounds an hour or so before he means to make his attack. He can implant his footprints. He can give the shutters a pull to make sure they are in order. Then he can alarm the household — get them to chase him — get any convenient witnesses on his trail. He can rush into the pavilion, as though wildly, a long distance ahead of them. The shoes in which he made the tracks are now buried somewhere in the grounds; he wears his own shoes. He can lock the door. He can fire two shots; one a miss, one killing his victim. He can fling up one of the west windows and toss the Browning outside. When the pursuers arrive, there he is: a man who has tried to murder — *and failed*. A real murder, instead, has been done by someone who fired from a window, and jumped out; someone who wore shoes that are not White's shoes and carried a gun White could not have carried. In short, White was blackening his character in order to whitewash it. He was admitting he intended murder; at the same time he was showing he could not have done it. He was creating a phantom. He would not get off scot-free; he was in danger; but he could not possibly be convicted, because in any court there would loom large that horned and devilish discomfort known as the Reasonable Doubt. His deliberate walking into the hangman's noose was the only sure way of making certain it never tightened round his neck."

Page turned round toward White, and again there was a subtle alteration on the young man's face. Though the same ugliness still moved behind the eyes, his handsome face had almost a smile of urbanity and charm. He had drawn himself upright.

"There is still a reasonable doubt, my dear old chap," said Lord Edward Whiteford lightly. "I didn't kill him, you know."

"Look here, Marquis, I am trying to keep my head," thundered Travers. "But I don't see this. Even if this is true, *how did the real murderer get out of the room?* We're as badly off as we were before. And why was White such an ass, or his accomplice such an ass, as to go through with the old scheme when the windows *hadn't* been altered? You say Carolyn is the murderer. I can't believe that —"

"Many thanks, Andrew," interrupted Carolyn mockingly. She shifted her position and walked forward with quick jerky steps. It was clear that she had not got herself completely under control: she could master her intellect, but she could not master her rage, which was a rage at all the world.

"Don't let them force you into admitting anything, Gabriel," she went on almost sweetly. "They are bluffing, you know. They haven't a scrap of real evidence against me. They accuse me of killing Father, but they don't seem to realize that in order to do it I must have made myself invisible; and they won't dare go to a jury unless they can show how Father really was killed. Besides, they'll make fools of themselves as it is. You spotted it, Andrew. If Gabriel and I were concerned in any such wild scheme, we should have known the windows were sealed up—"

A hoarse voice said: "Miss Carolyn, I lied to you."

Robinson had taken off his hat at last and he was kneading it in his hands. He continued: "I lied to you. I been on hot bricks all day; I been nearly crazy; but, so help me, I'm glad now I lied to you. You—the tall gent—you, sir; a couple of nights ago she gave me a five-pun note if I would sneak down here and put one of them windows right, so it could be opened, anyhow. And I went. But the judge caught me. And he said he'd skin me. And I went back to you; and I wanted that five-pun note; so I lied and said I'd fixed the window. I know I swore on the Bible to you I'd never mention it to anybody, and you said I wouldn't be believed if I told it, but I ain't going to be hanged for anybody. . . ."

"*Catch her, Page,*" snapped Marquis.

But it was not necessary to restrain her. She turned round to face them with a smiling calmness.

"Go on," she said.

"You and White planned this together, then," said Colonel Marquis. "I think you hated the judge almost as much as he did: his every mannerism, his very mildness.

Also, I am inclined to believe you were getting into desperate straits over your earlier affair with Ralph Stratfield the blackmailer. If your father ever heard of that, you would be unlikely to get a penny under the will. And you needed money for your various fancy men like Stratfield — and Gabriel White.

"Of course, it was plain from the start that White had an accomplice here in the house. He could not have known so much, got so much, unless that were so. It was also clear that his accomplice was a woman. The case had what Inspector Page described as a woman's touch in it: and no other possible accomplice in the house had any adequate motive except yourself — and your sister. That, I admit, bothered me. I did not know which of you it was. I was inclined to suspect Ida, until it became obvious that all these apparent attempts to throw suspicion on you were really intended against her and one other. . . . What size shoes do you wear, Travers?"

"Tens," said Sir Andrew grimly. "I'm rather bulky, as you've noticed."

"Yes. And it was your pistol; above all, it was your known afternoon to visit the judge. That was why White delayed so long, hoping you would appear. You are — um — associated with Ida Mortlake. Yes; you were the combination intended to bear the suspicion, you two.

"In the scheme as planned, Carolyn Mortlake was to have no hand in the actual murder. But she must have an alibi. For they were going to create a mystery, you see. Anybody might be suspected in addition to Travers and they must keep their own skirts absolutely clean. Hence the trick: 'Ralph Stratfield' was to be used as a blind, in a brilliant alibi which was all the more strong for being a discreditable alibi. Gabriel White should put through a phone call to the house, saying to go to such-and-such an (imaginary) address and ask for a letter. You, Carolyn Mortlake, *were really intended to go*. It was an ingenious sham plot: there was no such address and you and White knew it; but it would serve more strikingly to call attention to you later, when you wandered up and down a street for the inspection of later witnesses, and had an alibi for half an hour in *any* direction, no matter what time White should kill the judge. It would, in other words, give you an excuse for wandering all over the place under the eyes of certain witnesses. Also, you were to refuse to answer any questions about it: knowing quite well that the police would find it and that the invaluable Millie Reilly, the maid, was listening in to all phone conversations. She would report it. You could afford to have the apparent truth, the 'alibi,' dragged out of you. It was exactly like White's plan: you too were blackening your character in order to whitewash it.

"But you did not go to Hastings Street after all." Marquis stopped. He looked at her curiously, almost gently; then he nodded toward White. "You are very much in love with him, aren't you?"

"Whether I am or not," she told him, "is none of your business and has no connection with this case."

She was quite pale nevertheless. What puzzled Page throughout this was the gentle, aloof, almost indifferent air of Gabriel White himself, who had none of the bounce or fire which had characterized him in the morning. He stood far away on a polar star.

"Yes," Colonel Marquis said sharply, "it has a great deal of connection with the matter. You were afraid for him. You thought him, and you think him, weak. You were afraid he would lose his nerve; or that he would grow flurried and bungle the business. And above all you were afraid—fiercely afraid—*for* him, because you love him. You wished to remain behind here. Yet you are, I venture to think, a cold-hearted young devil, almost as cold-hearted as that smirking Adonis there. And yet you wanted that alibi. Opportunity knocked at your door yesterday afternoon: you interviewed a batch of applicants for the maid's position—?"

"Well?"

"And one of them looked like you," said the Assistant Commissioner. He glanced at Page. "Surely you noticed it, Inspector, in Sara Samuels? The short, plump figure; the dark good looks? She wasn't by any means a double, but she was near enough for the purpose. Suppose the Samuels girl were sent to Hastings Street? It was a dark, rainy day; the girl could put her collar up, as she was instructed; and to a casual witness she would later appear to *be* Carolyn Mortlake. It might be a case of 'Oh, you badly want a job, do you? Then I'll test you. Go to Hastings Street—' and the rest of it—'otherwise you get no job.' The girl would agree.

"If later the Samuels girl came to suspect something . . . well, you weren't much afraid: you have great faith in the power of blackmail and of saying 'You daren't speak now; they'd arrest you.' But it was unlikely the Samuels girl ever would come into it. She was not to take over her job until next month. There was absolutely no reason why the police should think of her at all.

"And there was your plot, all cooked up in ten minutes. You could remain behind now—and even kill the old man yourself if White wavered.

"That, I think, was why you went down to the pavilion before you ostensibly 'left' the grounds. It wasn't that you wanted money. But you did want the gun in your father's desk. To get it without his knowing might have been difficult. But you yourself, unfortunately, gave a clue as to how you might have stolen it, when you were so eager to throw suspicion toward Sir Andrew Travers by stressing the point of his being expected there. You mentioned to your father that the electric fire wasn't turned on in the living room; and that it would be freezing cold, and that the tea things were not set out. We have heard from others about his extremely finicky nature and how he would not allow others to touch things he manipulated himself. He would, to prevent your doing it, go into the living room, turn on the fire, and set out the kettle. In his absence you, in this room, would steal the Erckmann air pistol out of the drawer.

"I don't know whether it occurred to you to shoot him through the heart then and there, and so prevent White's bungling. But you realized the chances against you and you were wise enough not to do it. In one place you erred: you forgot to look closely at the west window, to make sure Robinson had repaired it as he had sworn. Well, you left the grounds after that.

"Meantime, White is talking to your sister at a tea-shop. He didn't want to see her, really; it was a bad chance meeting; but since it couldn't be avoided, he tried to pile it on thickly by raving out threats against your father so as to strengthen his position. But, unfortunately, he went too far. He scared her. He scared her to such an extent that when she went home, she phoned the police. You two conspirators did not want the police—emphatically not; it was too dangerous. White wanted to run into that pavilion pursued by a servant, or seen by a few servants; no more.

"When Ida had gone home, White followed and let himself in through the tradesmen's entrance with the duplicate key. It was foresight to have had that key, for he couldn't have known in the ordinary way that Ida would order the gate locked. By the way, my friend White: you told a foolish lie when you said you got into the grounds in her car. That was not only foolish, it was unnecessary. And I am tolerably sure it was done to direct attention toward her, making us wonder just how innocent she might have been in the rest of it.

"For consider—I am still following you, White— what you did then. Once in the grounds you set about prowling round the pavilion. You made your tracks. When you touched the shutters of the west window they still seemed tolerably solid: which bothered you. You went round and threw a pebble at one of the front windows, so as to draw the judge and Penney (who was with him then) to the front of the pavilion. And then you would be able to get a closer look at the shutters on the west window. Unfortunately, the judge only opened the front window and looked out; you didn't draw him away at all. But you thought, as Carolyn had assured you on Robinson's word, that the west window would open easily from inside.

"Presently you went to the house. In the yarn you told us there was one truth: you did get into the house through a side window, after a long failure to penetrate anywhere else. The purpose was to appear suddenly in the house before the servants; to run out pursued by the redoubtable Davies; to be seen lurking and dashing, and leave a trail to the pavilion. But—when you got through a window at twenty minutes past five—you heard a terrible thing. You heard Ida Mortlake talking to the butler. I say, Davies: in that conversation did Miss Mortlake tell you anything else besides the fact that the judge was taking tea at the pavilion?"

Davies nodded glumly.

"Yes, sir. She said not to be alarmed if I saw any

policemen on the grounds. She said she had telephoned for them. I already knew it, as a matter of fact. Millie heard her on the phone extension."

Colonel Marquis snapped his fingers. "Good! Now see White's position. He is up in the air. He is wild. He doesn't want the police or he may lose his nerve. Or will he? He climbs out of the window and stands in the rain wondering like hell. And White omitted to tell us about that hiatus of ten minutes next day; he placed the conversation at close on half-past five, thereby neatly throwing suspicion on Ida Mortlake when we learned the real time of it. Thus he stands in the rain, and finally he goes to the pavilion, still wild and weak and undecided. But thunder and lightning inspired him and he makes up his mind to be a god. He makes up his mind to kill the judge in front of all the police in the world . . . just as lightning shows him two policemen in the path. . . .

"But," snapped Marquis grimly, "let's not forget Miss Carolyn Mortlake, for hers is now the most important part in the story.

"She has come back into the grounds, unknown to White. (She was almost locked out unexpectedly; and, if White hadn't conveniently left the tradesmen's entrance unlocked when *he* went through, she wouldn't have been able to get in at all.) She is watching, and I am inclined to think she is praying a little. And what does she hear? At close on half-past five, near the lodge gates, she hears Robinson arguing with a couple of police officers who have just arrived.

"This must seem like the end. She runs back toward the pavilion before they can get there. There are trees round that pavilion. There is one particular tree, a dozen or more feet out from one of the front windows, and she hides behind that. And she sees two things in the lightning—the policemen running for the pavilion and a distracted Gabriel White running for it ahead of them.

"There is now no question about worrying whether he might lose his nerve; she *knows* he has lost his nerve and will smash all their plans like china, if he goes ahead now. The worst of it is that she cannot stop him. He will be caught and hanged for a certainty. Is there any way she can keep him from being caught for a murder which has now become a foolery? There is none . . . but she is given one.

"She is now in front of the tree, between it and the pavilion, hidden from Page's view by the bole of the tree. But at Sergeant Borden's yell the providential occurs. The curtains are pushed back. Mr. Justice Mortlake opens the window halfway, thrusts out his head, and shouts. There is her stepfather, facing her ten feet away, illuminated like a target in the window. There is one thing, my lads, you have forgotten. If a Browning .32 bullet can fly out of an open window, *an Erckmann air-pistol bullet can fly in!*

"She lifts the Erckmann and fires. There is no flash. There is no noise, nothing which would not be drowned out easily by the storm. The Erckmann bullet was in Mr. Justice Mortlake's chest about one second before Gabriel White threw open the door of the study. She has only to draw to the other side of the tree and the Inspector will not see her as he runs past."

Sir Andrew Travers put out his hand like a man signaling a bus.

"You mean that it was the *first* shot? That both the other two were fired afterward?"

"Of course I do. And now you will understand. Struck in the chest, he barely knows what has happened when White bursts into the room. Remember, the doctor told us that death was not instantaneous; that

Mortlake could have taken several steps, or spoken, before he collapsed. He turned round when he heard White enter. And then . . .

"You will be able to see what turned our friend White witless and inhuman, and why he had on his face an expression of bewilderment which no actor could produce. White lifted the Browning and fired; but on the instant he fired or even before, his victim took a few sideways steps and fell across the writing table. Well, has he shot the judge or hasn't he? What is more, he has no time to find out. He has forgotten that window. He has bolted the door, but now they may be in and catch him before he can make his second-to-second plans. He runs to the window to throw out the Browning. And the universe collapses, for the window will not budge. There is only one thing he can do; he simply drops the Browning, and it goes into the vase. Now all he wants to do is strike back, for he hears Page's footsteps within ten paces of the window. He swings round with the .38 revolver and fires blindly again. Was it with the intention of completing his story and his plan somehow? Yes. For, whatever happens, he has got to stick to his story. The worst and most devilish point is this: he does not really know whether he has killed the judge. He does not know it until this morning.

"But now you will be able to see why Inspector Page, running for that window, swore no bullet could have been fired past him into the tree, or he would have heard signs of it. It was because the bullet which struck the tree was the first of the two fired by White, and was fired when the Inspector was seventy feet away from the tree. You also see why Page saw no woman or no footprints. She had already run away. But she came back, after he had climbed through the window. She hid behind the tree and peered round it, in order to get a

direct view into the room. That was how she slipped—
you noticed the blurred toeprint on one shoe—and
planted that smashing heavy footprint (all unknow-
ingly) in the soft soil. It is a great irony, gentlemen. For
that was a perfectly genuine footprint. We must assume
that she remembered it and destroyed the slippers
afterward.

"We must assume many things, I think, until I
prove them in the case of Sara Samuels. When you went
out this afternoon, Miss Mortlake, did you see the
Samuels girl on her way here? Did you realize that she
knew the trap alibi she had fallen into and that she was
coming here to betray you? Did you dodge here ahead
of her, through that invaluable tradesmen's entrance
now unlocked? Did you get into the house unobserved
and find the knife and the hammer? Did you wish to
make her unrecognizable, so that it should never be
observed that she looked like you and thus betray the
alibi? Only you had interviewed her, you know, and
Robinson had no good description. It was blind panic.
You little devil, it was murderous panic. But at least you
did not err on the side of oversubtlety—as you have
done ever since you planted that air pistol in your own
bureau drawer, and so conveniently made out that your
sister was trying to throw suspicion on you."

Carolyn Mortlake opened and shut her hands. She
remained under the brilliant light by the table; but
abruptly she flung round toward White. She did not
scream, because her voice was very low, but her words
had the effect of a scream of panic.

"Aren't you going to do anything?" she cried to
White. "Aren't you going to say anything? Deny it? Do
something? Are you a man? Don't stand there like a
dummy. For God's sake don't stand there smirking.

They haven't got any evidence. They're bluffing. There's not one piece of real evidence in anything he's said."

White spoke in such a cool, detached voice that it was like a physical chill on the rest of them.

"Terribly sorry, old girl," he said, with a grotesque return of the old school tie; "but there really isn't much I can say, is there?"

She stared at him.

"After all, you know, that attack on the girl—that was a nasty bit of work," he went on, frowning. "I couldn't be expected to support that. It's like this. Rotten bad luck for you, but I'm afraid I shall have to save my own skin. *Sauve qui peut,* you know. I didn't commit the murder. Under the circumstances I'm afraid I shall have to turn King's evidence. I must tell them I saw you shoot the old boy through the window; it can't hurt you any more than their own evidence, now that the murder's out, and it may do me a bit of good. Sorry, old girl; there it is."

He adjusted his shabby coat, looked at her with great charm, and was agreeable. Page was so staggered that he could not speak or even think. Carolyn Mortlake did not speak. She remained looking at him curiously. It was only when they took her away that she began to sob.

"So," said Colonel Marquis formally, "you saw her fire the shot I take it?"

"I did. No doubt about that."

"You make that statement of your own free will, knowing that it will be taken down in writing and may be used as evidence?"

"I do," said White with the air of a martyr. "Rotten bad luck for her, but what can I do? How does one go about turning King's evidence?"

"I am happy to say," roared Colonel Marquis, suddenly rising to his full height, "that you can't. Making a statement like that will no more save your neck than it saved William Henry Kennedy's in 1928. You'll hang, my lad, you'll hang by the neck until you are dead; and if the hangman kicks your behind all the way to the gallows, I can't say it will weigh very heavily on my conscience."

Colonel Marquis sat at the writing table under the dragon lamp. He looked pale and tired and he smoked a cigarette as though it were tasteless. In the room now there were left only Ida Mortlake, Sir Andrew Travers, and Page busy at his notebook.

"Sir," said Travers in his most formal fashion, "my congratulations."

Marquis gave him a crooked grin. "There is one thing," he said, "on which you can enlighten me. Look here, Travers: why did you tell that idiotic lie about there being no way out of your rooms at the Temple except through the front? No, I'll change the question: what were you really doing at five-thirty yesterday afternoon?"

"At five-thirty yesterday afternoon," Travers replied gravely, "I was talking on the telephone with the Director of Public Prosecutions."

"Telephones!" said Marquis bitterly, striking the desk. Then he looked up with an air of inspiration. "Ha! I see. Yes, of course. You had an absolutely watertight alibi, but you didn't care to use it. You spun out all that cloud of rubbish because—"

"Because I was afraid you suspected Miss Ida Mortlake," said Travers. Page, glancing up, thought that he looked rather a stuffed shirt. "I—hum—there were times when I was afraid she might have been—" He grew honest. "Fair is fair, Marquis. She might have done it, especially as I thought she might have stolen my gun. So I directed your attention toward me. I thought if the hounds kept on my trail for a while, I could devise something for her whether she were guilty or whether she were innocent. I had a sound alibi, in case you ever arrested me. You see, I happen to be rather fond of Miss Mortlake."

Ida Mortlake turned up a radiant and lovely face.

"*Oh, Andrew,*" she said — and simpered.

If a hand grenade had come through the window and burst under his chair, Page could not have been more astounded. He looked up from his notebook and stared. The sudden gush of those words, no less than the simper, caused a sudden revulsion of feeling to go through him. And it was as though, in his sight, a blurred lens came into focus. He saw Ida Mortlake differently. He compared her with Mary O'Dennistoun of Loughborough Road, Brixton. He thought again. He was glad. He fell to writing busily, and thinking of Mary O'Dennistoun. . . .

"In one way this has been a very remarkable case," said Colonel Marquis. "I do not mean that it was exceptionally ingenious in the way of murders, or (heaven knows) that it was exceptionally ingenious in the way of detection. But it has just this point: it upsets a long-established and domineering canon of fiction. Thus. In a story of violence there are two girls. One of these girls seems dark-browed, sour, cold-hearted, and vindictive, with hell in her heart. The other is pink-and-white, golden of hair, innocent of intent, sweet of disposition, and (ahem) vacant of head. Now by the rules of sensational fiction there is only one thing that can happen. At the end of the story it is proved that the sullen brunette, who snarls all the way through, is really a misjudged

innocent who wants a lot of children and whose hard-
boiled worldly airs are a cloak for a modern girl's sweet
nature. The baby-faced blonde, on the other hand, will
prove to be a raging, spitting demon who has murdered
half the community and is only prevented by arrest from
murdering the other half. I glorify the high fates, we
have here broken that tradition! We have here a dark-
browed, sour, cold-hearted girl who really *is* a mur-
deress. We have a roseleaf, injured, generous innocent
who really *is* innocent. Play up, you cads! *Vive le roman
policier! Ave Virgo!* Inspector Page, gimme my hat and
coat. I want a pint of beer."

BOOKTAKER
by Bill Pronzini

*Bill Pronzini is best known for his "Nameless Detective"
series about a San Francisco private eye who collects pulp
magazines. His protagonist has no name because neither the
author nor his editor could think of one that fit, although
"Nameless" resembles Mr. Pronzini in a number of ways.
The series began with* The Snatch *in 1971 and has continued
through some fifteen adventures, including* Blowback
(1977), Scattershot (1982), *and* Deadfall (1985). *Many
critics believe that* Quicksilver (1984) *is the best of the series
to date, but others would vote for* Hoodwink (1981) *which
involves "Nameless" with the attendees at a pulp magazine
convention, and won a Shamus Award as Best Novel of 1981
from the Private Eye Writers of America.*

*Pronzini has been a prolific full-time writer since 1969
and also writes as Jack Foxx and William Jeffrey. He has
written science fiction and fantasy as well as mystery and
suspense, and is also an accomplished novelist of the Old
West. Also noteworthy are his collaborations with Barry N.
Malzberg, especially* The Running of Beasts (1976) *and*
Night Screams (1979), *and one with Marcia Muller,*
Double (1985). *He is one of the best anthologists in the
history of mystery fiction.*

*A long-time resident of San Francisco, he now lives in
Sonoma, California.*

It was a Thursday afternoon in late May, and it was
gloomy and raining outside, and I was sitting in my
brand-new offices on Drumm Street wishing I were
somewhere else. Specifically, over at Kerry's apartment
on Diamond Heights, snuggling up with her in front of
her nice big fireplace. Thoughts like that seemed to come
into my head all the time lately. I had known Kerry
Wade only a couple of weeks, but it had already developed into a pretty intense relationship. For me, anyhow.

But I was not going to get to snuggle up with her tonight. Or tomorrow night either. She worked as a copywriter for Bates and Carpenter, a San Francisco advertising agency, and when I'd called her this morning she'd said she was in the middle of an important presentation; she was going to have to work late both nights in order to finish it to deadline. How about Saturday night? I said. Okay, she said. So I had a promise, which was better than nothing, but Saturday was two long days away. The prospect of spending the next forty-eight hours alone, cooped up here and in my Pacific Heights flat, made me feel as gloomy as the weather.

My flat wasn't so bad, but these shiny new offices left a great deal to be desired. They consisted of two rooms, one waiting area and one private office, with pastel walls, beige carpeting, some chrome chairs with beige corduroy cushions and venetian blinds on the windows. The bright yellow phone somebody in the telephone company had seen fit to give me looked out of place on my battered old desk. The desk looked out of place, too, in the sterile surroundings. And so did I: big hulking guy, overweight, shaggy-looking, with a face some people thought homely and other people—me included, when I was in a good mood—thought of as possessing character. Sort of like the late actor Richard Boone.

I didn't belong in a place like this. It had *no* character, this place; it was just a two-room office in a newly renovated building down near the waterfront. It could have been anybody's office, in just about any profession. My old office, on the other hand, the one I had occupied for better than twenty years before moving here two weeks ago, had had too much character, which was the main reason I had made up my mind to leave it. It had been located in a frumpy old building on the fringe of the Tenderloin, one of the city's high-crime areas, and with the neighborhood worsening, I had finally accepted the fact that prospective clients wouldn't be too keen about hiring a private investigator with that sort of address.

This place had been the best I could find for what I could afford. And so here I was, all decked out with a new image, and the phone still didn't ring and clients still didn't line up outside my door. So much for transitioning upscale and all the rest of that crap. So much for detective work in general.

I was starting to depress myself. What I needed was to get out of here the rest of today and all day tomorrow; what I needed was work. So why doesn't somebody come in? I thought. I looked out across the anteroom to the access door. Well? I thought. Come on in, somebody.

And the door opened and somebody came in.

I blinked, startled. It was enough to make you wonder if maybe there was something after all to the theory of solipsism.

My visitor was a man, and I was on my feet when he limped through my private office and stopped in front of the desk. "I don't know if you remember me," he said. "I'm John Rothman."

"Yes, sir, sure I do. It's good to see you again. Mr. Rothman."

I had recognized him immediately even though I hadn't seen him in more than a year; I have a cop's memory for faces. He was the owner of San Francisco's largest secondhand bookshop—an entire building over on Golden Gate Avenue near the Federal Building, three floors and a basement full of every kind of used book, from reading copies of popular fiction and nonfiction to antiquarian books, prints and the like. I had first met him several years ago, when pulp magazines were still reasonably cheap and there were only a few serious collectors like myself around; he had acquired, through an estate sale, about a thousand near-mint issues of *Black Mask, Dime Detective, Dime Mystery, Thrilling Detective* and other pulps from the thirties and forties, and because I happened to be fairly solvent at the time, I'd been able to buy the entire lot at not much more than a dollar an issue. Those same thousand copies today would cost more than I made most years.

On four or five occasions since then, whenever a new batch of pulps came his way, Rothman had contacted me. I hadn't bought much from him, what with escalating prices, but I had purchased enough to keep my name in his files and in his memory.

But it wasn't his profession that had brought him here today; it was mine. "I've got a serious problem at the bookshop," he said, "and I'd like to hire you to get to the bottom of it."

"If I can be of help, I'll be glad to do what I can."

I waited until he was seated in one of the two clients' chairs and then sat down again myself. He was in his fifties, tall and aristocratic-looking, with silvering hair and cheekbones so pronounced they were like sharp little ridges. His limp was the result of some sort of childhood disease or accident—he had once made a vague reference to it—and he needed the use of a cane; the one he hooked over the arm of the chair was thick and gnarled and black, with a knobby handle. Its color matched the three-piece suit he wore.

"I'll get right to the point," he said. "I've been plagued by thefts the past few months, and I'm damned if I can find out who's responsible or how they're being done."

"What is it that's been stolen?"

"Valuable antiquarian items. Rare books at first; more recently, etchings, prints and old maps. The total value so far exceeds twenty thousand dollars."

I raised an eyebrow. "That's a lot of money."

"It is, and my insurance doesn't cover it all. I've been to the police, but there doesn't seem to be much they can do, under the circumstances. There seldom is in cases like this."

"You mean book thefts are a common occurrence?"

"Oh, yes," Rothman said. "Thieves are a thorn in the side of every bookseller. I lose hundreds, if not thousands, of dollars of stock to them each year. No matter how closely we watch our customers, the experienced thief can always find a way to slip a book into a concealed pocket or inside his clothing, or to wrap a print or an old map around himself under a coat. A few years ago an elderly gentleman, very distinguished, managed to steal a first edition of Twain's *Huckleberry Finn,* even though I can still swear I had my eyes on him the whole time."

"Do these people steal for profit—to resell the items?"

"Sometimes," he said. "Others are collectors who don't have the money or the inclination to pay for something they desperately want. A much smaller percentage are kleptomaniacs. But this is an unusual case because of the number and value of the thefts, and because of the circumstances surrounding them, and I'm fairly certain the motive is resale for profit. Not to other dealers, but to unscrupulous private collectors who don't care how the items were obtained and who don't ask questions when they're offered."

"Then you think the thief is a professional?"

"No. I think he's one of my employees."

"Oh? Why is that?"

"For several reasons. All of the items were taken from the Antiquarian Room on the third floor, a room that is kept locked at all times. I have a key and so do—or did—two of my employees; no customer has ever been allowed inside without one of us present. And after the first two thefts—a fine copy of T.S. Arthur's temperance novel, *Ten Nights in a Bar Room,* and an uncommon children's book, Mary Wollstonecraft's *Original Stories from Real Life*—I ordered the Antiquarian Room out of bounds to customers unless they were personally known to me. I also had a sensor alarm installed on the front entrance. You know what that is, of course?"

I nodded. It was an electronic gateway, similar to the metal detectors used in airports, through which customers had to pass on their way out. Any purchases they made were cleared by rubbing the items across a sensor strip. If someone tried to leave the premises with something that hadn't been paid for and cleared, an alarm would sound. A lot of bookstores used the device these days; so did most libraries.

"Three weeks later," Rothman said, "a sixteenth-century religious etching attributed to one of the pioneers of printmaking, Albrecht Dürer, disappeared. It was one of two I had recently purchased, and extremely valuable; if it had been authenticated, it would be priceless. Even so, I was in the process of realizing several thousand dollars from a collector in Hillsborough when it vanished." He paused. "The point is, I checked the Antiquarian Room that morning, before I went out to lunch, as I regularly do; the Dürer was still there at that time. But it had vanished when I checked the room again late that afternoon—and no customer had been permitted inside in the interim, nor had the door lock been tampered with."

"Did you take any further precautions after that theft?"

"Yes. I confiscated the other two keys to the Antiquarian Room. But that didn't stop him either. There have been four other thefts since then, at increasingly frequent intervals — all of them between eleven and two o'clock, evidently when I was away from the shop. The second Dürer etching, two seventeenth-century Japanese color prints and a rare map of the Orient; the map disappeared two days ago."

"The thief could have had a duplicate key made before you confiscated the originals," I suggested.

"I know; I thought of that, too. Any of my four employees could have had a duplicate made, in fact, not just the two who had keys previously. On occasion those two gave their keys to the other two, when they needed something from the Antiquarian Room and were too busy to get it themselves."

"Did you consider changing the lock?"

"I did, yes. But I decided against it."

"Why?"

"As clever as the thief is," Rothman said, "I suspect he'd have found a way to circumvent that obstacle, too. And I don't just want to stop the thefts; I want the person responsible caught and punished, and I want to know how he's getting the stolen items out of the shop so I can take steps to prevent it from ever happening again. The *how* of it bothers me almost as much as the thefts themselves."

"Couldn't the thief have simply cleared the items through the sensor when no one was looking and walked out with them later under his clothing?"

"No. The only sensor strip is located at the cashier's desk, and none of my people had access to it on the days of the thefts except Adam Turner. Adam is the only one of my people I trust implicitly; he's been with me twenty years, and he's loyal and honest to a fault. He'd taken to guarding the sensor since the thefts began, and on at least two of the days he swears he never left the desk for even a moment."

"Do you deactivate the alarm system when you close up for the day?"

"Yes."

"Well, couldn't the thief have stashed the items somewhere in the store and left with them after the alarm was shut off?"

Rothman shook his head. "I'm the last person to leave nearly every day. And when I'm not, Adam does the locking up. No one but the two of us has a key to the front door. Not only that, but each of the others has to pass through the alarm gateway on his way out, before it's shut off; that is a strict rule and there have been no exceptions."

I did some ruminating. "Is it possible the thief could have slipped out through another entrance during working hours? He wouldn't have to have been gone more than a couple of minutes; he could even have passed the stolen items to a confederate. . . ."

Rothman was shaking his head again. "All the other entrances to the shop—first-floor rear and fire-escape doors on the second and third floor—are kept locked and are protected by separate alarm systems."

"How many people have keys to those entrances?"

"Only myself. And even if one of the others managed to get hold of it and have a duplicate made, the alarm would still ring if any of the doors were opened."

"Where is the control box for those alarms located?"

"Behind the cashier's desk. But it's also kept locked, and Adam guards it as zealously as he does the sensor strip."

"What about a window?" I asked. "Are there alarms on those, too?"

"No, but they are all securely locked and also painted shut. None of them has been touched."

I ruminated again. "I can think of one other possibility," I said at length. "Suppose the thief *hasn't* got the stolen items out of the shop? Suppose he hid them somewhere with the idea of making off with them later, because he *hasn't* figured out a way to beat the alarms?"

"I'm afraid that's not the answer either," Rothman said. "For one thing, Adam and I have searched the shop on more than one occasion; it's quite large, granted, but I'm sure we would have found the missing pieces if they were there. And for another thing, at least one item—the first Dürer etching—appears to have surfaced in the collection of a man named Martell in Chicago."

"You've heard rumors, you mean?"

"More than just rumors. After each theft I notified other antiquarian booksellers throughout the country and in Europe, as well as *AB Bookman's Weekly* and other publications in the trade; that's standard procedure whenever anything of value is stolen. A dealer in Chicago called me not long after I publicized the theft of the first Dürer, to say that he'd heard Martell had intimated to another collector that he had acquired it. Admittedly, that's secondhand information. But I know of Martell; he's a passionate collector of fifteenth- and sixteenth-century religious etchings, and he has a reputation of being unscrupulous about it. My colleague in Chicago knows Martell personally and says that if he has bragged about having the Dürer etching, he really does have it."

"Did you try to contact Martell?"

"I did. He denies possession, of course."

"Isn't there anything you can do to prove otherwise?"

"No. Without proof that he bought it, there is no legal way I can have his premises searched or force him to admit to its current ownership."

"So the only way to get that proof," I said, "is to find out who stole it from you and sold it to Martell."

"That's correct."

"Do you suspect any one employee more than the others?"

"Not really. I've ruled out Adam Turner, as I told you; it could be any of the other three."

I had been taking notes as we talked; I flipped over to a clean page on my pad. "Tell me about those three."

"Tom Lennox has been with me the longest, next to Adam. Four years. He's quiet, intense, knowledgeable—a good bookman. He hopes to open his own antiquarian shop someday."

"So you'd say he's ambitious?"

"Yes, but not overly so."

"Is he one of the two who had keys to the Antiquarian Room?"

"Yes. Adam was the other. They both gave up their keys willingly."

"Uh-huh. Go ahead, Mr. Rothman."

"Harmon Boyette," he said, and spelled the last name. "He has worked for me a little more than two years, ever since he moved here from Seattle. He owned a bookstore there for several years, but he went bankrupt when his wife divorced him. He seems quite bitter about it."

"Do you consider him dependable?"

"Most of the time. But he does have an alcohol problem. Not that he drinks on the job—I wouldn't stand for that—but he comes in badly hungover on some mornings, and has missed days now and then."

"Does money seem to be important to him?"

"If so, he's never said anything about it. Nor has he ever said anything about wanting to go into business for himself again."

"And the third man?"

"Neal Vining. A Britisher, born in London. His father is a bookseller there. He married an American girl and came to San Francisco about eighteen months ago. I hired him because he has considerable expertise in English and European books, both antiquarian and modern. He learned the business from his father, and in a remarkably short time; he's only twenty-six."

"Is *he* ambitious, would you say?"

"Yes. He's eager, always asking questions, gathering more knowledge. His only apparent fault is that he tends to be a bit egotistical at times."

I took a moment to go back over my notes. "The thefts began how long ago?"

"Approximately five months."

"Were there many valuable items stolen in, say, the year prior to that?"

"Two books, as I recall." He frowned. "Are you thinking the same person might have stolen those, too?"

"It's possible," I said. "The man responsible could have started off in a small way at first and then decided to risk stealing items on a more regular basis. Particularly if he feels he has an undetectable method. Impatience, greed, a feeling of power—all those things could be driving him."

Rothman nodded speculatively. "Now that I think

of it," he said, "an inscribed first edition of Henry Miller's *Black Spring* disappeared about three months after Neal Vining came to work for me."

"Lennox and Boyette are just as likely to be guilty, from what you've told me. Lennox could have been taking rare books off and on for four years, Boyette off and on for two."

"Yes, you're right." He ran spread fingers through his silvering hair. "How will you handle your investigation?"

"Well, first of all I'll run a background check on each of the three suspects. And it would be a good idea if I spent some time in the store, especially since the thief seems to be getting bolder; I might be able to spot something that'll tell us how he's doing it. You could introduce me as a new employee, give me some work to do and let me take it from there."

"Fine. Can you start right away?"

"This afternoon, if you like. But I think it would look better if I came in first thing in the morning. That way, I can spend the rest of today making those background checks."

Rothman agreed. He gave me addresses for Lennox, Boyette and Vining, after which we settled on my fee and I made out one of my standard contract forms and had him sign it. We also settled on what my job would be at the book shop — I would come in as a stock clerk, which entailed shelving books, filling customer orders and the like, and which would allow me to move freely around the shop — and on the name I would be using: Jim Marlowe, in honor of Raymond Chandler. Then we shook hands, and he limped out, and I got to work.

I called a guy I knew in Records and Identification at the Hall of Justice; he promised me he's run the three names through his computer and the FBI hookup, to see if any of them had a criminal record, and get back to me before five o'clock. The next order of business was to get a credit report on each of the three, so I called another friend who worked for a leasing company and asked him to pull TRW's on the trio. He also said he'd have the information by five.

I got out my copy of the reverse directory of city addresses and looked up the street numbers I had for Lennox, Boyette and Vining. All three of them lived in apartment buildings, which made things a little easier for me. I made a list of the names and telephone numbers of all the other residents of those buildings; then I called them one by one, telling each person who answered that I was a claims representative for North Coast Insurance and that I was conducting a routine check in connection with a substantial insurance policy. Human nature being what it is, that was a ploy that almost always put people at their ease and got them to open up about their neighbors.

Two of Lennox's neighbors said that he kept pretty much to himself, had no apparent bad habits and seemed to be more or less happily married. A third person, who knew him a little better, had a somewhat different opinion of Lennox's marital status; this woman said that his wife, Fran, was a complainer who constantly nagged him about money matters. The woman also said that Lennox had a passion for books and that his apartment overflowed with them. She didn't know if any of the books were valuable; she didn't have time for such foolishness as reading, she said, and didn't know anything about books except that they were dust collectors.

Harmon Boyette's neighbors confirmed that he was a heavy drinker; most of his imbibing was done at home, they said, and he tended to be surly when he was tight. They didn't seem to like him much. Nobody knew if he had money to spend, or what he spent it on if he did. None of them had ever been inside his apartment.

Neal Vining, on the other hand, was friendly, gregarious, enjoyed having people in for small parties and was well liked. So was his wife, Sara, whose father owned a haberdashery shop in Ghirardelli Square that specialized in British imports; she and Vining had met during one of the father's buying trips to London. I also learned that Vining was the athletic type — jogged regularly, played racquetball — and that he liked to impress people with his knowledge of books and literary matters. As with Lennox and Boyette, he didn't seem to have a great deal of money and he didn't spend what he had indiscriminately.

There was nothing in any of this, at least so far as I could tell, that offered a clue as to which of the three men might be guilty. I considered running a check on Adam Turner, even though Rothman had seemed certain of Turner's innocence; I like to be thorough. But I decided to let Rothman's judgment stand, at least for the time being.

The guy at R and I called back at four-thirty, with a pretty much negative report: none of the three suspects had a criminal record, and with the exception of Boyette, none of them had ever been arrested. Boyette had been jailed twice, overnight both times, on drunk-and-disorderly charges.

Just before five, my friend at the leasing company came through with the credit reports. Not much there either. Vining had a good credit rating, Lennox a not very good one and Boyette none at all. The only potentially interesting fact was that Lennox had defaulted on an automobile loan nine months ago, with the result that the car—a new Mercedes—had been repossessed. Up until then, Lennox's credit rating had been pretty good. It made me wonder why he had decided to buy an expensive car like a Mercedes in the first place; he couldn't have been paid a very hefty salary. But then, it might have been his wife's doing, if what I'd been told about her was true.

By the time I looked over everything again, reread the notes I'd taken during my talk with Rothman and put it all away in a file folder, it was five-twenty and I was ready to pack it in for the day. I was feeling considerably better than I had been before Rothman's arrival; I had a job, and I would not have to spend tomorrow sitting around this damned office watching it rain and waiting for something to happen and pining away for Kerry.

The telephone was ringing when I let myself into my flat an hour later. I hustled into the bedroom, where I keep the thing, and hauled up the receiver and said hello.

"Hi," Kerry's voice said. "You sound out of breath."

"I just came in. *You* sound tired."

"I am. And the way it looks, I'm not going to get out of here until nine o'clock."

"How's the presentation going?"

"Pretty good. I'll probably have to work Saturday morning, but I should be finished by noon."

"We're still on for Saturday night, aren't we?"

"We are. What did you have in mind?"

"Well, I've been wondering—"

"Oh, damn," she said. "Can you hold on a minute? I'm being paged by the boss."

"Sure."

There was a clicking noise as she put me on hold. I shrugged out of my damp overcoat, tossed it on the floor and sat down on the rumpled bed. While I waited I occupied myself by visualizing Kerry in my mind. She was something to look at, all right. Not pretty in any classic sense, but strikingly attractive: coppery hair worn shoulder-length; animated face marked with humor lines; generous mouth; greenish eyes that seemed to change color, like a chameleon, according to her moods. And a fine willowy body, with the kind of legs men stared at and most women envied.

I wondered again, as I had on several occasions, what she saw in me. I was fifty-three to her thirty-eight and not much to look at, but she thought I was pretty hot stuff all the same. Sexy, she'd said once. Which was all a crock, as far as I was concerned, but I loved her for feeling that way.

I *did* love her, that was the thing, even though we'd only known each other a couple of weeks. I'd met her during a pulp-magazine convention, which she'd attended because both her parents—Ivan and Cybil Wade—were ex-pulp writers who had been well known in the forties, Ivan for his fantasy/horror stories in *Weird Tales* and *Dime Mystery,* Cybil for a hardboiled detective series under the male pseudonym of Samuel Leatherman. The pulp angle had been part of my attraction to her in the beginning, just as part of hers for me had been the fact that, as a result of her mother's writing, she'd always been intrigued by private detectives. So we'd struck up an immediate friendship, and had become lovers much sooner than I could have hoped for.

Meanwhile, things had been happening at the convention that culminated in murder, and I had found myself in an investigation that had almost got me killed.

When it was finished I had asked her to marry me, surprising myself as well as her. She hadn't said no; in fact, she'd said that she loved me, too, after her fashion. But she'd been married once, a bad marriage, and she just wasn't sure if she wanted to try it again. She needed more time to think things over, she said. And that was where things stood now.

Not for long, though, I hoped. I had never been as sure of anything as I was that I wanted Ms. Kerry Wade, she of the fine legs and the wonderful chameleon eyes, to be my wife.

There was another noise as the line reopened, and she said, "You still there?"

"Would I hang up on a gorgeous lady like you?"

"Gorgeous," she said. "Hah. What were you saying about Saturday night?"

"I was just wondering," I said, "how you felt about snuggling up at your apartment in front of a nice hot fire?"

"Oh ho. So that's it."

"Yep. So how *do* you feel about it?"

"Well, I might be persuaded. Providing, of course, that you take me out first and ply me with good food."

"Done. How about Oaxaca's over on Mission?"

"Mmm, yes. We could spend the afternoon together, too. Drinks in Sausalito, maybe?"

"Sounds terrific," I said. "Only I think I may be tied up during the afternoon. I picked up a job today." I told her about John Rothman and what he had hired me to do. "So unless I can wrap things up tomorrow, which doesn't seem likely, I'll be at the book shop all day Saturday. The place closes at six, though. I could pick you up around seven."

"Fine," she said. "Right now, I'd better get back to work. Call me tomorrow night? I'll be here late again."

"Okay. And Kerry . . . I love you."

"Me, too," she said, and she was gone.

Smiling, feeling chipper, I went out into the kitchen and opened myself a beer and made a couple of salami-and-cheese sandwiches. Kerry wouldn't have approved; she was of the opinion that my eating habits left something to be desired. Well, she could change them when she became my wife. I had been a bachelor too long to want to change them on my own.

After I finished eating I curled up on the couch in my cluttered living room—another thing Kerry disapproved of, and that she could change if she was of a mind to, was my sloppy housekeeping habits—with Volume One, Number One of *Strange Detective Mysteries,* dated October 1937. Norville Page's lead novel, "When the Death-Bat Flies," kept me amused for an hour, and stories by Norbert Davis, Wayne Rogers, Paul Ernst and Arthur Leo Zagat took care of the rest of the evening.

I got down to Rothman's book shop, dressed in a sports shirt and a pair of old slacks instead of my usual suit and tie, at five minutes to nine on Friday morning. The building, a big old structure with a Victorian facade, was sandwiched between an auction gallery and a Chinese restaurant. A pair of wide plate-glass windows flanked the entrance; behind them were display racks of books of various types. Both windows bore the same legends in dark red lettering:

J. ROTHMAN, BOOKSELLER
Fine Books — Used, Rare, Antiquarian

The front door was locked; I rapped on the glass panel. Pretty soon a stooped, elderly guy, coatless but wearing a white dress shirt and a bow tie, appeared inside. When he got to the door he peered out at me through rimless glasses and then threw the bolt lock and opened up.

"My name is Jim Marlowe," I told him. "I'm the new man Mr. Rothman hired yesterday."

"Oh, yes." He gave me his hand and I took it. "Turner, Adam Turner. Assistant manager."

"Pleased to meet you, Mr. Turner."

He nodded, stepped aside to let me come in. While he was relocking the door I glanced around the main floor. The cashier's desk was on the left, flanked by the wide gateway for the sensor alarm; you had to go through the gateway both entering and leaving, because there was a six-foot-high partition on the right-hand side. Beyond, several long display tables filled with sale books and recent arrivals were arranged for easy browsing. Floor-to-ceiling shelves covered the side walls, and stacks with narrow aisleways between them took up the rear half of the room. Off to one side toward the back, a flight of stairs led up to the second floor and another down to the basement.

I let Turner precede me through the gateway. He looked to be in his mid-sixties, nondescript and mild; but his rheumy blue eyes were alert and intelligent, and I thought that they would not miss much.

I asked him, "Is Mr. Rothman here?"

"Yes. He's in his office, upstairs on the second floor. He asked me to send you right up; he'll show you around personally."

"Thanks."

Most of the second floor was given over to stacks; according to a number of neatly painted signs, all of the books here were used hardcover fiction—general novels, mysteries, Western and science fiction. Another flight of stairs led to the third floor, but there was a chain drawn across the bottom and a sign that said, *No Admittance*. A wider corridor than the aisleways between the stacks extended the length of the far wall, and when I got over there I saw three doors, the middle one standing open. I stopped in front of the open one. Inside was a good-sized office — Rothman's, probably, judging from the size of the desk and the big old-fashioned safe in one corner — but nobody was in it.

I was standing there looking in when I heard a toilet flush. Then the third door opened and Rothman appeared. He saw me, caught up his cane from where it was leaning against the wall and limped over to me.

"One of the signs of advancing age is a weak bladder," he said, and gave me a rueful smile. "Have you been waiting long?"

"No, I just came up."

"You spoke to Adam, of course. I didn't tell him you were a detective; I thought it would be best if only you and I know your real purpose here."

I nodded. "Does he always come in this early?"

"Most days, yes. Sometimes he's here before I am, and I usually arrive by eight-thirty. His wife died a few years ago; he's lonely, and the shop is a second home to him."

"I see."

"Would you like to see the Antiquarian Room before I show you the rest of the shop?"

"Yes, please."

We went back to the stairs, and Rothman unlocked the chain and led me up to the third floor. There was a door at the top of the stairs; he unlocked it with his key, switched on the lights inside.

The Antiquarian Room was divided into two sections — the first and larger one containing several hundred books and pamphlets, the other one about a fifth as many prints, etchings, engravings, broadsides and maps. Half of the items were in glass display cases or inside glass-doored bookcases; the rest were openly shelved, most of those being sets of books: encyclopedias, histories, the collected works of nineteenth- and early twentieth-century authors. Refectory tables were set in the middle of each section, presumably so potential buyers could sit down and inspect whatever they were interested in. The good, musty smell of old books and old leather bindings was strong in the room.

I asked, "Are all the things in here valuable?"

"Comparatively, no," Rothman said. "Some are worth less than fifty dollars; they're kept here because of their age and because they're of interest only to serious collectors. I transferred a dozen or so of the most valuable items to my office safe several months ago, but there are still quite a few here worth a thousand dollars or more."

"Are most of those prints and the like?"

"No. Books."

"But the prints and engravings and maps that were stolen were worth more, weren't they?"

"Only in the case of the two Dürer etchings."

"Then why would the thief have taken prints and maps instead of the more expensive books?"

"I suppose because the people he's selling them to specialize in that sort of thing."

I moved around the room, examining the cases. Most of them were locked, but the locks were pretty flimsy; once the thief had got in here, it wouldn't have taken long to break them open. The lock on one in the print section had scratches on it, as if it had been picked with a sharp instrument. That was the case, Rothman told me, which had contained the Orient map that had disappeared three days ago.

When I was done looking around, Rothman locked the door again and we descended to the second floor. He gave me a brief tour of the fiction section; took me down to the first floor, where most of the nonfiction was kept; and pointed out the location of the various categories. With the exception of a wall devoted to Western and regional Americana, and to travel books, the basement was full of trade and mass-market paperbacks of various types and back-issue magazines. There was also a stockroom down there, at the rear.

By the time we came back up to the main floor, it was a quarter to ten and the other employees were beginning to arrive. The first of the three to show up was Harmon Boyette. He was about forty, gaunt, with curly black hair, ascetic features and a bushy mustache. Judging from his bloodshot eyes and splotchy skin, the faint trembling of his hands, he'd had another rough night with the bottle.

Rothman introduced us. Boyette gave me a brief, appraising look, seemed to decide I was nobody he was much interested in and said he was glad to meet me without meaning it. He didn't offer to shake hands.

Neal Vining came in five minutes later. Rothman had excused himself and gone back upstairs to answer another call of nature, so it was Adam Turner who performed the introductions this time. Vining had brown eyes, lank brown hair, a bright smile with a lot of teeth in it and one of those lean, athletic bodies that make you think of long-distance runners. He was dressed in a sports jacket and slacks, very spiffy, and he looked older than the twenty-six Rothman had told me he was.

"Marlowe," he said, pumping my hand. "English name. But you don't look a bit English, I'm afraid."

"My mother was Italian," I said truthfully.

"Lovely people, the Italians. Have you ever been?"

"To Italy? No, I haven't."

"You should go someday, if you have the chance. Do you know books well, Jim?"

"Not as well as I'd like to."

"You'll learn them here, then. Won't he, Adam?"

"If he chooses," Turner said.

I did not get to meet Tom Lennox right away because he hadn't shown up yet when Turner hustled me down into the basement stockroom and put me to work. There were a couple of hundred newly acquired paperbacks on a table; my job was to sort them into categories and shelve them alphabetically in the proper sections. I figured I had better complete that task, to make the proper impression, before I did any roaming around. It took me more than an hour, and the place was full of customers when I finally went back upstairs.

Vining was over in the Occult section, trying to sell a fat woman a book on witchcraft; I could hear him regaling her with esoteric information on the subject when I passed. Turner was behind the cashier's desk, and so was a short, stocky guy with not much hair who was talking on the telephone. I didn't see any sign of Boyette.

The stocky guy finished his conversation and replaced the receiver as I came up. He was around thirty, freckled, with sad eyes and the sad, jowly face of a hound; what hair he had was a dark reddish color. I thought he must be Tom Lennox, and Turner confirmed it when he introduced us.

"Good to have you with us, Mr. Marlowe," Lennox said. He had a soft, cultured voice that belied his appearance.

"Thanks. I'm glad to be here."

"You've had previous bookstore experience, have you?"

"Some," I said. "I'm also a collector."

"Oh? What do you collect?"

"Pulp magazines."

He wasn't impressed. Maybe he was a literary snob, or maybe he just had no interest in pulps; in any case, he said, "You have plenty of company these days. The prices tend to be highly overinflated."

"I know," I said. "Supply and demand. That's why I collect the more inexpensive variety."

Lennox nodded and turned away. So much for me, and so much for pulp magazines.

Turner asked me if I'd finished shelving the paperbacks, and I told him I had. Then he said, "Harmon is upstairs working in hardcover fiction. I'd like you to go up and give him a hand."

When I got upstairs I found Boyette in the mystery section, weeding out the stock—evidently to make room for new acquisitions. Books were stacked on the floor to one side.

"Mr. Turner sent me up to give you some help," I said.

"I don't need any help."

"Well, those were my instructions."

He ran a hand over his splotchy face; he was sweating and he looked sick. "All right, then. Take that stack of books downstairs and put them out front in the bargain bins. But make sure you stop at the desk first."

"Why is that?"

"So Turner can clear them before you go out. They told you about the alarm, didn't they?"

"Oh, right. I guess that's a pretty good safeguard, the alarm system."

"Is it?"

"It prevents thefts, doesn't it?"

"Sometimes," he said. "Not always."

"You mean people can still manage to steal books? I don't see how."

"There are ways."

"What ways?"

"Didn't anybody tell you about the thefts we've been having?"

"No," I said. "What sort of thefts?"

"Valuable items from the Antiquarian Room upstairs. A half-dozen over the past few months. Nobody knows how it's been done." His mouth turned sardonic. "Rothman thinks one of us is responsible."

"One of the employees?"

"That's right."

"Is that what you think, too?"

"I don't get paid to think," Boyette said. "Personally, I don't give a damn who's responsible. Whoever it is can steal Rothman blind for all I care."

"You sound as though you don't like Mr. Rothman much."

"Maybe I've got reason not to like him."

"He seems like a decent sort to me. . . ."

"He is if you suck up to him. I've got five times as much bookselling experience as Lennox and Vining, but I'm the one who gets all the scut work around here. That's because I don't brownnose anybody."

"But Lennox and Vining do?"

"Lennox goes to garage sales, buys books and resells them to Rothman for a few cents apiece. Vining gives him fancy presents from his father-in-law's store. All I give him is a good eight hours of work."

"That ought to be enough."

"It isn't," he said bitterly. He narrowed his eyes at me. "What about you, Marlowe? Are *you* a brownnoser?"

"No."

"Then we're in the same boat. But I wouldn't care if you were. I wouldn't even care if you went to Rothman and told him everything I just said."

"I wouldn't do that—"

"He could fire me tomorrow and I wouldn't give a damn. I don't like him and I don't like this place and I don't like being under suspicion all the time."

"If you feel that way, why don't you quit?"

"That's just what I intend to do. As soon as I can find another job."

A customer came clumping up the stairs just then and over into the aisle where we were, and that put an end to the conversation. Boyette said, "Go ahead and take those books downstairs," and returned his attention to the shelves.

I carried the stack of books down to the cashier's desk, waited while Turner cleared them across the sensor strip and then took them outside to where two rolling bins of bargain items were set in front of the display windows. When I got back to the second floor I tried to talk to Boyette again, to see if I could get anything else out of him, but he had lapsed into a moody silence. He didn't have more than a dozen words to say to me over the next two hours.

Rothman went out for lunch at twelve-thirty, Vining around one and Boyette at one-thirty. Lennox and Turner ate brown-bag lunches on the premises, Turner right there at the desk. I also ate lunch in the shop—I'd made myself a couple of sandwiches before leaving my flat that morning—up on the second floor where I could watch the stairs to the Antiquarian Room. Rothman had told me that all of the thefts had occurred between eleven and two; I didn't want to leave, even for a half-hour, and risk missing something.

But there was nothing to miss. Nobody went near the Antiquarian Room and nobody did anything else of a suspicious nature, at least as far as I could tell.

Boyette came back at two-fifteen. He no longer looked quite so sick; his face was flushed and his eyes were a little glassy. I was downstairs when he came in, working in the section marked *Belles Lettres*. Lennox happened to be nearby, and I moved over to him as Boyette climbed the stairs to the second floor.

"Looks as though Harmon drank his lunch," I said.

Lennox made a disapproving noise. "He generally does."

"An alcoholic?"

"That's rather obvious, isn't it?"

"I guess it is. He seems to be a pretty bitter man, from some of the things he said to me this morning."

"Don't pay any attention to him," Lennox said. "The man has a chip on his shoulder. He thinks he deserves better than his present lot, and he can be damned unpleasant at times."

"Do you think he's honest?"

Lennox frowned. "What sort of question is that?"

"Well, he told me about the thefts from the Antiquarian Room," I said. "He says Mr. Rothman believes one of the employees is responsible."

"He had no business talking to you about that," Lennox said stiffly. "The thefts are none of your concern."

"Maybe not, but I do work here now —"

"Yes. And if you want to continue working here, you'll do well to tend to your work and mind your own affairs."

He stalked away toward the cashier's desk. As he did, Neal Vining appeared around the corner of the near stack and came up beside me; he had a fat book on archaeology in one hand. "Harmon isn't the only fellow who can be unpleasant," he said. "Tom's a bit tight-assed himself, you know."

"You overheard?"

"Accidentally, yes."

"What's Lennox's problem?"

"Oh, he takes himself and his work much too seriously. One would think *he* owned the shop, the way he acts."

"Those thefts do seem pretty serious," I said.

"They are, of course. Nasty business. I expect we're all on edge because of them."

"Do you agree with Mr. Rothman that someone who works here is responsible?"

He shrugged. "So it would seem, under the circumstances."

"Who do you think it might be?"

"I really don't have any idea," Vining said. "For all *I* know, Mr. Rothman himself could be slipping out with the spoils. Not that I believe that's the case, you understand," he added hastily. "He's quite above reproach. The point is, the thief could be anyone."

"Even Adam Turner?"

"Adam? I hardly think so. But then, two of the missing items were etchings attributed to Albrecht Dürer, and Adam does have considerable expertise in that area. He once wrote an article on Dürer's work. He was also the person who arranged for Mr. Rothman to purchase the two etchings from the estate of a private collector."

"Oh? How was he able to do that?"

"The collector was an acquaintance of Adam's," Vining said. "They struck up a correspondence when the article was published."

Lennox returned and called Vining away to the

telephone, so I didn't have a chance to press him for any more information. But what he'd told me was food for thought. If Turner was the guilty party, there was no real mystery in how he'd managed the thefts. He could have cleared the stolen pieces through the sensor at any time, working as he did on the cashier's desk, and walked out with them hidden in his clothes. Or he could have simply arrived early in the morning, as Rothman had told me he did periodically, and removed them from the store before Rothman showed up.

I decided that on Monday I would run a background check on Turner, after all.

The rest of the afternoon passed uneventfully. I spent most of it on the main floor, with occasional trips upstairs to check on Boyette. He was still uncommunicative, and by four o'clock, when the drinks he'd had for lunch had worn off, he had turned surly; he snapped at me and at a customer who asked him a question abut a book. When closing time rolled around, he was the first one out the door.

I stayed until six-fifteen, making myself look busy; Vining and Lennox were gone by then. When Rothman came down he sent Turner and me on our way so he could shut off the sensor alarm and lock up as he usually did. I waited around for him outside. The rain had stopped and there were patches of clear sky among the clouds to the east; with any luck, the weather would be good for my weekend with Kerry.

Rothman came out a couple of minutes later. "Where's your car?" he asked when he finished locking the front doors.

"In the lot two blocks down."

"That's my direction. We can talk as we walk."

He set off at a brisk pace, in spite of his game leg. I asked him, "Everything okay in the Antiquarian Room?"

"Yes, I checked it this morning, and again tonight before I came down. Nothing's been touched. Have you found out anything so far?"

"Nothing specific, no," I said. I saw no purpose in telling him about Boyette's references to him, in making trouble for Boyette, unless it turned out to have some bearing on my investigation. And I didn't want to press him on Turner until I ran the background check. "I'm afraid this is the kind of job that may take some time, Mr. Rothman."

"I don't expect you to perform miracles," he said. "Time isn't important to me; finding out which of them is guilty, and how he's doing it, is what matters."

We had gone a block, and when we crossed the street Rothman stopped in front of a building that bore a sign reading: *Pacific Health Club*. "This is where I'm going," he said.

"You belong to a health club?"

He smiled. "I don't lift weights or play racquetball with Neal Vining, if that's what you're thinking. Mostly I use the Jacuzzi; it helps me relax and eases the pain in my leg."

"Oh, I see."

"You can join me if you like. Guests are permitted."

"No, thanks. I think I'll head home. I like to do my relaxing with a cold beer."

He glanced at my protruding belly. "So I see," he said, gently, without censure.

We said good night, and he entered the building and I went and got my car and drove home. I drank two cans of Schlitz — the hell with health clubs and the hell with my belly — and then called Kerry at Bates and Carpenter. But she was busy and couldn't talk more than a couple of minutes. She did say that the presentation was going according to schedule and that she still expected to be done with it by noon tomorrow.

"Is it all right if I stop by the book shop when I'm finished?" she asked. "I like bookstores; and I'd love to see you shlepping books around."

"I don't see why not. As long as you don't tell anybody I'm really a private eye on a case."

"I'll try to restrain myself. See you tomorrow, then."

"Lovely lady, I'll count the minutes."

"Phooey," she said, and rang off.

I made myself something to eat, read for a while and turned in early. It had been a reasonably productive day and I was satisfied with it. I had learned a few things; maybe I would learn a few more tomorrow that would establish some kind of pattern. Maybe tomorrow would turn out, I thought, to be an even more productive day.

Saturday was a productive day, all right.

The thief hit the Antiquarian Room again, and he did it right under my damn nose.

It happened, as before, sometime between eleven-twenty, when Rothman checked the room before going out for an early lunch, and two o'clock, when he went up to check it again. I was on the main floor talking to Kerry at the time he made the discovery. She had been there about a half-hour, browsing, looking terrific in a black suit and a frilly white blouse; she was about to buy a book she'd found—a scarce old one of her father's, one of his early novels—and she was telling me how pleased he was going to be because he was down to only two file copies of that particular title.

I didn't like Ivan Wade—Ivan the Terrible, I called him—any more than he liked me; he was overprotective of Kerry, supercilious, humorless and something of a jerk. So I said, "I'm thrilled for him."

"Now don't be that way," she said. "*The Redmayne Horror* really is a scarce book. And they only want fifteen dollars."

"*The Redmayne Horror* is a dumb title," I said.

"It was a pulp serial, originally. That was the kind of title they put on weird fiction back in the forties, in the pulps and in book editions; you know that."

"It's still a dumb title."

"Oh, stick it in your ear," she said, and made a face at me. "Can't you see I'm excited about this? I almost knocked over a man with a cane upstairs when I found it."

"That would be Mr. Rothman. Nice going."

"Well, I'm sorry. But I —"

And that was when Mr. Rothman appeared on the stairs and beckoned to me urgently. I left Kerry and followed him up to his office, and as soon as he shut the door he told me about the latest theft.

"It was another rare map," he said. His face was flushed and his knuckles showed white where they gripped the head of his cane. "A sixteenth-century map by the Flemish cartographer and geographer Gerhardus Mercator."

"Valuable?"

"Very. Damn, I should have put it in my safe months ago."

"Where was it kept?"

"In one of the glass display cases. The lock was broken, just as in the other thefts."

"Whichever of them it is, he's bold and he's quick," I said. "I've been on this floor off and on ever since you left for lunch. He couldn't have spent much time up there; he had to know exactly what he was after."

"What do we do now?"

"What did you do after you discovered the other thefts?"

"Asked the customers to leave, closed up shop for the day, then gathered my people together and questioned them."

"All right. Do the same thing this time, only let me get rid of the customers. When you start the questioning, ask everybody if they mind being searched. If any of them refuses, press him on it. Then designate me to do the searching."

"Do I tell them you're a detective?"

"No. We won't get anywhere by blowing my cover. Just say you want me to do the searching because I'm new and you don't have any reason to suspect me."

"The thief won't have the map on his person," Rothman said grimly. "He's too clever for that."

"I know. But I want to see how they react and what they might be carrying in their pockets. I don't think he'll have the duplicate key on him either — he's probably got it stashed somewhere in the shop — but it's worth checking for."

"And if none of that does any good?"

"Then you'll have to let them go home. And you and I'll search this place from top to bottom. If none of them can leave with the map, then it's still got to be here somewhere."

We went downstairs together. Kerry was still waiting; when I joined her she said, "What's the matter? You look upset."

"Trouble. Another theft. You'd better go now; we're closing the shop."

"Oh boy. Will you still be able to make our date tonight?"

"I hope so. If I can't I'll call you."

It took twenty minutes to clear the store of customers and to get the front door locked. Turner and the others knew right away what was going on; none of them had much to say at first, and I could see them giving each other faintly mistrustful glances. Lennox looked aggrieved, as if he took the thefts personally and the money was coming straight out of his pocket. Boyette seemed more angry than anything else, but it was a put-on kind of anger; he was suffering another hangover and his bloodshot eyes said the last thing he wanted to deal with was another crisis. Vining was subdued, the set of his face grave and concerned. Turner wore an expression of mingled agitation and worry— the look of a loyal company man whose boss is in trouble. None of the four seemed nervous. Or any more guilty, on the surface, than I was.

The six of us gathered near the cashier's desk. Rothman started off by explaining what it was that had been stolen this time. Then he asked if anyone had seen anyone else go up to the Antiquarian Room; nobody had. Had anyone seen anything of a suspicious nature between eleven-thirty and two o'clock? Nobody had. Who had left the store during that time period? Boyette had, and so had Lennox. But Turner had seen them both leave, through the alarm gateway as always, and nothing had happened.

Rothman said then, "I'm sorry, gentlemen, but these thefts have become intolerable; getting to the bottom of them calls for extreme measures. Do any of you object to being searched?"

The only one who did was Boyette. "Why the hell should I stand for that?" he said. "Even if I were guilty, I wouldn't be stupid enough to have the map on my person."

Lennox said, "Then you shouldn't object to being searched."

"I've had enough of this crap. Thefts, suspicion, body searches — pretty soon it'll be accusations. I won't stand for it; I'm leaving right now and I'm not coming back."

"If you do, Harmon," Vining said, "it will make you look guilty, you know."

"I don't care," Boyette said. He looked mean and belligerent; there was a pugnacious thrust to his jaw. "Is anyone going to try to stop me?"

Rothman glanced at me, but I gave him a faint headshake. I had no right to restrain Boyette, or to search him, without some proof of guilt; if any of us tried, it would leave us open to a lawsuit.

"All right, Harmon," Rothman said coldly. "Consider your employment terminated. I'll mail you what I owe you in salary. Adam, let him out."

Turner went through the gateway and unlocked the front door. The alarm was still operational, and when Boyette stomped through after him the bell didn't go off. It was still possible that he was guilty, but he wasn't walking out of here with the Mercator map.

When Turner relocked the door and came back to join the rest of us, Rothman said, "Does anyone else feel the same way? Or will you all submit to a search?"

There were no more objections. Rothman designated me to do the searching, as we'd agreed, and I frisked each man in turn. Turner first, because I knew he wasn't carrying the map; he'd gone through the gateway just as Boyette had. Then Vining, and then Lennox. No map. All three men had keys — no loose ones, though; they were all on rings or in cases — and Rothman examined each one stoically. His silence told me that none of the keys was the duplicate to the Antiquarian Room door.

There was nothing to do then but let the three of them leave, too. Turner was the last to go, and he went reluctantly. "If you're planning to search the shop, Mr. Rothman," he said, "I can help. . . ."

"No, you go ahead. Marlowe will help me this time."

As soon as Turner was gone, Rothman and I began our search. We started with the Antiquarian Room; it wasn't likely that the thief would have hidden the Mercator map in there, but we gave it a good going-over just the same. No map. We went down to the second floor and searched the stacks, the storage room next to Rothman's office, the bathroom. No map. We combed the first-floor stacks and shelves, the display tables, the cashier's desk, even the window displays. No map. In the basement we searched the paperback sections, the Americana and travel shelves, the stockroom. No map.

We covered every inch of that building, from top to bottom. There was no way the map could have been gotten out, and yet there was no place an item of its size and fragility could have been hidden inside the shop that we had overlooked.

So what *had* happened to it?

Where the hell was the missing map?

It was ten of seven when Rothman and I finally called it quits, left the shop and went our separate ways. I was almost as frustrated as he was by then. On the drive home to my flat, I kept gnawing at the question, the seeming impossibility of the theft, like a dog gnaws at a bone. And the more I gnawed, the more I felt as if I were close to the marrow of the thing.

The answer was something clever and audacious,

yes, but I also sensed that it was something simple. And that I had heard enough and seen enough the past three days to put it all together — a lot of little things that just needed to be shifted around into the right order. Damn it, I could almost taste the marrow. . . .

I gave Kerry a brief call, to tell her I would be late, and then showered the bookstore dust off me and put on my suit. Dusk was settling by the time I got up to Diamond Heights. The weather had cleared and the view from up there was spectacular; you could see both bridges, the wide sweep of the bay, the Oakland hills and the Pacific Ocean in the opposite direction. It was too nice an evening, I told myself, to let my frustration spoil things with Kerry, and as I parked the car in front of her building I decided I wouldn't let that happen.

I went into the vestibule and rang her bell, and she buzzed me in right away. When I got upstairs she was waiting for me in a shimmery green dress with plenty of cleavage — a dress designed to knock your optic out, as the pulp private eyes used to say.

"Sorry I'm so late," I said, admiring her. "It was some afternoon."

"That's okay. Did you catch the thief?"

"No. He swiped another rare map and managed to get it out of the store again, past the alarm system. I ought to be able to figure out which one of them it is and how he did it, but I can't seem to do it."

"Uh-oh. Does that mean you're going to be moody tonight?"

"No. I am not going to be moody tonight."

"You're *already* moody," she said.

"Bah. Let's go eat."

We went down to the car. Kerry said, "I'm starved. You must be, too."

"Yeah. They do a fine chorizo-and-peppers dish at the Oaxaca, very hot and spicy."

"So of course you have to drink a lot of beer with it."

"Sure. What's Mexican food without cold Mexican beer?"

"You put away more beer than any man I've ever known," she said. "I swear, sometimes I think you've got a hollow leg."

I leaned forward to switch on the ignition. Then I stopped with my hand on the key and stared at her. "What did you say?"

"I said sometimes I think you've got a hollow leg. What's the matter?"

"That's it," I said.

"What's it?"

"The answer."

"I don't know what you're talking about. . . ."

I waved her quiet, started the car, switched on the headlights — it was full dark now — and pulled away from the curb; I tended to think more clearly while I was driving. By the time we approached Diamond Heights Boulevard, I had most of it put together. And when we were headed down the steep, curving boulevard, nearing Glen Canyon, I had the rest of it. All I needed was confirmation of one thing, and Kerry herself could give me that.

But before I could ask her about it, there was a roar of noise outside and the interior of the car was bathed in the bright glare of headlights. Another car had come boiling up behind us, so close that its lights were like huge staring eyes framed in the rear window. Damn tailgater, I thought, and took my foot off the accelerator and tapped the brake pedal gently, just enough to let the other driver see the flash of the brake lights.

Only he didn't slow down; he just kept coming. And his front bumper smacked into my rear bumper, hard enough to jolt the car and almost wrench the wheel loose from my hands.

Kerry twisted around on the seat. "My God! What's the matter with him? What's he *doing*?"

"Hang on!"

The other car jarred into us again, harder than before, shattering one or both of the taillights. Even though I was ready for it, I had to fight the wheel and feather the brakes to keep my car from fishtailing into a skid. The tires made screaming noises on the pavement; I could smell the burning rubber and the sudden sour odor of my own sweat.

The road had steepened and hooked over toward the long, narrow, tree-choked expanse of Glen Canyon; for a stretch of maybe five hundred yards, Diamond Heights Boulevard paralleled the canyon's eastern rim. In the reach of my headlights I could see that there was no guardrail, just a sidewalk and some knee-high brown grass on a strip of bank and then the drop-off, sheer, almost straight down. If we went off there, there wasn't much chance that we'd survive.

And that was just what the driver of the other car wanted, all right. It wasn't a drunk back there, or kids playing dangerous games; it was somebody bent on mayhem.

Downhill to the left, on the other side of the curve, a residential street cut away uphill. I yelled at Kerry again to hang on and got set to drop the transmission lever into low gear so I could make a fast, sharp left-hand turn into the other street. There was nothing else I could do with the trailing car hanging on my bumper the way it was.

But the driver saw the street, too, and before I got

close enough to make the turn, his headlights flicked out to the left, into the uphill lane. In my side mirror I could see the bulky shape of the car outlined behind the glare; then he accelerated and pulled up abreast. I glanced over at him, but all I could make out was one person, his face a white smear in the darkness. Then I put my eyes back on the road and kept them there, muscles tensed, hands tightened on the wheel, because I sensed what he was going to try to do next.

It was only a couple of seconds before he did it, just as I started into the wide left-hand curve along the rim of the canyon: he pulled slightly ahead and then whipped over into me, hard along the front fender. There was a crunching sound, and Kerry cried out, and the car shimmied and the right front tire scraped against the curb on that side. But I was able to maintain control, even though we were still crowded together and he was trying to use his momentum to shove us up and over the bank.

I came down hard on the brake pedal, bracing myself, throwing my right arm out in front of Kerry to keep her from flying into the windshield. The tires shrieked again; we bucked and slid through the curve, losing speed. The other car glanced off, with another tearing-metal noise, yawing at a slight angle in front of me. Then the driver got it straightened out and braked as I had, swinging back full into the other lane so he could try ramming us again.

He would have done it, too, if it hadn't been for the third car that came sailing around another curve below, headed uphill.

I saw the oncoming headlights sweep through the scattered eucalyptus that grew inside the canyon further down, but the other driver was too intent on me to notice them because he didn't try to swing back into the downhill lane. Frantically I stood on the brake and got ready to yank on the emergency brake, if that was what it took to bring us to a stop; it seemed sure there would be a collision and all I could think was: Kerry might be hurt, I can't let her get hurt.

There was no collision. The driver of the third car saw what was happening, leaned hard on the horn, and managed to swerve up onto the sidewalk and across somebody's front lawn. But the guy who'd tried to kill Kerry and me had run out of luck. He saw the third car in time to swerve himself, back into the downhill lane, only he did it too sharply; he missed the third car, all right, by at least twenty feet—and he missed hitting mine by the same distance when he veered in front of me—but the rear end of his car broke loose and he wasn't able to fight through the skid and pull it out.

His car went out of control, spun all the way around, and then hit the curb and bounced up into the air like something made out of rubber. Its headlights sprayed the trees as it hurtled toward them, sideways. In the next second it was gone, and in the second after that the explosive sound of buckling metal and breaking glass and splintering wood erupted from inside the canyon.

I managed to bring my car to a stop. When I took my hands off the wheel they were as wet as if I'd dunked them in water.

"God," Kerry said, in a soft, trembly voice.

"Are you all right?"

"Yes. I . . . just give me a minute. . . ."

I touched her arm, and then opened the door and got out. People were spilling from houses in the vicinity, running toward the canyon; the driver of the third car, a heavyset woman, was slumped against her front fender, not moving, looking dazed. I ran up onto the sidewalk and ahead to where the other car had gone over. It was wrapped around one of the eucalyptus about a third of the way down the slope; the upper part of the tree had been sheared off and was canted at a drunken angle. From the mangled appearance of the wreckage, I didn't see how the guy inside could have survived.

But I was wrong about that. When I got there along with a couple of other people, and we dragged him out, he was alive. Unconscious and pretty badly cut up, but unless he had internal injuries, it looked as though he'd make it all right.

It did not surprise me when I saw who he was. Because he was the same person who had committed the thefts in John Rothman's book shop — the same clever, greedy, *stupid* young man.

Neal Vining.

Three hours later, I was sitting in a room at the Hall of Justice with Kerry, John Rothman and an inspector I knew named Jack Logan, who had been the investigating officer when Rothman first reported the thefts. Vining was in the hospital under police guard. He'd already been charged with attempted vehicular homicide, and had been coherent enough and frightened enough to confess to that, and when I got done with my explanations he would also be charged with several counts of grand larceny.

I was saying, "I knew even before Vining tried to run us off the road that he was the thief. And I know how he got the stolen items out of the store, too. It was a combination of things I'd seen and heard; and when Kerry made a comment about me having a hollow leg, because I like to drink beer, it triggered an association that put it all together."

"Hollow leg?" Rothman said. "I don't understand what—"

"You'll see what I mean in a minute. The whole thing is really pretty simple; it was Vining himself, in fact, who told me how he pulled off the thefts, either without realizing what he was saying or, more likely, because he was so sure of himself that it was his way of bragging. He said yesterday, "For all I know, Mr. Rothman himself could be slipping out with the spoils.""

They were all staring at me, Rothman with a look of incredulity. "Are you saying *I* took the items out of the shop for him? That's preposterous—"

"No, it isn't," I said. "You took them out, all right; that's the beauty of his scheme. He made you an unwitting accomplice."

"How could he possibly have done that?"

"By putting the stolen items inside your cane," I said.

"My *cane?*"

"Vining gave it to you, didn't he? Some months ago? Harmon Boyette told me Vining was in the habit of giving you presents from his father-in-law's haberdashery."

"Yes, but . . ." Rothman seemed a little nonplussed. He reached for the cane, propped against the side of the chair, and gawped at it as if he'd never seen it before.

Logan said, "You mean the cane's hollow?"

"Yes. That's the significance of Kerry's hollow-leg comment. And that's why Vining stole only etchings, prints and maps, instead of books that were more valuable, since you installed the alarm system: they could be rolled up and inserted inside the cane. They still make canes like that over in England; people keep money and other small valuable items inside them—as a safeguard against theft, ironically enough. It wouldn't have been difficult for Vining to have one imported through his father-in-law's store."

Rothman was running his fingers over the thick barrel of the cane, peering at it. "How does the damn thing work?"

"I don't know. But it shouldn't take us long to find out."

It took us about two minutes. The catch was well concealed, and so was the long hinged opening; you couldn't see either with the naked eye, you couldn't feel the grooves with your fingers and it wasn't likely that you could open it by accident. Fine British craftsmanship. Logan was the one who finally found the catch, and when the hinges released I saw what I expected to see: the hollow interior contained a rolled-up length of parchment.

Rothman took the parchment out and unrolled it gently. "My God," he said, "the Mercator map."

"Right where Vining put it this afternoon," I said, "after he stole it from the Antiquarian Room."

"But I keep the cane with me at all times; I need it to get around for any distance. I don't see how —"

"You don't take it into the bathroom with you, Mr. Rothman. When I got to the store yesterday morning, and went up to talk to you, you were in the bathroom; the cane was leaning against the wall outside. I remember you taking it from there when you came out."

Rothman nodded. "You're right, of course; I never took the cane into the bathroom because it was too cumbersome in that little cubicle. I always left it against the wall outside."

"And you used the bathroom fairly often during the day, didn't you? Because of your bladder problem?"

"Yes."

"So it was easy enough for Vining to put the stolen

items inside the cane. He committed each of his thefts while you were out to lunch or otherwise away from the store in the early afternoons so he could be sure you wouldn't catch him red-handed. Then he either hid the pieces somewhere, or kept them inside his clothes, until you returned and he saw an opportunity to put them inside the cane while you were in the bathroom and there was nobody else in the vicinity. It only took him a few seconds each time.

"The whole idea was to beat the sensor alarm. Everyone who left the store after one of the thefts had to pass through the alarm gateway *except you*; you were always the last one to leave on those days, and you always switched the alarm off before you went through the gateway yourself to lock up. The *only* person who could have taken the items out of the shop was you."

"But how did Vining retrieve them from the cane after I'd left?" Rothman asked. Then I saw understanding come to him and he answered his own question. "Well, I'll be damned. The Pacific Health Club."

"Right. Vining is a member, too, isn't he?"

"Yes, he is. How did you know?"

"You told me yourself, last night. You said you didn't go to the health club to lift weights or to play racquetball with Neal Vining; you wouldn't have phrased it that way unless he was also a member."

Logan asked, "How did Vining get the stuff out of the cane at the health club?"

"I go there every night to use the Jacuzzi," Rothman explained. "It's right off the locker room, so I've never taken the cane in there with me; there's no place to put it near the Jacuzzi."

"You left it inside your locker, is that it?"

"Yes. The locker has a combination lock, but I don't suppose it would have been difficult for Vining to get the combination. I remember him standing there talking to me on more than one occasion while I was opening it."

"So all he had to do," I said, "was to wait for you to go into the Jacuzzi and then open up your locker, transfer the stolen items from the cane to inside his clothing and walk out with them. Simple as that."

Rothman shook his head wonderingly. "The only other question I have," he said, "is why did Vining try to kill you and Miss Wade tonight?"

"He slipped up this afternoon at the store, while he was putting the Mercator map inside the cane. He'd been careful not to let anybody see him in the past; this time he wasn't so careful and somebody did see him."

"Me," Kerry said. "Well, I didn't exactly see him putting anything inside the cane; I just saw him with the cane in his hand."

"How did that happen?"

"I was browsing in the stacks at the rear of the fiction section. In the W's, along the rear wall directly behind the last stack, near what must be the bathroom. I guess he didn't see me when he looked down the aisles, so he didn't think anybody was around. I found an old scarce book of my father's — he's been a writer for forty years, you see — and I was excited about it; I grabbed it off the shelf and hurried out into the last aisle, and a man was standing there with that cane in his hand. I bumped right into him."

"She told me about that a few minutes later," I said. "At the time I naturally assumed the man she'd bumped into was Mr. Rothman. But later, I realized it could have been Vining. And it was."

"Then it was Miss Wade he was after tonight?"

Rothman asked. "Because he was afraid she'd seen him put the Mercator map inside the cane?"

"Not exactly," I said. "Vining was trying to kill both of us. He was afraid Kerry had seen him with the map, yes, and he wanted to know who she was; from what he told the police at the hospital a little while ago, he hadn't formed any definite plans about her at that time. He'd followed her downstairs and overheard her talking to me, about the date we had tonight, so he knew we were friends. After he left the shop he waited around until I left at seven o'clock and then followed me until I led him to Kerry's apartment building. I was so preoccupied when I went inside to get her that I left my car unlocked. Vining looked inside and found out from the registration that I'm a detective. That really unnerved him. So when I drove away with Kerry a little while later, he followed us again—maybe with the intention of committing murder, maybe not. He said he didn't plan to try forcing us off the road; he just did it on impulse. Whether it was premeditated or not is up to a jury to decide."

And that was about it. Rothman still had the problem of recovering the other stolen items, but with a full confession from Vining—and it seemed probable the police would get one—he would know to whom they had been sold, and the chances were good that he would be able to force their return.

Saturday night may have been a bust as far as my date with Kerry had gone, but early Sunday morning at her apartment was something else again. Early Sunday morning was terrific.

"I love to watch you work," she said once. "You're a pretty good detective, you know that?"

"Well," I said modestly, "I do the best I can."

"Yes, you do. No matter what you're doing."

"The fire's getting low. Shall I get up and put another log on?"

"The heck with the fire," she said.

Neither of us noticed when it finally went out.

FROM ANOTHER WORLD
by Clayton Rawson

Born in Elyria, Ohio, Clayton Rawson (1906–1971) graduated from Ohio State University and also attended the Art Institute of Chicago. He had a long association with both magazine and book publishing, working in editorial positions at True Detective *and* Master Detective *magazines and as the Mystery Editor for the Ziff-Davis chain of magazines from 1942 to 1947. He later held such important posts as Director of the Unicorn Mystery Book Club and Editor of Simon & Schuster's Inner Sanctum Mystery series, and also served as the Managing Editor of* Ellery Queen's Mystery Magazine *from 1963 to 1970.*

As an author, he is best known as the creator of "The Great Merlini," perhaps the most famous magician detective in history. His short stories featuring Merlini can be found in the The Great Merlini : The Complete Stories of the Magician Detective *(1979). An accomplished magician himself and the author of several important non-fiction books on the subject, he brought a great deal of technical accuracy to his well-plotted novels, the best known of which are* Death From a Top Hat *(1938),* The Headless Lady *(1940), and* No Coffin for the Corpse *(1942).*

Like his novels, his short stories frequently involve an "impossible" crime of one sort or another, including the locked-room type.

It was undoubtedly one of the world's strangest rooms. The old-fashioned roll-top desk, the battered typewriter, and the steel filing cabinet indicated that it was an office. There was even a calendar memo-pad, a pen and pencil set, and an overflowing ashtray on the desk, but any resemblance to any other office stopped right there.

The desk top also held a pair of handcuffs, half a

dozen billiard balls, a shiny nickel-plated revolver, one celluloid egg, several decks of playing cards, a bright green silk handkerchief, and a stack of unopened mail. In one corner of the room stood a large, galvanized-iron milk-can with a strait jacket lying on its top. A feathered devil mask from the upper Congo leered down from the wall above and the entire opposite wall was papered with a Ringling Bros. and Barnum & Bailey twenty-four sheet poster.

A loose-jointed dummy-figure of a small boy with pop-eyes and violently red hair lay on the filing cabinet together with a skull and a fish-bowl filled with paper flowers. And in the cabinet's bottom drawer, which was partly open and lined with paper, there was one half-eaten carrot and a twinkly-nosed, live white rabbit.

A pile of magazines, topped by a French journal, *L'Illusioniste,* was stacked precariously on a chair, and a large bookcase tried vainly to hold an even larger flood of books that overflowed and formed dusty stalagmites growing up from the floor—books whose authors would have been startled at the company they kept. Shaw's *Joan of Arc* was sandwiched between Rowan's *Story of the Secret Service* and the *Memoirs of Robert Houdin*. Arthur Machen, Dr. Hans Gross, William Blake, Sir James Jeans, Rebecca West, Robert Louis Stevenson, and Ernest Hemingway were bounded on either side by Devol's *Forty Years a Gambler on the Mississippi* and Reginald Scott's *Discoverie of Witchcraft*.

The merchandise in the shop beyond the office had a similar surrealistic quality, but the inscription on the glass of the outer door, although equally strange, did manage to supply an explanation. It read: *Miracles For Sale*—THE MAGIC SHOP, *A. Merlini, Prop.*

And that gentleman, naturally, was just as unusual as his place of business. For one thing, he hadn't put a foot in it, to my knowledge, in at least a week. When he finally did reappear, I found him at the desk sleepily and somewhat glumly eyeing the unopened mail.

He greeted me as though he hadn't seen another human being in at least a month, and the swivel chair creaked as he settled back in it, put his long legs up on the desk, and yawned. Then he indicated the card bearing his business slogan — "Nothing Is Impossible" — which was tacked on the wall.

"I may have to take that sign down," he said lazily. "I've just met a theatrical producer, a scene designer, and a playwright, all of whom are quite impossible. They came in here a week before opening night and asked me to supply several small items mentioned in the script. In one scene a character said, 'Begone!' and the stage directions read: 'The genie and his six dancing girl slaves vanish instantly.' Later an elephant, complete with howdah and princess, disappeared in the same way. I had to figure out how to manage all that and cook up a few assorted miracles for the big scene in heaven, too. Then I spent thirty-six hours in bed. And I'm still half-asleep." He grinned wryly and added, "Ross, if you want anything that is not a stock item, you can whistle for it."

"I don't want a miracle," I said. "Just an interview. What do you know about ESP and PK?"

"Too much," he said. "You're doing another magazine article?"

"Yes. And I've spent the last week with a queer assortment of characters, too — half a dozen psychologists, some professional gamblers, a nuclear physicist, the secretary of the Psychical Research Society, and a neurologist. I've got an appointment in half an hour with a millionaire, and after that I want to hear what you think of it."

"You interviewed Dr. Rhine at Duke University, of course."

I nodded. "Sure. He started it all. He says he's proved conclusively that there really are such things as telepathy, mind-reading, clairvoyance, X-Ray vision, and probably crystal-gazing as well. He wraps it all up in one package and calls it ESP—meaning Extra Sensory Perception."

"That," Merlini said, "is not the half of it. His psychokinesis, or PK for short, is positively miraculous—and frightening." The magician pulled several issues of the *Journal of Parapsychology* from the stack of magazines and upset the whole pile. "If the conclusions Rhine has published here are correct—if there really is a tangible mental force that can not only reach out and influence the movements of dice but exert its mysterious control over other physical objects as well—then he has completely upset the apple-cart of modern psychology and punctured a whole library of general scientific theory as well."

"He's already upset me," I said. "I tried to use PK in a crap game Saturday night. I lost sixty-eight bucks."

My skepticism didn't disturb Merlini. He went right on, gloomier than ever. "If Rhine is right, his ESP and PK have reopened the Pandora's box in which science thought it had forever sealed Voodoo and witchcraft and enough other practices of primitive magic to make your hair stand on end. And *you're* growling about losing a few dollars—"

Behind me a hearty, familiar voice said, "I haven't got anything to worry about except a homicidal maniac who has killed three people in the last two days and left absolutely no clues. But can I come in?"

Inspector Homer Gavigan of the New York City Police Department stood in the doorway, his blue eyes twinkling frostily.

Merlini, liking the Cassandra role he was playing, said, "Sure, I've been waiting for you. But don't think that PK won't give you a splitting headache, too. All a murderer would have to do to commit the perfect crime—and a locked room one at that—would be to exert his psychokinetic mental force from a distance against the gun trigger." He pointed at the revolver on the desk. "Like this—"

Gavigan and I both saw the trigger, with no finger on it, move.

Bang!

The gun's report was like a thunderclap in the small room. I knew well enough that it was only a stage prop and the cartridge a blank, but I jumped a foot. So did Gavigan.

"Look, dammit!" the Inspector exploded, "how did you—"

The Great Merlini grinned. He was fully awake now and enjoying himself hugely. "No," he said, "that wasn't PK, luckily. Just ordinary run-of-the-mill conjuring. The Rising Cards and the Talking Skull are both sometimes operated the same way. You can have the secret at the usual catalog price of—"

Like most policemen Gavigan had a healthy respect for firearms and he was still jumpy. "I don't want to buy either of them," he growled. "Do we have a date for dinner—or don't we? I'm starved."

"We do," Merlini said, pulling his long, lean self up out of the chair and reaching for his coat. "Can you join us, Ross?"

I shook my head. "Not this time. I've got a date just now with Andrew Drake."

In the elevator Merlini gave me an odd look and asked, "Andrew Drake? What has he got to do with ESP and PK?"

"What doesn't he have something to do with?" I replied. "Six months ago, it was the Drake Plan to Outlaw War; he tried to take over the UN singlehanded.

Two months ago he announced he was setting up a fifteen-million dollar research foundation to find a cancer cure in six months. 'Polish it off like we did the atom bomb,' he says. 'Put in enough money and you can accomplish anything.' Now he's head over heels in ESP with some Yogi mixed in. 'Unleash the power of the human mind and solve all our problems.' Just like that."

"So that's what he's up to," Merlini said as we came out on to 42nd Street, half a block from Times Square, to face a bitterly cold January wind. "I wondered."

Then, as he followed Gavigan into the official car that waited and left me shivering on the curb, he threw a last cryptic sentence over his shoulder.

"When Drake mentions Rosa Rhys," he said, "you might warn him that he's heading for trouble."

Merlini didn't know how right he was. If any of us had had any clairvoyant ability at all, I wouldn't have taken a cab up to Drake's; all three of us would have gone — in Gavigan's car and with the siren going full blast.

As it was, I stepped out all alone in front of the big 98th Street house just off Riverside Drive. It was a sixty-year-old mansion built in the tortured style that had been the height of architectural fashion in the '80's but was now a smoke-blackened monstrosity as coldly depressing as the weather.

I nearly froze both ears just getting across the pavement and up the steps where I found a doctor with his finger glued — or frozen perhaps — to the bell push. A doctor? No, it wasn't ESP; a copy of the *A.M.A. Journal* stuck out his overcoat pocket, and his left hand carried the customary small black case. But he didn't have the medical man's usual clinical detachment. This doctor was jumpy as hell.

When I asked, "Anything wrong?" his head jerked around, and his pale blue eyes gave me a startled look. He was a thin, well-dressed man in his early forties.

"Yes," he said crisply. "I'm afraid so." He jabbed a long forefinger at the bell again just as the door opened.

At first I didn't recognize the girl who looked out at us. When I had seen her by daylight earlier in the week, I had tagged her as in the brainy-but-a-bit-plain category, a judgment I revised somewhat now, considering what the Charles hair-do and Hattie Carnegie dress did for her.

"Oh, hello, doctor," she said. "Come in."

The doctor began talking even before he crossed the threshold. "Your father, Elinor — is he still in the study?"

"Yes, I think so. But what —"

She stopped because he was already gone, running down the hall toward a door at its end. He rattled the doorknob, then rapped loudly.

"Mr. Drake! Let me in!"

The girl looked puzzled, then frightened. Her dark eyes met mine for an instant, and then her high heels clicked on the polished floor as she too ran down the hall. I didn't wait to be invited. I followed.

The doctor's knuckles rapped again on the door. "Miss Rhys!" he called. "It's Dr. Garrett. Unlock the door!" There was no answer.

Garrett tried the doorknob once more, then threw his shoulder against the door. It didn't move.

"Elinor, do you have a key? We must get in there — quickly!"

She said, "No. Father has the only keys. Why don't they answer? What's wrong?"

"I don't know," Garrett said. "Your father phoned me just now. He was in pain. He said, *Hurry! I need you.*

*I'm—'"*The doctor hesitated, watching the girl; then he finished " *'—dying.'* After that—no answer." Garrett turned to me. "You've got more weight than I have. Think you can break this door in?"

I looked at it. The door seemed solid enough, but it was an old house and the wood around the screws that held the lock might give. "I don't know," I said. "I'll try."

Elinor Drake moved to one side and the doctor stepped behind me. I threw myself against the door twice and the second time felt it move a bit. Then I hit it hard. Just as the door gave way I heard the tearing sound of paper.

But before I could discover what caused that, my attention was held by more urgent matters. I found myself staring at a green-shaded desk lamp, the room's only source of light, at the overturned phone on the desk top, and at the sprawled shape that lay on the floor in front of the desk. A coppery highlight glinted on a letter-opener near the man's feet. Its blade was discolored with a dark wet stain.

Dr. Garrett said, "Elinor, you stay out," as he moved past me to the body and bent over it. One of his hands lifted Andrew Drake's right eyelid, the other felt his wrist.

I have never heard a ghost speak but the sound that came then was exactly what I would expect—a low, quivering moan shot with pain. I jerked around and saw a glimmer of white move in the darkness on my left.

Behind me, Elinor's whisper, a tense thread of sound, said, "Lights," as she clicked the switch by the door. The glow from the ceiling fixture overhead banished both the darkness and the spectre—but what remained was almost as unlikely. A chair lay overturned on the carpet, next to a small table that stood in the center of the room. In a second chair, slumped forward with her head resting on the tabletop, was the body of a young woman.

She was young, dark-haired, rather good-looking, and had an excellent figure. This latter fact was instantly apparent because—and I had to look twice before I could believe what I saw—she wore a brief, skin-tight, one-piece bathing suit. Nothing else.

Elinor's eyes were still on the sprawled shape on the floor. "Father. He's—dead?"

Garrett nodded slowly and stood up.

I heard the quick intake of her breath but she made no other sound. Then Garrett strode quickly across to the woman at the table.

"Unconscious," he said after a moment. "Apparently a blow on the head—but she's beginning to come out of it." He looked again at the knife on the floor. "We'll have to call the police."

I hardly heard him. I was wondering why the room was so bare. The hall outside and the living room that opened off it were furnished with the stiff, formal ostentation of the overly-rich. But Drake's study, by contrast, was as sparsely furnished as a cell in a Trappist monastery. Except for the desk, the small table, the two chairs, and a three-leaf folding screen that stood in one corner, it contained no other furniture. There were no pictures on the walls, no papers, and although there were shelves for them, no books. There wasn't even a blotter or pen on the desk top. Nothing but the phone, desk lamp—and, strangely enough, a roll of gummed paper tape.

But I only glanced at these things briefly. It was the large casement window in the wall behind the desk that held my attention—a dark rectangle beyond which, like a scattered handful of bright jewels, were the lights of

Jersey and, above them, frosty pinpoints of stars shining coldly in a black sky.

The odd thing was that the window's center line, where its two halves joined, was criss-crossed by two-foot strips of brown paper tape pasted to the glass. The window was, quite literally, sealed shut. It was then that I remembered the sound of tearing paper as the lock had given way and the door had come open.

I turned. Elinor still stood there—motionless. And on the inside of the door and on the jamb were more of the paper strips. Four were torn in half, two others had been pulled loose from the wall and hung curled from the door's edge.

At that moment a brisk, energetic voice came from the hall. "How come you leave the front door standing wide open on the coldest day in—"

Elinor turned to face a broad-shouldered young man with wavy hair, hand-painted tie, and a completely self-assured manner. She said, "Paul!" then took one stumbling step and was in his arms.

He blinked at her. "Hey! What's wrong?" Then he saw what lay on the floor by the desk. His self-confidence sagged.

Dr. Garrett moved to the door. "Kendrick," he said, "take Elinor out of here. I'll—"

"No!" It was Elinor's voice. She straightened up, turned suddenly and started into the room.

But Paul caught her. "Where are you going?"

She tried to pull away from him. "I'm going to phone the police." Her eyes followed the trail of blood-stains that led from the body across the beige carpet to the overturned chair and the woman at the table. "She—killed him."

That was when I started for the phone myself. But I

hadn't taken more than two steps when the woman in the bathing suit let out a hair-raising shriek.

She was gripping the table with both hands, her eyes fixed on Drake's body with the rigid, unblinking stare of a figure carved from stone. Then, suddenly, her body trembled all over, and she opened her mouth again — But Garrett got there first.

He slapped her on the side of the face — hard.

It stopped the scream, but the horror still filled her round dark eyes and she still stared at the body as though it were some demon straight from hell.

"Hysteria," Garrett said. Then seeing me start again toward the phone, "Get an ambulance too." And when he spoke to Paul Kendrick this time, it was an order. "And get Elinor out of here — quickly!"

Elinor Drake was looking at the girl in the bathing suit with wide, puzzled eyes. "She — she killed him. Why?"

Paul nodded. He turned Elinor around gently but swiftly and led her out.

The cops usually find too many fingerprints on a phone, none of them any good because they are superimposed on each other. But I handled the receiver carefully just the same, picking it up by one end. When Spring 7-1313 answered, I gave the operator the facts fast, then asked him to locate Inspector Gavigan and have him call me back. I gave Drake's number.

As I talked I watched Dr. Garrett open his black case and take out a hypodermic syringe. He started to apply it to the woman's arm just as I hung up.

"What's that, Doc?"

"Sedative. Otherwise she'll be screaming again in a minute."

The girl didn't seem to feel the needle as it went in.

Then, noticing two bright spots of color on the table, I went across to examine them closely and felt more than ever as though I had stepped straight into a surrealist painting. I was looking at two rounded conical shapes each about two inches in length. Both were striped like candy canes, one in maroon against a white background, the other in thinner brilliant red stripes against an opalescent amber.

"Did Drake," I asked, "collect seashells, too?"

"No." Garrett scowled in a worried way at the shells. "But I once did. These are mollusks, but not from the sea. *Cochlostyla,* a tree snail. Habitat: The Philippines." He turned his scowl from the shells to me. "By the way, just who are you?"

"The name is Ross Harte." I added that I had had an appointment to interview Drake for a magazine article and then asked, "Why is this room sealed as it is? Why is this girl dressed only in—"

Apparently, like many medical men, Garrett took a dim view of reporters. "I'll make my statement," he said a bit stiffly, "to the police."

They arrived a moment later. Two uniformed prowl-car cops first, then the precinct boys and after that, at intervals, the homicide squad, an ambulance interne, a fingerprint man and photographer, the medical examiner, an assistant D.A. and later, because a millionaire rates more attention than the victim of a Harlem stabbing, the D.A. himself, and an Assistant Chief Inspector even looked in for a few minutes.

Of the earlier arrivals the only familiar face was that of the Homicide Squad's Lieutenant Doran—a hard-boiled, coldly efficient, no-nonsense cop who had so little use for reporters that I suspected he had once been bitten by one.

At Dr. Garrett's suggestion, which the interne

seconded, the girl in the bathing suit was taken, under guard, to the nearest hospital. Then Garrett and I were put on ice, also under guard, in the living room. Another detective ushered Paul Kendrick into the room a moment later.

He scowled at Dr. Garrett. "We all thought Rosa Rhys was bad medicine. But I never expected anything like this. Why would *she* want to kill him? It doesn't make sense."

"Self-defense?" I suggested. "Could he have made a pass at her and —"

Kendrick shook his head emphatically. "Not that gal. She was making a fast play for the old man — and his money. A pass would have been just what she wanted." He turned to Garrett. "What were they doing in there — more ESP experiments?"

The doctor laid his overcoat neatly over the back of an ornate Spanish chair. His voice sounded tired and defeated. "No. They had gone beyond that. I told him that she was a fraud, but you know how Drake was — always so absolutely confident that he couldn't be wrong about anything. He said he'd put her through a test that would convince all of us."

"Of what?" I asked. "What was it she claimed she could do?"

The detective at the door moved forward. "My orders," he said, "are that you're not to talk about what happened until after the Lieutenant has taken your statements. Make it easy for me, will you?"

That made it difficult for us. Any other conversational subject just then seemed pointless. We sat there silent and uncomfortable. But somehow the nervous tension that had been in our voices was still there — a foreboding, ghostly presence waiting with us for what was to happen next.

A half hour later, although it seemed many times that long, Garrett was taken out for questioning, then Kendrick. And later I got the nod. I saw Elinor Drake, a small, lonely figure in the big hall, moving slowly up the wide stairs. Doran and the police stenographer who waited for me in the stately dining room with its heavy crystal chandelier looked out of place. But the Lieutenant didn't feel ill at ease; his questions were as coldly efficient as a surgeon's knife.

I tried to insert a query of my own now and then, but soon gave that up. Doran ignored all such attempts as completely as if they didn't exist. Then, just as he dismissed me, the phone rang. Doran answered, listened, scowled and then held the receiver out to me. "For you," he said.

I heard Merlini's voice. "My ESP isn't working so well today, Ross. Drake is dead. I get that much. But just what happened up there, anyway?"

"ESP my eye," I told him. "If you were a mind-reader you'd have been up here long ago. It's a sealed room — in spades. The sealed room to end all sealed rooms."

I saw Doran start forward as if to object. "Merlini," I said quickly, "is Inspector Gavigan still with you?" I lifted the receiver from my ear and let Doran hear the "Yes" that came back.

Merlini's voice went on. "Did you say sealed room? The flash from headquarters didn't mention that. They said an arrest had already been made. It sounded like a routine case."

"Headquarters," I replied, "has no imagination. Or else Doran has been keeping things from them. It isn't even a routine sealed room. Listen: A woman comes to Drake's house on the coldest January day since 1812 dressed only in a bathing suit. She goes with him into

his study. They seal the window and door on the inside
with gummed paper tape. Then she stabs him with a
paper knife. Before he dies, he knocks her out, then
manages to get to the phone and send out an S.O.S.

"She's obviously crazy; she has to be to commit
murder under those circumstances. But Drake wasn't
crazy. A bit eccentric maybe, but not nuts. So why
would he lock himself in so carefully with a homicidal
maniac? If headquarters thinks that's routine I'll—"
Then I interrupted myself. There was too much silence
on the other end of the wire. "Merlini! Are you still
here?"

"Yes," his voice said slowly. "I'm still here. Headquarters was much too brief. They didn't tell us her
name. But I know it now."

Then, abruptly, I felt as if I had stepped off into
some fourth-dimensional hole in space and had dropped
on to some other nightmare planet.

Merlini's voice, completely serious, was saying,
"Ross, did the police find a silver denarius from the time
of the Caesars in that room? Or a freshly picked rose, a
string of Buddhist prayer beads—perhaps a bit of damp
seaweed—?"

I didn't say anything. I couldn't.

After a moment, Merlini added, "So—they did.
What was it?"

"Shells," I said dazedly, still quite unconvinced that
my conversation could sound like this. "Philippine tree
snail shells. Why, in the name of—"

Merlini cut in hastily. "Tell Doran that Gavigan and
I will be there in ten minutes. Sit tight and keep your
eyes open—"

"Merlini!" I objected frantically, "if you hang up
without—"

"The shells explain the bathing suit, Ross—and

make it clear why the room was sealed. But they also introduce an element that Gavigan and Doran and the D.A. and the Commissioner are not going to like at all. I don't like it myself. It's even more frightening as a murder method than PK."

He hesitated a moment, then let me have both barrels.

"Those shells suggest that Drake's death might have been caused by even stranger forces—evil and evanescent ones—from another world!"

My acquaintance with a police inspector cut no ice with Doran; he ordered me right back into the living room.

I heard a siren announce the arrival of Gavigan's car shortly after, but it was a long hour later before Doran came in and said, "The Inspector wants to see all of you—in the study."

As I moved with the others out in the hall I saw Merlini waiting for me.

"It's about time," I growled at him. "Another ten minutes and you'd have found me D.O.A., too—from suspense."

"Sorry you had to cool your heels," he said, "but Gavigan is being difficult. As predicted, he doesn't like the earful Doran has been giving him. Neither do I." The dryly ironic good humor that was almost always in his voice was absent. He was unusually sober.

"Don't build it up," I said. "I've had all the mystery I can stand. Just give me answers. First, why did you tell me to warn Drake about Rosa Rhys?"

"I didn't expect murder, if that's what you're thinking," he replied. "Drake was elaborating on some of Rhine's original experiments aimed at discovering whether ESP operates more efficiently when the subject is in a trance state. Rosa is a medium."

"Oh, so that's it. She and Drake were holding a séance?"

Merlini nodded. "Yes. The Psychical Research Society is extremely interested in ESP and PK—it's given them a new lease on life. And I knew they had recommended Rosa, whom they had previously investigated, to Drake."

"And what about the Roman coins, roses, Buddhist prayer beads—and snail shells? Why the bathing suit and how does that explain why the room was sealed?"

But Doran, holding the study door open, interrupted before he could reply.

"Hurry it up!" he ordered.

Going into the room now was like walking onto a brightly lighted stage. A powerful electric bulb of almost floodlight brilliance had been inserted in the ceiling fixture and its harsh white glare made the room more barren and cell-like than ever. Even Inspector Gavigan seemed to have taken on a menacing air. Perhaps it was the black mask of shadow that his hat brim threw down across the upper part of his face; or it may have been the carefully intent way he watched us as we came in.

Doran did the introductions. "Miss Drake, Miss Potter, Paul Kendrick, Dr. Walter Garrett."

I looked at the middle-aged woman whose gayly frilled, altogether feminine hat contrasted oddly with her angular figure, her prim determined mouth, and the chilly glance of complete disapproval with which she regarded Gavigan.

"How," I whispered to Merlini, "did Isabelle Potter, the secretary of the Psychical Research Society, get here?"

"She came with Rosa," he answered. "The police found her upstairs reading a copy of Tyrell's *Study of Apparitions*." Merlini smiled faintly. "She and Doran don't get along."

"They wouldn't," I said. "They talk different languages. When I interviewed her, I got a travelogue on the other world — complete with lantern slides."

Inspector Gavigan wasted no time. "Miss Drake," he began, "I understand the medical foundation for cancer research your father thought of endowing was originally your idea."

The girl glanced once at the stains on the carpet, then kept her dark eyes steadily on Gavigan. "Yes," she said slowly, "it was."

"Are you interested in psychical research?"

Elinor frowned. "No."

"Did you object when your father began holding séances with Miss Rhys?"

She shook her head. "That would only have made him more determined."

Gavigan turned to Kendrick. "Did you?"

"Me?" Paul lifted his brows. "I didn't know him well enough for that. Don't think he liked me much, anyway. But why a man like Drake would waste his time —"

"And you, doctor?"

"Did I object?" Garrett seemed surprised. "Naturally. No one but a neurotic middle-aged woman would take a séance seriously."

Miss Potter resented that one. "Dr. Garrett," she said icily, "Sir Oliver Lodge was not a neurotic woman, nor Sir William Crookes, nor Professor Zoëllner, nor —"

"But they were all senile," Garrett replied just as icily. "And as for ESP, no neurologist of any standing admits any such possibility. They leave such things to you and your society, Miss Potter—and to the Sunday supplements."

She gave the doctor a look that would have split an atom, and Gavigan, seeing the danger of a chain reaction if this sort of dialogue were allowed to continue, broke in quickly.

"Miss Potter. You introduced Miss Rhys to Mr. Drake and he was conducting ESP experiments with her. Is that correct?"

Miss Potter's voice was still dangerously radioactive. "It is. And their results were gratifying and important. Of course, neither you nor Dr. Garrett would understand—"

"And then," Garrett cut in, "they both led him on into an investigation of Miss Rhys's psychic specialty—apports." He pronounced the last word with extreme distaste.

Inspector Gavigan scowled, glanced at Merlini, and the latter promptly produced a definition. "An apport," he said, "from the French *apporter,* to bring, is any physical object supernormally brought into a séance room—from nowhere usually or from some impossible distance. Miss Rhys on previous occasions—according to the Psychical Society's *Journal*—has apported such objects as Roman coins, roses, beads, and seaweed."

"She is the greatest apport medium," Miss Potter declared somewhat belligerently, "since Charles Bailey."

"Then she's good," Merlini said. "Bailey was an apport medium whom Conan Doyle considered *bona fide.* He produced birds, oriental plants, small animals, and on one occasion a young shark eighteen inches long which he claimed his spirit guide had whisked instantly via the astral plane from the Indian Ocean and projected, still damp and very much alive, into the séance room."

"So," I said, "that's why this room was sealed. To make absolutely certain that no one could open the door or window in the dark and help Rosa by introducing—"

"Of course," Garrett added. "Obviously there could be no apports if adequate precautions were taken. Drake also moved a lot of his things out of the study and inventoried every object that remained. He also suggested, since I was so skeptical, that I be the one to make certain Miss Rhys carried nothing into the room on her person. I gave her a most complete physical examination—in a bedroom upstairs. Then she put on one of Miss Drake's bathing suits."

"Did you come down to the study with her and Drake?" Gavigan asked.

The doctor frowned. "No. I had objected to Miss Potter's presence at the séance and Miss Rhys countered by objecting to mine."

"She was quite right," Miss Potter said. "The presence of an unbeliever like yourself would prevent even the strongest psychic forces from making themselves manifest."

"I have no doubt of that," Garrett replied stiffly. "It's the usual excuse, as I told Drake. He tried to get her to let me attend but she refused flatly. So I went back to my office down the street. Drake's phone call came a half hour or so later."

"And yet"—Gavigan eyed the two brightly colored shells on the table—"in spite of all your precautions she produced two of these."

Garrett nodded. "Yes, I know. But the answer is fairly obvious now. She hid them somewhere in the hall outside on her arrival and then secretly picked them up again on her way in here."

Elinor frowned. "I'm afraid not, doctor. Father

thought of that and asked me to go down with them to the study. He held one of her hands and I held the other."

Gavigan scowled. Miss Potter beamed.

"Did you go in with them?" Merlini asked.

She shook her head. "No. Only as far as the door. They went in and I heard it lock behind them. I stood there for a moment or two and heard Father begin pasting the tape on the door. Then I went back to my room to dress. I was expecting Paul."

Inspector Gavigan turned to Miss Potter. "You remained upstairs?"

"Yes," she replied in a tone that dared him to deny it. "I did."

Gavigan looked at Elinor. "Paul said a moment ago that your father didn't like him. Why not?"

"Paul exaggerates," the girl said quickly. "Father didn't dislike him. He was just—well, a bit difficult where my men friends were concerned."

"He thought they were all after his money," Kendrick added. "But at the rate he was endowing medical foundations and psychic societies—"

Miss Potter objected. "Mr. Drake did *not* endow the Psychic Society."

"But he was seriously considering it," Garrett said. "Miss Rhys—and Miss Potter—were selling him on the theory that illness is only a mental state due to a psychic imbalance—whatever that is."

"They won't sell me on that," Elinor said and then turned suddenly on Miss Potter, her voice trembling. "If it weren't for you and your idiotic foolishness Father wouldn't have been—killed." Then to Gavigan, "We've told all this before—to the Lieutenant. Is it quite necessary—"

The Inspector glanced at Merlini, then said, "I think that will be all for now. Okay, Doran, take them back. But none of them are to leave yet."

When they had gone, he turned to Merlini. "Well, I asked the questions you wanted me to, but I still think it was a waste of time. Rosa Rhys killed Drake. Anything else is impossible."

"What about Kendrick's cab driver?" Merlini asked. "Did your men locate him yet?"

Gavigan's scowl, practically standard operating procedure by now, grew darker. "Yes. Kendrick's definitely out. He entered the cab on the other side of town at just about the time Drake was sealing this room and he was apparently still in it, crossing Central Park, at the time Drake was killed."

"So," I commented, "he's the only one with an alibi."

Gavigan lifted his eyebrows. "The only one? Except for Rosa Rhys they *all* have alibis. The sealed room takes care of that."

"Yes," Merlini said quietly, "but the people with alibis also have motives while the one person who could have killed Drake has none."

"She did it," the Inspector answered. "So she's got a motive — and we'll find it."

"I wish I were as confident of that as you are," Merlini said. "Under the circumstances you'll be able to get a conviction without showing motive, but if you don't find one, it will always bother you."

"Maybe," Gavigan admitted, "but that won't be as bad as trying to believe what she says happened in this room."

That was news to me. "You've talked to Rosa," I asked.

"One of the boys did," Gavigan said sourly. "At the hospital. She's already preparing an insanity defense."

"But why," Merlini asked, "is she still hysterical with fright? Could it be that she's scared because she really believes her story—because something like that really did happen in here?"

"Look," I said impatiently, "is it top secret or will somebody tell me what she says happened?"

Gavigan glowered at Merlini. "Are you going to stand there and tell me that you think Rosa Rhys actually believes—"

It was my question that Merlini answered. He walked to the table in the center of the room. "She says that after Drake sealed the window and door, the lights were turned off and she and Drake sat opposite each other at this table. His back was toward the desk, hers toward that screen in the corner. Drake held her hands. They waited. Finally she felt the psychic forces gathering around her—and then, out of nowhere, the two shells dropped onto the table one after the other. Drake got up, turned on the desk light, and came back to the table. A moment later it happened."

The magician paused for a moment, regarding the bare, empty room with a frown. "Drake," he continued, "was examining the shells, quite excited and pleased about their appearance when suddenly, Rosa says, she heard a movement behind her. She saw Drake look up and then stare incredulously over her shoulder." Merlini spread his hands. "And that's all she remembers. Something hit her. When she came to, she found herself staring at the blood on the floor and at Drake's body."

Gavigan was apparently remembering Merlini's demonstration with the gun in his office. "If you," he warned acidly, "so much as try to hint that one of the people outside this room projected some mental force that knocked Rosa out and then caused the knife to stab Drake—"

"You know," Merlini said, "I half expected Miss Potter would suggest that. But her theory is even more disturbing." He looked at me. "She says that the benign spirits which Rosa usually evoked were overcome by some malign and evil entity whose astral substance materialized momentarily, killed Drake, then returned to the other world from which it came."

"She's a mental case, too," Gavigan said disgustedly. "They have to be crazy if they expect anyone to believe any such —"

"That," Merlini said quietly, "may be another reason Rosa is scared to death. Perhaps she believes it but knows you won't. In her shoes, I'd be scared, too." He frowned. "The difficulty is the knife."

Gavigan blinked. "The knife? What's difficult about that?"

"If I killed Drake," Merlini replied, "and wanted appearances to suggest that psychic forces were responsible, you wouldn't have found a weapon in this room that made it look as if I were guilty. I would have done a little de-apporting and made it disappear. As it is now, even if the knife was propelled supernaturally, Rosa takes the rap."

"And how," Gavigan demanded, "would you make the knife disappear if you were dressed, as she was, in practically nothing?" With sudden suspicion, he added, "Are you suggesting that there's a way she could have done that — and that you think she's not guilty because she didn't?"

Merlini lifted one of the shells from the table and placed it in the center of his left palm. His right hand covered it for a brief moment, then moved away. The shell was no longer there; it had vanished as silently and as easily as a ghost. Merlini turned both hands palms outward; both were unmistakably empty.

"Yes," he said, "she could have made the knife disappear—if she had wanted to. The same way she produced the two shells." He made a reaching gesture with his right hand and the missing shell reappeared suddenly at his fingertips.

Gavigan looked annoyed and relieved at the same time. "So," he said, "you do know how she got those shells in here. I want to hear it. Right now."

But Gavigan had to wait.

At that moment a torpedo hit the water-tight circumstantial case against Rosa Rhys and detonated with a roar.

Doran, who had answered the phone a moment before, was swearing profusely. He was staring at the receiver he held as though it were a live cobra he had picked up by mistake.

"It—it's Doc Hess," he said in a dazed tone. "He just started the autopsy and thought we'd like to know that the point of the murder knife struck a rib and broke off. He just dug out a triangular pointed piece of—steel."

For several seconds after that there wasn't a sound. Then Merlini spoke.

"Gentlemen of the jury. Exhibit A, the paper knife with which my esteemed opponent, the District Attorney, claims Rosa Rhys stabbed Andrew Drake, is a copper alloy—and its point, as you can see, is quite intact. The defense rests."

Doran swore again. "Drake's inventory lists that letter opener, but that's all. There is no other knife in this room. I'm positive of that."

Gavigan jabbed a thick forefinger at me. "Ross, Dr. Garrett was in here before the police arrived. And Miss Drake and Kendrick."

I shook my head. "Sorry. There was no knife near

the door and neither Elinor nor Paul came more than a foot into the room. Dr. Garrett examined Drake and Rosa, but I was watching him, and I'll testify that unless he's as expert at sleight-of-hand as Merlini, he didn't pick up a thing."

Doran was not convinced. "Look, buddy. Unless Doc Hess has gone crazy too, there was a knife and it's not here now. So somebody took it out." He turned to the detective who stood at the door. "Tom," he said, "have the boys frisk all those people. Get a policewoman for Miss Drake and Miss Potter and search the bedroom where they've been waiting. The living room, too."

Then I had a brainstorm. "You know," I said, "if Elinor is covering up for someone—if three people came in here for the séance instead of two as she says—the third could have killed Drake and then gone out—with the knife. And the paper tape could have been . . ." I stopped.

"—pasted on the door *after* the murderer left?" Merlini finished. "By Rosa? That would mean she framed herself."

"Besides," Gavigan growled, "the boys fumed all those paper strips. There are fingerprints all over them. All Drake's."

Merlini said, "Doran, I suggest that you phone the hospital and have Rosa searched, too."

The Lieutenant blinked. "But she was practically naked. How in blazes could she carry a knife out of here unnoticed?"

Gavigan faced Merlini, scowling. "What did you mean when you said a moment ago that she could have got rid of the knife the same way she produced those shells?"

"If it was a clasp knife," Merlini explained, "she could have used the same method other apport mediums have employed to conceal small objects under test conditions."

"But dammit!" Doran exploded. "The only place Garrett didn't look was in her stomach!"

Merlini grinned. "I know. That was his error. Rosa is a regurgitating medium—like Helen Duncan in whose stomach the English investigator, Harry Price, found a hidden ghost—a balled-up length of cheese-cloth fastened with a safety pin which showed up when he X-rayed her. X-rays of Rosa seem indicated, too. And search her hospital room and the ambulance that took her over."

"Okay, Doran," Gavigan ordered. "Do it."

I saw an objection. "Now *you've* got Rosa framing herself, too," I said. "If she swallowed the murder knife, why should she put blood on the letter opener? That makes no sense at all."

"None of this does," Gavigan complained.

"I know," Merlini answered. "One knife was bad. Two are much worse. And although X-rays of Rosa before the séance would have shown shells, I predict they won't show a knife. If they do, then Rosa needs a psychiatric examination as well."

"Don't worry," Gavigan said gloomily. "She'll get one. Her attorney will see to that. And they'll prove she's crazier than a bedbug without half trying. But if that knife isn't in her . . ." His voice died.

"Then you'll never convict her," Merlini finished.

"If that happens," the Inspector said ominously, "you're going to have to explain where that knife came from, how it really disappeared, and where it is now."

Merlini's view was even gloomier. "It'll be much worse than that. We'll also have an appearing and van-ishing murderer to explain—someone who entered a sealed room, killed Drake, put blood on the paper knife to incriminate Rosa, then vanished just as neatly as any of Miss Potter's ghosts—into thin air."

And Merlini's predictions came true.

The X-ray plates didn't show the slightest trace of a knife. And it wasn't in Rosa's hospital room or in the ambulance. Nor on Garrett, Paul, Elinor Drake, Isabelle Potter—nor, as Doran discovered, on myself. The Drake house was a mess by the time the boys got through taking it apart—but no knife with a broken point was found anywhere. And it was shown beyond doubt that there were no trapdoors or sliding panels in the study; the door and window were the only exits.

Inspector Gavigan glowered every time the phone rang—the Commissioner had already phoned twice and without mincing words expressed his dissatisfaction with the way things were going.

And Merlini, stretched out in Drake's chair, his heels up on the desk top, his eyes closed, seemed to have gone into a trance.

"Blast it!" Gavigan said. "Rosa Rhys got that knife out of here somehow. She had to! Merlini, are you going to admit that she knows a trick or two that you don't?"

The magician didn't answer for a moment. Then he opened one eye. "No," he said slowly, "not just yet." He took his feet off the desk and sat up straight. "You know," he said, "if we don't accept the theory of the murderer from beyond, then Ross must be right after all. Elinor Drake's statement to the contrary, there must have been a third person in this room when that séance began."

"Okay," Gavigan said, "we'll forget Miss Drake's testimony for the moment. At least that gets him into the room. Then what?"

"I don't know," Merlini said. He took the roll of

gummed paper tape from the desk, tore off a two-foot length, crossed the room, and pasted it across the door and jamb, sealing us in. "Suppose I'm the killer," he said. "I knock Rosa out first, then stab Drake—"

He paused.

Gavigan was not enthusiastic. "You put the murder knife in your pocket, not noticing that the point is broken. You put blood on the paper knife to incriminate Rosa. And then—" He waited. "Well, go on."

"Then," Merlini said, "I get out of here." He scowled at the sealed door and at the window. "I've escaped from handcuffs, strait jackets, milk cans filled with water, packing cases that have been nailed shut. I know the methods Houdini used to break out of safes and jail cells. But I feel like he did when a shrewd old turnkey shut him in a cell in Scotland one time and the lock—a type he'd overcome many times before—failed to budge. No matter how he tried or what he did, the bolt wouldn't move. He was sweating blood because he knew that if he failed, his laboriously built-up reputation as the Escape King would be blown to bits. And then . . ." Merlini blinked. "And then . . ." This time he came to a full stop, staring at the door.

Suddenly he blinked. "Shades of Hermann, Kellar, Thurston—and Houdini! So that's it!"

Grinning broadly, he turned to Gavigan. "We will now pass a miracle and chase all the ghosts back into their tombs. If you'll get those people in here—"

"You know how the vanishing man vanished?" I asked.

"Yes. It's someone who has been just as canny as that Scotch jailer—and I know who."

Gavigan said, "It's about time." Then he walked across the room and pulled the door open, tearing the paper strip in half as he did so.

Merlini, watching him, grinned again. "The method by which magicians let their audiences fool themselves—the simplest and yet most effective principle of deception in the whole book—and it nearly took me in!"

Elinor Drake's eyes still avoided the stains on the floor. Paul, beside her, puffed nervously on a cigarette, and Dr. Garrett looked drawn and tired. But not the irrepressible Potter. She seemed fresh as a daisy.

"This room," she said to no one in particular, "will become more famous in psychic annals than the home of the Fox sisters at Lilydale."

Quickly, before she could elaborate on that, Merlini cut in. "Miss Potter doesn't believe that Rosa Rhys killed Drake. Neither do I. But the psychic force she says is responsible didn't emanate from another World. It was conjured up out of nothing by someone who was—who had to be—here in this room when Drake died. Someone whom Drake himself asked to be here."

He moved into the center of the room as he spoke and faced them.

"Drake would never have convinced anyone that Rosa could do what she claimed without a witness. So he gave someone a key—someone who came into this room *before* Drake and Rosa and Elinor came downstairs."

The four people watched him without moving— almost, I thought, without breathing.

"That person hid behind that screen and then, after Rosa produced the apports, knocked her out, killed Drake, and left Rosa to face the music."

"All we have to do," Merlini went on, "is show who it was that Drake selected as a witness." He pointed a lean forefinger at Isabelle Potter. "If Drake discovered how Rosa produced the shells and realized she was a fraud, you might have killed him to prevent an exposure and save face for yourself and the Society; and you might have framed Rosa in revenge for having deceived you. But Drake would never have chosen you. Your testimony wouldn't have convinced any of the others. No. Drake would have picked one of the skeptics — someone he was certain could never be accused of assisting the medium."

He faced Elinor. "You said that you accompanied Rosa and your father to the study door and saw them go in alone. We haven't asked Miss Rhys yet, but I think she'll confirm it. You couldn't expect to lie about that and make it stick as long as Rosa could and would contradict you."

I saw Doran move forward silently, closing in.

"And Paul Kendrick," Merlini went on, "is the only one of you who has an alibi that does not depend on the sealed room. That leaves the most skeptical one of the three — the man whose testimony would by far carry the greatest weight.

"It leaves you, Dr. Garrett. The man who is so certain that there are no ghosts is the man who has conjured one up!"

Merlini played the scene down; he knew that the content of what he said was dramatic enough. But Garrett's voice was even calmer. He shook his head slowly.

"I am afraid that I can't agree. You have no reason to assume that it must be one of us and no one else. But I would like to hear how you think I or anyone else could have walked out of this room leaving it sealed as it was found."

"That," Merlini said, "is the simplest answer of all. You walked out, but you didn't leave the room sealed. You see, *it was not found that way!*"

I felt as if I were suddenly floating in space.

"But look—" I began.

Merlini ignored me. "The vanishing murderer was a trick. But magic is not, as most people believe, only a matter of gimmicks and trapdoors and mirrors. Its real secret lies deeper than a mere deception of the senses; the magician uses a far more important, more basic weapon—the psychological deception of the mind. *Don't believe everything you see* is excellent advice; but there's a better rule: Don't believe everything you *think*."

"Are you trying to tell me," I said incredulously, "that this room wasn't sealed at all? That I just thought it was?"

Merlini kept watching Garrett. "Yes. It's as simple as that. And there was no visual deception at all. It was, like PK, entirely mental. You saw things exactly as they were, but you didn't realize that the visual appearance could be interpreted two ways. Let me ask you a question. When you break into a room the door of which has been sealed with paper tape on the inside, do you find yourself still in a sealed room?"

"No," I said, "of course not. The paper has been torn."

"And if you break into a room that had been sealed but from which someone has *already gone out,* tearing the seals—what then?"

"The paper," I said, "is still torn. The appearance is—"

"—*exactly the same!*" Merlini finished.

Garrett's voice was a shade less steady now. "You forget that Andrew Drake phoned me—"

Merlini shook his head. "I'm afraid we only have your own statement for that. You overturned the phone and placed Drake's body near it. Then you walked out, returned to your office where you got rid of the knife—probably a surgical instrument which you couldn't leave behind because it might have been traced to you."

Doran, hearing this, whispered a rapid order to the detective stationed at the door.

"Then," Merlini continued, "you came back immediately to ring the front-door bell. You said Drake had called you, partly because it was good misdirection; it made it appear that you were elsewhere when he died. But equally important, it gave you the excuse you needed to break in and find the body without delay—*before Rosa Rhys should regain consciousness and see that the room was no longer sealed!*"

I hated to do it. Merlini was so pleased with the neat way he was tying up all the loose ends. But I had to.

"Merlini," I said. "I'm afraid there is one little thing you don't know. When I smashed the door open, I heard the paper tape tear!"

I have seldom seen the Great Merlini surprised, but that did it. He couldn't have looked more astonished if lightning had struck him.

"You—you *what?*"

Elinor Drake added, "I heard it, too."

Garrett added, "And I."

It stopped Merlini cold for a moment, but only a moment.

"Then that's more misdirection. It has to be." He hesitated, then suddenly looked at Doran. "Lieutenant, get the doctor's overcoat, will you?"

Garrett spoke to the inspector. "This is nonsense. What possible reason could I have for—"

"Your motive was a curious one, doctor," Merlini said. "One that few murderers—"

Merlini stopped as he took the overcoat Doran

brought in and removed from its pocket the copy of the AMA *Journal* I had noticed there earlier. He started to open it, then lifted an eyebrow at something he saw on the contents listing.

"I see," he said, and then read: "*A Survey of the Uses of Radioactive Tracers in Cancer Research* by Walter M. Garrett, M.D. So that's your special interest?" The magician turned to Elinor Drake. "Who was to head the $15-million foundation for cancer research, Miss Drake?"

The girl didn't need to reply. The answer was in her eyes as she stared at Garrett.

Merlini went on. "You were hidden behind the screen in the corner, doctor. And Rosa Rhys, in spite of all the precautions, successfully produced the apports. You saw the effect that had on Drake, knew Rosa had won, and that Drake was thoroughly hooked. And the thought of seeing all that money wasted on psychical research when it could be put to so much better use in really important medical research made you boil. Any medical man would hate to see that happen, and most of the rest of us, too.

"But we don't all have the coldly rational, scientific attitude you do, and we wouldn't all have realized so quickly that there was one very simple but drastic way to prevent it—murder. You are much too rational. You believe that one man's life is less important than the good his death might bring, and you believed that sufficiently to act upon it. The knife was there, all too handy, in your little black case. And so—Drake died. Am I right, doctor?"

Doran didn't like this as a motive. "He's still a killer," he objected. "And he tried to frame Rosa, didn't he?"

Merlini said, "Do you want to answer that, doctor?"

Garrett hesitated, then glanced at the magazine Merlini still held. His voice was tired. "You are also much too rational." He turned to Doran. "Rosa Rhys was a cheap fraud who capitalized on superstition. The world would be a much better place without such people."

"And what about your getting that job as the head of the medical foundation?" Doran was still unconvinced. "I don't suppose that had anything to do with your reasons for killing Drake?"

The doctor made no answer. And I couldn't tell if it was because Doran was right or because he knew that Doran would not believe him.

He turned to Merlini instead. "The fact still remains that the cancer foundation has been made possible. The only difference is that now two men rather than one pay with their lives."

"A completely rational attitude," Merlini said, "does have its advantages if it allows you to contemplate your own death with so little emotion."

Gavigan wasn't as cynical about Garrett's motives as Doran, but his police training objected. "He took the law into his own hands. If everyone did that, we'd all have to go armed for self-protection. Merlini, why did Ross think he heard paper tearing when he opened that door?"

"He did hear it," Merlini said. Then he turned to me. "Dr. Garrett stood behind you and Miss Drake when you broke in the door, didn't he?"

I nodded. "Yes."

Merlini opened the medical journal and riffled through it. Half a dozen loose pages, their serrated edges showing where they had been torn in half, fluttered to the floor.

Merlini said, "You would have made an excellent

magician, doctor. Your deception was not visual, it was auditory.'

"That," Gavigan said, "tears it."

Later I had one further question to ask Merlini.

"You didn't explain how Houdini got out of that Scottish jail, nor how it helped you solve the enigma of the unsealed door."

Merlini lifted an empty hand, plucked a lighted cigarette from thin air and puffed at it, grinning.

"Houdini made the same false assumption. When he leaned exhaustedly against the cell door, completely baffled by his failure to overcome the lock, the door suddenly swung open and he fell into the corridor. The old Scot, you see, hadn't locked it at all!"

DAY OF THE WIZARD
by Edward D. Hoch

Edward D. Hoch is widely acclaimed as a leading writer of short mystery stories and is almost certainly the only writer who makes a living from short fiction. He has now written 650 stories: he has had a story in every issue of Ellery Queen's Mystery Magazine for some thirteen years.

Hoch has five memorable series characters: Dr Sam Hawthorn, a New England doctor who solves "impossible crimes" in stories set in the 1920s and '30s; Nick Velvet, a thief who steals only objects which have no value (collected as The Thefts of Nick Velvet (1979)); Rand, a retired spy who solves crimes connected with codes (The Spy and the Thief (1971) is a collection with stories about both Velvet and Rand); Simon Ark who may be a two-thousand-year-old Coptic priest (collected in The Judges of Hades (1971), City of Brass (1971) and The Quests of Simon Ark (1985)); and Captain Leopold, the leading character in many of Hoch's police procedurals (featured in Leopold's Way (1985)).

Hoch has also published several novels. Perhaps the best one is The Shattered Raven (1979) about a murder at the annual banquet of the Mystery Writers of America.

Yesterday it was like this.

The big four-engined bomber coming in low over the Red Sea, catching now and then the glint of sunlight on the water and the sand below. The crew singing and joking, because they were nearly home, near to the home-away-from-home where the bombers no longer waited, and the world no longer stood still for the falling bombs and the screaming men and the cities glowing brightly in the flame of war.

For the war was over. Here against the quiet of the desert and everywhere the world around, there was no war any longer. The legions of Hitler had long since surrendered, and Tokyo had announced acceptance of the surrender terms only a few days earlier. So the men sang, and occasionally one of them would go back to check on the very special cargo that was bringing this plane almost halfway around the world.

The sky was empty that day, dotted only with occasional puffs of cloud so rare against the desert sun. No longer were there the dangerous tiny specks on the horizon, specks that grew into Nazi-fighter planes on the prowl. But there was another danger here, even in the empty sky. The pilot had time for nothing but the half-formed thought of a silent prayer; and then in an instant the great silver bird was screeching, flaming, screaming its swan-song to the silent skies, plunging, billowing in under waiting blankets of sand and stone; digging its own grave in a world untouched by any civilized man till now.

Somewhere nearby, a desert scorpion tensed at the sound of the dying, curling itself into a tiny defenseless ball. But then no sound followed the first, gradual setting of the silent dust cloud of sand, and soon the scorpion uncurled to continue its journey across the changeless, ever-changing sands. . . .

That was how it must have been, back on that August day in 1945. At least that was the picture which formed itself in my own mind as I listened to the man across the table from me. He was a youngish sort, perhaps in his mid-thirties, and I had the distinct feeling of superiority that four or five years of prior existence can give one—superiority that went far towards outweighing the official-looking cards he carried in his wallet.

"You want *me* to go?" I asked, not quite believing the words he'd just spoken.

"We need Simon Ark," the man from Washington answered simply and truthfully. "You're probably the only person on Earth who can find him for us. You know him, you know where he is."

I snorted a bit at that. "Does anyone really know him? Certainly I don't. Besides, that plane of yours went down nearly seventeen years ago, in one of the remotest areas on Earth. For all you know, the plane might even be at the bottom of the Red Sea."

But the man from Washington only shook his head with a tired smile. He dipped into his briefcase and came out holding a dull, rusty piece of metal. "Our man in Cairo found this three weeks ago in a little curio shop."

"What is it?"

"At one time it was a cigarette case. The man in the shop apparently figured he could sell it to some stupid tourist. Open it and look at the engraving."

The thing I hold in my hand might have been a hundred or more years old. Only the familiar trademark of the American manufacturer told me it must be of more recent vintage. *"Carey W. Lindhurst,"* I read with difficulty. *"U.S. Army Air Force."*

The man across the table nodded. "Lindhurst was the pilot, a major. It was a million-to-one chance finding that thing in Cairo after all these years."

"So the plane is out there somewhere in the desert. So what?" I lit another cigarette and thought about all the business piling up on my desk during this long lunch hour.

"There was . . . something on it," he said. "Something that would be out there still."

"What?"

But he only spread his hands flat on the soiled tablecloth and frowned slightly. "I'm not at liberty to say."

"You want me to fly halfway around the world, find Simon Ark, get him to tramp through the desert for a couple of months, and dig out an old airplane—and you won't even tell me what's in it?" I sipped my drink to cool off a bit. "What am I supposed to do, close my eyes when we find it?"

"Naturally, if and when the plane is found, you will be made aware of its contents. Till then, I have my orders."

They always had their orders. "Is it an atomic bomb?"

"No. Nothing like that."

"How do you know the people who found the cigarette case didn't make off with your treasure too?"

"It isn't the sort of thing anybody would want to take," he answered mysteriously. "It must still be there."

"Look," I said, on the last legs of my argument, "I'm forty years old. Tramping through the desert is for younger guys."

"We're certainly not asking you to attempt the journey alone. All we really want is a contact with Simon Ark. He knows the region and he knows the people. If that plane is out there anyplace, he can find it for us."

"Simon Ark can be a tough man to locate."

The man nodded. "We know. That's why we came to you. He's in the Middle East, probably in Cairo, and if anybody can contact him, you can. We'll arrange for you to fly to Egypt, where you'll be met by one of our men. As soon as you place him in contact with Simon Ark, your job is done."

It had been many months since I'd last seen Simon, and then only briefly for dinner one night in New York. Egypt, I supposed, was his home if he had a home, and I wasn't surprised to hear that he'd returned there. I knew

I could find him, or let him find me, among the shadowed streets of Cairo or Alexandria. "All right," I agreed suddenly, for no real reason except a desire to see Simon once more. "I'll go, but only for a week. If I haven't contacted him in seven days I'll have to get back to work."

"Fair enough," the man from Washington said. And that was the beginning of it. . . .

Cairo in summer is hot and horrible, with a peculiar odor all its own. The streets for the most part are filled with shuffling white-robed figures, blending with and overpowering what European manners or influence had penetrated this far East. Truly the British were gone, departed with the ebb of empire, and what remained in their place seemed only a shadow of existence, a modern city struggling against the past but not really winning the struggle.

I made it somehow into the city from the airport, and found the promised room awaiting me at the new Shepherd's Hotel. The first thing I wanted was a cold shower, but my preparations for it were interrupted by the arrival of my contact. He was a tall, handsome chap in his early thirties, with rippling muscles in all the right places. When he spoke, it was with a quick alertness which extended to his eyes. "Blake's the name," he said, offering his hand. "Harry Blake, assigned to the American Embassy."

"Oh," I said, probably showing my surprise. "I hadn't really expected a State Department man."

"It gives me an excuse for being around," he explained with a smile. "I can be other things on occasion."

"Glad to hear it."

"I understand you're a friend of this Ark fellow."

"I've known him for many years. I suppose if he has any friends I'm one of them."

"Odd sort of guy, isn't he? Claims to be a couple thousand years old?"

I offered him a cigarette and took one myself. "It's actually closer to fifteen hundred years. And whether you believe him or not, he's certainly a man of vast knowledge."

"He was once a Coptic priest, here in Egypt?"

"Something like that. If anybody knows this part of the world, it's Simon Ark."

Blake smiled, a friendly sort of smile that made you like him. "I don't go along with this supernatural stuff, but if Ark can find that plane, he's the man we need."

"I must warn you that Simon is far more interested in Satanism and evil than in the quirks of modern warfare. Even if I find him, there's no assurance that he'll do the job for you. He may very well be working on something he considers more important. After all, if we don't even know what's on this plane that makes it so valuable after seventeen years . . ."

But I could see I wasn't going to get any more out of Blake than I had from the man back in New York. He simply shrugged. "Let's just say it's a lot of money, gold bricks or something."

"It isn't, though. They wouldn't still be there if someone had found the plane already."

Another shrug. "Who knows? But let's get down to business. Where do we find Simon Ark?"

I sighed and ground out my cigarette. Now that I was in Cairo, thousands of miles from home, how *was* I going to find Simon? It had all seemed so easy, flying over and registering at a hotel and finding him. Now somehow it wasn't so easy at all. The streets and alleys of the city teemed with white-robed Egyptians and mysterious-looking Europeans. Since the Suez trouble it was a far different city from the one I remembered during a brief war stay in the early forties. "I'll do the looking," I said finally. "You just keep in touch."

"We're anxious to get started on the journey."

"Journey?"

"To the crash site." Just like that.

"Well, I'll do the best I can. I have to be back in New York next week."

He nodded, shook hands, and promised to call that evening. I waited till he was gone and then slipped off my sticky clothes and stepped into the long-awaited shower. The coolness of the water helped relax me, and I had a few moments to think about Simon and the whole crazy business. But when I finished bathing and started to dress I still had no real plan for finding him.

I went out into the heat of the city, deciding to at least prowl the more likely places. Across the street from the hotel, a small band of noisy students scuffled with police, intent on starting some sort of demonstration. "Go home, American," one of them yelled in my direction, but I pretended I hadn't heard it.

The alleys of Cairo were strange to me after all these years, though here and there a half-remembered landmark still remained. Presently I found myself on a street hung with multi-colored banners, where tattered signs proclaimed in a half-dozen languages the merits of past and present attractions to be found at nearby theaters. It was here that one sign caught my eye, a blazing red thing with an unmistakable figure of Satan rising from the ashes of a smouldering fire like some great phoenix. Printed below the picture, in large Arabic characters with the English translation helpfully supplied, was the legend : *The Wizard — World's Greatest Magician.*

The Wizard. A simple name for a magician, though it looked somehow more imposing in Arabic. If Simon Ark were to be found anywhere in Cairo, I had the feeling it would be here. I located the bannered entrance to the theater in question and entered, past a sleepy ticketseller who hardly noticed me. The afternoon show was just beginning, playing to a depressingly empty house hot with the sweat of un-air-conditioned bodies.

The Wizard, when he appeared in a puff of pale smoke, proved to be amazingly good, even by American standards. He vanished a long series of beautiful Egyptian girls with all the ease of an old pro, and then settled down to some original versions of famous continental tricks. During the next hour he somehow managed to walk through a wall, eat fire and swallow swords, catch bullets in his teeth, and saw a girl quite convincingly in half. But even all this moved the audience to only mild applause, and I decided they must consider the Wizard just an American or some other despised foreigner.

After the show I made my way backstage, because the Wizard still seemed the best path I had to Simon Ark. I knocked on the dressing-room door and entered at his request, finding a man somewhat older than I'd expected. The pointed black beard he'd worn on stage was indeed phoney, but the face beneath his Satanic makeup was older than my own. I guessed him to be about forty-five. "Ah," he greeted me. "An American!"

The accent was unmistakably German, though the tone was friendly enough. I introduced myself as a New York publisher and got right to the point. "I'm looking for a friend, Mr. Wizard. I thought you might help."

"Mr. Wizard! Ha! I sound like someone on your American television, no?"

I smiled and kept going. "My friend is named

Simon Ark. He has an interest in magic and I thought you might know him."

"Simon? Simon Ark? A familiar name."

"You do know him?"

"I have heard of him. He is well known in the East."

"I think he might be in Cairo."

The Wizard shrugged and continued removing his makeup. "It is possible, though I have never met the man."

My heart sank a little at his words, but I still had a plan. "It's important that I find him before the week is out. I was wondering . . . You're not drawing much of a crowd here."

"No. It is the heat! But night shows are a little better."

"You could use some publicity in the local papers."

"The local papers are too full of threats of war, and hate-the-English, and Communist activities. There is no room for a poor but honest magician."

"There's room if you've got one good trick. If you make a direct challenge to Simon Ark, it would be good for some space. You said yourself his name is well known here."

"I have a good trick," the Wizard said simply. "Tell me a little more."

"We call in the reporters and announce that you are challenging the great mystic, Simon Ark, to solve your riddle. How's that? You get the publicity and I find Simon."

"You are a smart American. Smart, smart! I do it."

I sighed and pulled up a chair. That had been easy, and with Simon not far off this would surely bring him to me. "Start working on your trick, then," I told him. "I'll have the newsmen here tonight."

"On your way," he said with a mysterious smile,

"bring me a lock, a simple padlock of some sort. Buy one in a store."

"A padlock?" I made a note of it. "You need it for your trick?"

He nodded. "This is not a trick quite right for the stage, but I believe it will certainly baffle your friend Simon Ark."

"I don't know about that. But at least it should bring him into the open. See you tonight." I left him there, puttering about the dressing-room with the quaint mannerisms of an aging German professor, humming low to himself some half-remembered melody from Gilbert and Sullivan.

It was an easy job to round up some representatives of the Egyptian press, easier in fact than I'd expected. They seemed to think that anything concerning an American was news, and especially if the half-legendary Simon Ark was concerned. I gathered he was always good copy in the Cairo newspapers. They promised happily to appear at the theater at the appointed hour, and I went off in search of a padlock for the Wizard. I found one without much trouble, a standard model that seemed sturdy enough for most purposes. It came complete with two keys, and a small yellow tag which announced it had been *Made in Brooklyn, U.S.A.* I figured that should be good enough for any Wizard.

The crowd was a bit better at the evening show that night, sprinkled with a cross-section of foreign faces apparently taking in the sights of the city by night. A few were British, businessmen no doubt, trying hard to hold their ties with the slipping Middle Eastern markets. Others were French, German, American and even Russian. A group of girls just out of college giggled in a back row, obviously American, incongruously clashing with the surroundings. I stood quietly near the back of the darkened house, watching the Wizard run through his familiar àct on the nearly barren stage. The same raven-haired Egyptian girl was sawed once more in half, and now even the fire from the Wizard's fingertips seemed familiar and less frightening than before. When finally the curtain ran down, I found three of the reporters outside and led them backstage.

"Ah, good evening!" the Wizard greeted us. "I am waiting for you." The English was still a bit broken and the face was still aging as he patted his beard. "You brought the lock?"

I nodded and produced it from my pocket. He took it carefully from my fingers, turned it over once or twice as if studying it, and said finally, "Very good. We proceed."

One of the leathery-skinned newsmen, his stub of pencil poised in the best Manhattan manner, asked. "Do we understand that you are challenging Simon Ark to solve this trick?"

"You call·it a trick?" The Wizard scowled in the best stage tradition. "It is a miracle, a true miracle. Observe, gentlemen, this door to my closet."

We observed, seeing only a thick wooden door that swung open at his touch, revealing a closet that he'd apparently emptied only recently. "Step into it, examine it, assure yourself there is no secret panel or trickery. No trickery, only a miracle."

The little closet was certainly solid enough, with room for only one or two people. The walls, ceiling and floors resisted every effort at pounding or tapping. "It is solid," one of the reporters stated finally, and the others nodded in agreement.

"And empty," the Wizard said. "Completely empty."

"Completely empty."

"Now observe." He took the lock once more and clicked it into place on the closet door, securing the hasp to the metal staple in the frame. The door did not close tightly—there was a quarter-inch crack remaining—but for all practical purposes the closet was locked securely. The Wizard unlocked it with one of the keys and then clicked it shut again. He passed the keys to one of the reporters and allowed him to repeat his operation. The closet was opened, inspected once more, and finally the padlock was snapped shut by one of the newsmen. The keys were tested one final time to make certain the Wizard had not switched them.

"Keep the keys," the Wizard said with a smile. "And to make certain there is no trickery with the lock, suggest you put a bit of wax over the keyhole."

The newsmen agreed it was a good idea. With the Wizard's help the padlock's keyhole was plugged with a matchstick, which they broke off flush with the surface of the lock. Then a few drops of candle wax were allowed to drip onto this. It would be impossible to open the lock even with the proper keys. Both of these keys were then placed in a sealed envelope which each reporter in turn initialed on the flap. One of them was assigned to keep it in his office safe until it was needed.

"Now examine the hinges and the screws holding the hasp to the wood," the Wizard said. "Note how they are painted over. They will be the same tomorrow when you return." He gave a little chuckle. "And now—the miracle is yours, gentlemen. What shall the closet contain when you open it tomorrow night? Name anything you desire, and I will accomplish it."

It was a good stunt, one that even Simon couldn't help appreciating. "An elephant," one of the men said.

"Ah, too small a space," the magician answered sadly.

"A girl," I suggested with a laugh. "The most beautiful girl in Cairo."

"Spoken like a true American," the Wizard said with a quick smile. "So be it! Tomorrow night at this same hour—behold, the most beautiful girl in all of Cairo will be locked in my closet. And I challenge Simon Ark to explain how she passed through this locked door and these solid walls."

"It'll be something to see," one of the newsmen agreed, obviously aware that a touch of sex made this an even better story.

I parted from the reporters outside the theater and headed back to my hotel, not entirely convinced that my stunt would locate Simon. It might well be weeks before news of the Wizard's challenge and my part in it reached him, and by that time I would be back at my office in New York. And even if I found him, Simon wouldn't likely jump at the chance to go wandering about the desert in search of a lost plane. Feeling a bit discouraged, I checked at the hotel desk for calls and then went upstairs to my room. I was tired after my first day in Cairo, anxious for the hopeful coolness of my bed.

I unlocked the door and stepped into the room—and froze in the darkness. Someone was there waiting. "Who . . . ?"

"It is only I," a familiar voice said.

"Simon?" My heart skipped a beat.

"I understand you are looking for me, my friend."

"The United States government is looking for you," I answered, flipping on a light switch, seeing again the tall, stocky frame, the mysterious eyes shaded by lowered brows, the face not really old but somehow ancient. "How are you, Simon?"

"Very well." He sighed softly and settled back into his chair. "Excuse me if I startled you, but there are others who seek me for less friendly purposes."

It was good to see him once more, to talk with him again, and for the moment all thought of returning home left my mind. I lit a cigarette and settled down to tell him of my mission. "They want you to find an airplane for them, an army plane that crashed in the desert back in 1945."

He smiled a bit at this. "I search for Satan, not for missing airplanes. And the shifting sands of time would certainly have covered this wreckage long before now."

"Maybe it's uncovered again." I told him about the cigarette case and the rest of it.

"What would be on the plane to cause interest after so long a time?" Simon wondered, half to himself.

"That's a mystery. Nobody's talking."

"You can introduce me to the American agent?"

I nodded. "He's a man named Harry Blake. Seems like a nice enough fellow. Actually, he said he'd call me tonight. Let me ring for a couple of drinks whle we're waiting." Simon nodded in agreement and I called downstairs for some scotch. Then I told Simon of my meeting with the Wizard and the trick with the locked closet. "It'll probably be all over the papers in the morning. You really should go there tomorrow night."

He chuckled a bit. "Most interesting."

"You think he'll really produce her inside the closet?"

Simon nodded. "There are at least five ways in which the trick could be accomplished. I only wonder which one he plans to use."

The telephone rang at that point and I picked it up,

knowing it must be the unsleeping Blake. I was right. "Harry Blake here. Anything from our man?"

"He's sitting across the room from me right this minute, looking like the Sphinx itself."

"You found him?"

"He found me. Come on over."

And so the post-midnight conference was held in my hotel room, with Simon Ark, Harry Blake and me hunched over a coffee-table studying maps of Egypt and reproductions of yellowed flight charts. Blake told what little they knew of the mysterious crash, and through it all Simon listened intently, sometimes questioning, more often only nodding. And, at the end of it, came the question I'd been awaiting. "Tell me, Mr. Blake, just what is on this plane that makes it suddenly so valuable?"

Blake gave his usual shrug. "Call it gold."

"From what I know of the American government, even a few million dollars in gold would not call for measures such as this."

"I can't tell you any more," Blake said firmly. "Locate the plane and then you'll know for yourself what's inside."

Simon Ark leaned back from the table with a smile. "You awaken my curiosity. Very well, I'll do it."

Blake smiled broadly and turned to me. "Will you be going too?"

"On no. I'll be on a plane to New York in the morning!"

Simon wrinkled his brow in my direction. "Might I remind you of the most beautiful girl in Cairo? Surely she is worth waiting for."

"Might I remind you of my wife back in Westchester?"

"It would be like old times, my friend."

"Sure! Out in the desert searching for some damned plane!"

"You must at least remain for the Wizard's trick tomorrow night."

"All right," I agreed. "But then it's back to New York. I'm too old for this chasing around." With that, the meeting broke up. Simon and Blake were to leave by car in some thirty hours, driving to the southern desert area near the place where the plane might be. Where the roads ran out, they would switch to camels.

They left me, and I slept. But the morning's sun brought with it a vaguely troubled feeling which I could not pinpoint. Perhaps it was only the unfamiliar food of this strange land. I spent the afternoon seeing the city, forming my own opinions about its most beautiful girl, finally deciding there was no such thing — at least not in public. Finally, after dinner, I made my way back to the little theater where the Wizard was appearing. Simon was standing in the shadows awaiting me. "Have you seen the show?" I asked him.

He shook his head. "Magic is unchanging, like the climate of Hell. I see magic every day, all about me, and there is no need to see it bartered in the marketplace. It is only the Wizard's one trick which interests me."

We moved together down an alley which seemed to circle the building, coming at last to the dimly-lit rear entrance. As I'd expected, the reporters were already waiting inside. There was a brief flurry of excitement as they recognized Simon Ark, and then we headed for the Wizard's dressing-room in a body. He stood in the doorway awaiting us, one hand stroking his pointed beard in a Mephistophelian gesture. "Ah! The reporters and the American — and the famous Simon Ark! This is surely a pleasure." The accent seemed a little less German tonight, as if he were forgetting about it.

We crowded once more into his dressing-room, as he prepared for his master trick. The closet door was exactly as I remembered it, with padlock in place and keyhole jammed shut. Both the door hinges and the screws of the hasp remained painted over and obviously untouched. Surely the door had not been opened since the previous night. "Here's the key," one of the Egyptian reporters said, producing the familiar envelope with its initialed flap. The others inspected it in turn, and then ripped it open, revealing the two keys which had come with the lock when I purchased it. But of course there was no easy way to undo the padlock now. The wax was scraped away but there was still the broken matchstick to contend with. The keys were useless.

One of the less sedate reporters picked up a sturdy iron bar that the Wizard used for some bit of magic and set to work prying open the locked door. A grunt and a tug from the dark-skinned newsman and the door snapped open, the hasp and its ancient screws pulled loose with a splintering of wood. And there, inside the tiny closet, huddled on the floor against the back wall, was a girl. She might have been the most beautiful in Cairo, but she certainly wasn't Egyptian. She was English or American, a blonde in her early twenties. "Get her out of there," Simon Ark said suddenly, pushing the others aside. "That girl's sick!"

We helped her out of the closet and into the nearest chair. "What's the matter with her, Simon?" I asked.

"I believe she's been drugged." With these words all eyes turned towards the Wizard. "Was this quite necessary for your little trick, sir?"

"I . . ." The Wizard started to speak, then thought better of it.

"But how did he do it?" one of the reporters was asking. "We locked the door ourselves last night. It hasn't been opened since, and yet the girl was inside!" One of the other newsmen was once more inspecting the closet walls and floors and ceiling, but without success.

Simon Ark turned to the bearded magician. "Will you tell them or shall I?"

But the Wizard remained silent. "Tell us," one of the reporters urged, and Simon seemed about to.

But at that moment the girl struggled to regain her senses. She mumbled something and opened her eyes. "Where . . . what happened?"

"Are you all right?" I asked, pinpointing her accent as pure Boston.

"I think so. What happened to me?"

"We don't really know. We found you locked in that closet."

"He must have drugged me," she announced firmly. "I feel awful."

Simon Ark's voice boomed once more. "Who drugged you? This man?" His accusing finger pointed in the Wizard's direction.

"No. No, it was someone else, a man I'd never seen before. I was leaving the theater after today's matinee when he called to me from the alley. He wanted me to enter a beauty contest."

"Was he Egyptian?"

"No, he seemed European, perhaps German." She was gaining better control of herself now, and a bit of color was returning to her face.

"Who are you, miss?" one of the reporters asked.

"Rima Jackson. I'm a staff writer for *Fashion Week* magazine in New York. I'm on a vacation."

"Rima as in *Green Mansions?*" I asked.

She nodded with a smile. "My parents liked the book." Looking at her now that she'd partly recovered her composure, I could easily see why the Wizard might have picked her for his trick. Certainly no one could argue the choice. She was blonde, trim, and very very sleek — almost like a cover from *Fashion Week*.

"But what happened to you?" another of the reporters demanded, no doubt aware that his press time was fast approaching.

"He must have put something in my drink. We went into this little bar across the street, and that's the last I remember."

And now it was the Wizard's turn to step forward. "Gentlemen," he said in a clear voice, "I assure you I know nothing of this fantastic business, nothing at all."

"You didn't put the girl in your closet?"

"Certainly not! The girl I put in there was an Egyptian, and I didn't resort to drugs to accomplish it."

"Then how was it done?" someone asked. "How could *two* girls have passed through that locked door?"

But before Simon Ark could speak we were interrupted once more, this time by a terrified scream from the direction of the stage. We hurried out, with the bearded Wizard in the lead. Already a circle of performers had gathered in shocked silence about an ancient black woman with a broom, a cleaning woman who had stumbled upon something too horrible to sweep away. There, stretched out on the floor of the stage before one of the Wizard's multi-colored magic cabinets, was the body of a man. His throat had been cut clear across with a single deadly stroke, contorting his face in a final mask of startled pain.

But even more startling was the terrified gasp from the girl, Rima Jackson. "That's him! That's the man who drugged me . . ."

By noon the next day, the five of us found ourselves better than a hundred miles south of the city. That's right—the five of us. Rima Jackson and Harry Blake and the Wizard and Simon Ark and myself. In the middle of the damned desert.

How it happened was simple, I suppose. Harry Blake had pulled the right strings to rescue us from the questioning clutches of the Cairo police. By that time the decision had been made for me—either I accompanied Simon and Blake into the desert on their fantstic quest, or I spent the next week or so tied up in Cairo answering a lot of stupid questions about the murder of the nameless man. I chose the desert, and off we went. Five miles outside the city a little French car had overtaken us, and there were the Wizard and Rima, fleeing from police questioning themselves. They refused to turn back, and at this point there was no other course than to take them with us—much as Blake hated to do it. He probably had visions of official Washington popping its lid when the news got around that an American fashion writer and a German magician had accompanied us on a top-secret mission.

So there we were, by car and finally by camel, tramping across the sands on an obscure route that seemed to be known only to Simon. The first night out, we set up our tent on the edge of an oasis, and found a separate place for Rima to sleep among the palm trees. I could imagine the sort of magazine article that was already forming in her mind. Later, while the Wizard tried a few card tricks and Harry Blake checked his maps, Simon and I walked over to look at the camels. I would gladly have settled at that point for one of those trucks that can travel on sand, but we hadn't been lucky enough to obtain one. "Really, Simon, I'm too old to be riding one of these things," I told him. The nearest camel clicked its teeth at me, and I jumped back in alarm. "See what I mean? They hate me."

Simon Ark smiled into the night. "Our search for the lost plane is fast assuming a most complex nature, and the camels are the least of my worries at this point, my friend. It seems quite obvious to me that one of our unexpected companions — either the Wizard or Rima — was most anxious to accompany us on the quest. Certainly it was more than coincidence that they joined us."

"The police were after them."

"The police, even the Cairo police, would have a difficult time proving that Rima Jackson could have slit a man's throat while drugged and unconscious in a locked closet."

"Maybe the guy was killed earlier."

But Simon shook his head. "The magic cabinet was obviously used in the act, so the body wasn't put there till just after the show. Besides the blood indicated that our stranger had been dead only a short time."

"You think the Wizard killed him?"

"I really don't know. At least, not yet. Perhaps the girl was not really drugged."

I threw up my hands. "It's too much for me."

"Then there is the matter of the plane. And its contents. Were you aware of the fact that our Mr. Blake is an expert on Indian affairs? His previous assignment was in Goa, before the recent troubles there."

"Oh?" I found it interesting but not too startling.

"One of the Communists' fondest dreams is to

cause a split between the United States and Great Britain, and even now with its decade and more of independence behind it, India is still one place to do it. Are you familiar with a man named Subhas Bose?"

"I don't think so."

"He rates only a single line in Churchill's six-volume history of the Second World War, but he was quite a thorn in the side of the British. Wanted them out of India, even to the extent that he openly collaborated with the Germans and Japanese. If Japan had conquered India, Subhas Bose would have been its ruler."

"What happened to him?"

"He was reported killed several times, but always seemed to turn up alive. The last time was on Formosa, August 18, 1945. His followers in India were convinced he still lived, but apparently that was the end of it."

"So?"

"My sources tell me that while our friend Blake was in India and Goa, he was especially interested in the Bose affair."

"It was a long time ago."

Simon nodded. "But the ghost of Subhas Bose may still walk."

"You handle the politics, Simon. I'm just interested in finding the plane and being done with this business."

Simon Ark stared up at the thousands of twinkling stars, just out of reach. "Oh, I know where the plane is. I've known since yesterday."

I'd suspected as much from the careful route he seemed to have plotted for us, but his words still managed to surprise me. "What?"

"When Harry Blake told me about the cigarette case with Lindhurst's name on it, I naturally investigated the curio shop myself. Perhaps my ways were more effective than Blake's. In any event, I located the native who'd found the case. He gave me the location of the plane."

"Where is it?"

Simon stooped to trace some sandy lines with his finger. "Here is the Nile, running due south to Asyut, where we left the cars. We are now heading southeast, bypassing Qena and heading generally towards El Qoseir on the Red Sea. According to my information, the plane lies buried in the sand just north of there, some ten miles inland from the sea."

"Isn't there a great deal of activity in this region, with ships passing often?"

"Apparently not. And the plane over the years has become almost completely buried by the sand. In any event, another day's travel will bring us to the spot."

"Then what do we do with the Wizard and Rima?"

"One of them will have to make a move soon, if there is really a move to be made."

"What about the trick with the locked closet? How did the Wizard do it?"

"In good time I will tell you, my friend. There is a good reason for not telling you yet."

We strolled back to the others, who seemed to have retired for the night, and I was about to join them when I heard Rima Jackson call my name. I found my way to her side in the darkness, wondering what she could want at this time of night. She was still dressed in shirt and tapered slacks — a *Fashion Week* costume if I ever saw one — and she spoke urgently. "Tell me something, please. What is it you're all looking for?"

"Believe me, I have no idea. I do know, though, that this is no place for a girl like you. Why aren't you covering a fashion show at the Waldorf, for God's sake? Or strolling down Fifth Avenue with a hatbox?"

"I'm a reporter, and I smell a story. It may not be a

fashion story, but it could be something even bigger. Does that answer your question? After all, don't I have the right to it after being drugged and locked up in a closet?"

I watched the glow of her cigarette for a time in the darkness, and since I had no real answer for her argument, I finally went off to bed. She was a strange one, but then weren't we all?

The morning dawned with a fierce heat that promised to scorch away the chill of the desert night. By the time I'd dressed, the others were outside, fixing a meager breakfast on our little charcoal grill. The camels seemed fresh after the night's rest, and we made good time during the early hours. Simon was indeed leading us now, more obviously than before, and Blake especially seemed to sense that the prize was close at hand. Once during the morning we sighted a distant band of wandering nomads to the north, but otherwise we might have been the only five people on Earth. I wondered if it would seem like this to the first men on the moon.

Presently, as Simon Ark and Harry Blake rode slightly ahead of us, being the most experienced camel-drivers in the group, I dropped back to speak to the Wizard. He looked a bit younger today, even with the false beard which he insisted on wearing. Perhaps it, along with his heavy make-up, kept him from burning in the sun, but it certainly didn't keep him from sweating. "How much farther?" he asked in the odd German accent.

"Not long now."

"This sun is unbearable."

"Better than a jail cell."

He frowned at that. "You think I killed that stranger?"

"Somebody killed him."

"By now the police have probably solved it."

"Maybe," I said, lighting a cigarette.

"Your brilliant friend Simon Ark—he missed the oddest thing about the murder."

"What was that, Wizard?"

"The stranger's throat was cut, his face contorted and bloody. It is doubtful that his own mother would have recognized him immediately. And yet this girl Rima Jackson named him at once as a man she'd seen for only ten minutes or so. Think of that!"

It was a point, I had to admit. Maybe she'd been a bit too quick and sure with her identification, under the circumstances. "You think she's lying?"

He shrugged, and at that moment Simon Ark called a halt to our weird procession. I rode up to him and he said, "I think we are nearly there. Perhaps just over that next dune." He pointed towards a mound of sand a few miles distant.

The Wizard joined us, but his attention was diverted farther down the valley. "What's that cloud of dust?" he asked, of no one in particular. We followed his gaze and saw indeed that the distant sand was rising, swirling like a minor whirlpool, eddying gradually towards us.

"Sandstorm!" Blake shouted. "Everyone under cover!"

"Where?" I wondered. "Under the camels?"

"Somebody take care of the girl," Blake said, sliding off his animal. "Get these camels sitting down to protect us a little."

"I will help Rima," the Wizard said, but I got to her first.

"No thanks. You might just make her disappear." We were all down then, our faces pressed to the camel's hides, trying not to notice the foul odor. Rima was right next to me, and the Wizard was on the other side of her, the wind already billowing his white robe. Within a minute the sand was swirling around our heads, the camels were venting their fright with a queer gasping sort of sond, and nobody could see a thing. I kept a grip on Rima's arm, and I could feel her moving against me, struggling in her own private battle with the storm. I'd lost all track of Blake and Simon, but I knew they were somewhere near at hand.

As quickly as it came, the sandstorm seemed to subside. "It's letting up," Rima said, and I released my grip on her arm. I was starting to lift my head to verify her observation when it happened.

She gave a slight but audible gasp and that was all. I opened my eyes, shielding them against the dying force of sand, and looked around. Blake and Simon, and next to me the Wizard — *but Rima Jackson had vanished!*

It was impossible. But as the air cleared and the wind died away I saw that it was true. This girl who had been in my hands only a few seconds earlier, who had actually spoken to me, vanished now as completely as if the sand had swallowed her up. "Simon!" I shouted. "The girl is gone! She was just here and now she's gone!"

"One of the camels is missing too," Harry Blake said.

"Could she be under the sand somewhere?" I suggested, already clawing at the ground around me.

But Simon Ark remained surprisingly calm. "The camel could hardly be under there too," he said quietly, glancing curiously at the Wizard.

Harry Blake drew his gun, a wicked-looking .38 revolver. It was pointing in the Wizard's general direction. "She was here a minute ago," he said. "We all heard her speak. No one could have imitated her voice. And besides, the wind has died down enough now to show tracks in the sand. You can see there are no tracks. She couldn't have left."

"The Wizard did it," I accused, knowing this thought was in Blake's mind too. "I said he might make her disappear."

But the bearded man only smiled and said nothing. I took a step towards him, but Simon Ark's hand restrained me. "Careful, my friend. There is no mystery here."

"No mystery! Then where is Rima Jackson?"

Simon turned away, towards the distant dune which might mark our goal. "There is no time to spare. We must hasten to our goal. Explanations can come later."

But Harry Blake was waving his pistol. "This girl is an American citizen, Mr. Ark. We don't move till you tell me where she is."

Simon Ark gave a sigh. "Very well, sir, if you insist." And he took a step towards the Wizard. I thought for a moment he was going to strike out at the bearded magician, but he merely wrapped his long fingers into the hair of the false beard and tugged. There was a gasp of surprise from Blake and a little screech from the Wizard—and the beard came away and we were looking into the face of Rima Jackson.

"But . . . how?" I managed to gasp out. "If this is Rima, where's the Wizard?"

"No more questions," Simon ordered. "We must hurry."

Rima was busy pulling off the false hair and eyebrows she'd used to complete her brief disguise, and I helped her to pull off the loose white robe with which she'd covered her shirt and slacks. "What in hell was the idea of all this?" I asked her.

"I wanted to see if it could be done," she answered simply. "I'm becoming a bit of a detective myself."

"But where's the Wizard?"

"He took off his robe and make-up as soon as the storm started and left with one of the camels. I saw it and decided to try impersonating him. At least I fooled you and Blake."

"But *why?*"

"Ask your friend Simon Ark. I think he knows."

But Simon and Blake had already mounted their camels, and were urging them across the rippled sea of sand. Rima and I followed, with the question unanswered for the moment. Truly this was the day of the Wizard.

Finally we neared the dune Simon had pointed out, our eyes shielded against the blinding glare of the sun, our throats dry with thirst. And through it all Simon would say nothing more of Rima Jackson's strange actions, or the equally strange disappearance of the Wizard. Presently, though, we began to make out fresh tracks ahead of us in the sand, indicating the position of a rider at the time the sandstorm passed. "The Wizard?" I asked, pointing them out to Simon.

But he shook his head. "The Wizard is dead, my friend. These are the tracks of his murderer."

"What? Dead? But where is the body?"

"Back in Cairo," he answered quietly, studying the camel tracks in the sand. "The man with the slit throat was the real Wizard."

I started to protest, but Harry Blake had already reached the top of the dune and was urging us forward. There, not a half-mile ahead, was the tail section of a plane, all that remained above the level of the all-engulfing sands. "Is that it?" Rima asked.

Simon nodded, sliding down from his camel. "The final piece of the puzzle, I think."

"Will you tell us now?" Blake demanded. "Who killed that man? How did Miss Jackson get into that closet?"

But Simon only smiled. "Will you tell me the contents of that plane? Notice the camel down there, just the other side of the wreckage. Our friend is already on the scene."

"But who is he, if he isn't the Wizard?"

"Who?" We were moving slowly forward now, on foot, and Blake had drawn his gun once more. "Consider, my friends, and you will know. The Wizard was killed as he stepped off the stage following his act, and this man took his place. It had to be like that, because obviously the impostor could not have gone through a complex magic act. Also, we already established that the body was a fresh one."

"Wait a minute," I protested. "You say he killed the real Wizard, but I talked with the Wizard, both before and after the trick with the locked door. Wouldn't I have realized it was a different person?"

"You might have, my friend, but the fact is you didn't. As Miss Jackson aptly demonstrated just now, the false hair and beard made a most effective disguise. Stage magicians often use trickery involving bearded men. The audience sees the beard, not the man."

I still wasn't convinced. "But that first time, backstage, I saw the Wizard removing his beard. Why didn't I recognize him as the dead man when I saw the body?"

"Simple. His face was smeared with make-up and such when you first saw him, and quite horribly contorted when you saw him as a dead man. Rima Jackson recognized him because she'd sat and talked with him and seen his natural face, just before he drugged her. Then too, you had no reason to think the dead man might be the Wizard when we all saw the Wizard standing there with us."

"Then just what happened back at the theater?"

"The Wizard, seeking a beautiful girl for his closet trick, drugged Rima and locked her in there. He simply rushed out after the early show, without his beard and make-up, and lured her into having a drink with him. Probably an Egyptian girl would never have fallen for it, but Americans are more foolhardy. It was a shocking thing to do just for publicity, but he probably would have offered to pay her something later. Anyway, he locked her in the closet . . ."

"How?"

"What?"

"How did he get through that padlocked door?"

Simon Ark patted his camel's side, never taking his eyes from the remnant of wreckage ahead. "By a trick not even worthy of a good magician. He told you to purchase a common type of padlock. When he saw which make it was, he simply went out and bought another one just like it. He carefully filed off the original padlock without damaging the door, put the drugged girl inside and snapped the new lock into place. With the keyhole jammed and sealed, he knew you wouldn't be able to use your carefully guarded keys, and thus would never realize the switch."

"It seems so simple when you tell it, Simon."

"In the meantime, though, the false Wizard had read the publicity about the search for me and guessed the United States was seeking this missing plane. Unfortunately, I played into his hands by visiting the curio shop, but more about that in a moment. He figured the best way to join our little expedition was to kill the real Wizard and take his place. Remember, he didn't know you'd seen the magician without his beard. The thing must have seemed perfectly safe to him. He arrived at the theater after the evening show, slit the real Wizard's throat backstage among the props, and quickly donned his false hair and beard. Of course he knew nothing about Rima, so he was as surprised as the rest of us when the closet was opened."

"A good story, Mr. Ark," Blake said. "But how did you *know* all this?"

"There were numerous things. First, why did our Wizard keep his beard on during the entire journey through this heat? It made me suspicious from the start, and my suspicions grew when he didn't once mention the closet trick to me. The real Wizard couldn't have resisted gloating over it. Also, since leaving Cairo the supposed Wizard has amused us only with the simplest of card tricks, because he knew no others. Rima here was suspicious of him, which is why she tried the trickery with his beard after he made his escape."

We were only a hundred yards from the remains of the plane now, but still there was no sign of the man we sought, the man I still thought of as the Wizard. "Who is he, Simon? Who?"

"A man. A man who could do a reasonable imitation of the Wizard's German accent after sitting through just one show—though I believe you noticed a little difference yourself, my friend. He's a man a bit younger than the real Wizard—you noticed that too—and I would guess him to be about forty. He's a man familiar with this small area of desert, or he wouldn't have risked going off alone during the sandstorm. Yet he isn't a native of the country, or he wouldn't have felt it necessary to travel with us as far as he did. I told you the Communists were anxious to drive a wedge between

America and England. I believe this man is someone who fell in with them during the postwar years, and was sent on a mission now to make sure we don't destroy this plane and its secret. The Communists are just now deciding it's important."

"If he killed the magician, he'll kill us."

Simon Ark nodded. "He would have killed us during the sandstorm if he'd been certain of finding the plane himself. Now . . ."

There was the single crack of a pistol, and next to me Rima screamed. "He's shooting from behind the plane!" I hit the sand, pulling her down on top of me as the others followed.

"We're out of range," Blake said, but a second shot disproved him by kicking up sand a foot from his head.

"What now, Mr. Blake?" Simon asked.

"We've got to take him, before he kills us all." He got to his feet and started down the dune, urging one of the camels before him as a shield.

"Come," Simon told Rima and me, "perhaps we can circle around the other side." But two more shots whistled our way as we started to follow his lead. Ahead and to the right of us, Blake fired once at the unseen target hidden behind the wreckage.

We were still a good distance from the plane when the shooting stopped as suddenly as it had started. Blake must have guessed he was reloading, for he left the shelter of the camel and darted the rest of the distance on foot, running like the wind through the loose, clinging sand. He almost made it. But when he was a scant ten yards from the plane's tail, the enemy's head popped into view. He fired once and Harry Blake went down sliding in the sand.

"Come on!" Simon Ark urged. The killer turned his gun now in our direction and fired again. One of the camels started to go down in a heap before us, filling the air with a strange shrill cry of death.

And then there was nothing else between me and the gun. I looked across the sand and saw death written across the enemy's face. He raised the pistol once more, and a final shot split the desert quiet. The face above the gun shuddered and seemed to dissolve before my eyes. I shifted my gaze and saw Harry Blake on his knees, his .38 held tightly in two quivering hands.

"It is over," Simon Ark said.

"He . . . he looks almost like an American without the beard and make-up."

"He was an American," Simon said quietly. "The ways of the gods are strange at times, and the end of the quest is not always a pleasing one. The man before us, the man who killed the real Wizard and took his place, was the pilot of this plane, Major Carey Lindhurst . . ."

While Rima bandaged Harry Blake's flesh wound, the government man stared up at the hot and cloudless sky. "They'll be here soon," he said, almost to himself.

"They?"

"Navy helicopters to take us out of here. I've got a transmitter in my gear that's been sending out a radio signal since we started our trip. The Navy's been tracking us from a ship in the Red Sea."

"Why?" Rima asked.

Blake smiled. "In this business you don't take chances. I expected trouble of some sort. With the radio signal they'd have had the location of the wreckage even if we were all killed."

"It was important, wasn't it?" Simon asked.

"Important, yes. I suppose so. Tell me, Ark, how did you know Lindhurst was still alive after all these years?"

"He fitted. He was about the right age to take the Wizard's place, and as I said before he knew this part of the desert. He knew where to find the wreckage, once we got him to the general area. That made me suspect one of the crew. And when I saw the plane, buried up to its tail in sand, I knew no wandering native had accidentally come upon that cigarette case of Lindhurst's. And if the case hadn't been buried in that plane, perhaps the pilot hadn't been, either."

"A native could have dug the case up."

But Simon Ark shook his head. "Remember how rusty it was? I doubt if any rust could form in an area of desert as dry as this. No, I knew immediately that the cigarette case had spent those seventeen years somewhere else. I suppose the curio shop was linked to the Communists somehow. They felt it was Lindhurst's fault that the cigarette case fell into American hands after all these years, so he had to correct the error. About then they must have started to realize why the plane was important."

"Why did they tell you the location of the plane, Simon?"

"Just to get us out here, where Lindhurst could kill us once he was sure the plane could be located. Of course in the interests of deduction I must admit that our killer could have been some other crew member who was carrying Lindhurst's cigarette case at the time of the crash, but such a possibility was quite remote."

"But the man was an American officer!" Blake said.

"He was. I imagine he felt the plane crash was his fault, and couldn't bring himself to admit that he'd bungled an important mission that cost the lives of everyone but himself. The rest of course must be speculation now. He drifted to Cairo, and somehow during those seventeen years fell in with the Communists."

"Why the Communists?" I asked.

Simon shrugged. "Who else would profit from the secret of the plane?"

"What is the secret?" Rima asked. But no one answered her question. Overhead, distantly, came the beating of a helicopter's blades, and we could see it as a tiny growing speck on the horizon.

"They're coming for us," Blake said. "We'll have to take time to bury Lindhurst. Bury him right where he should have died in the first place."

When the helicopter had landed in the soft sand, and Rima and Blake had gone forward to meet it, I said to Simon, "That Indian you mentioned, Subhas Bose. He was killed in a plane crash, wasn't he?"

Simon smiled a bit and nodded. "In Formosa."

"But the dates were the same! Both plane crashes were on the same day! And you said yourself no one was ever sure of Bose's death on Formosa."

"Who is ever sure of anything on this Earth, my friend?"

"If the plane crash wasn't on Formosa . . . if it was here . . . if England's most hated enemy in India died on an American plane two days after the war ended . . ."

"If."

"But why, Simon? If Bose was on the plane, what was he doing there? Where were the Americans taking him?"

"I can only solve the puzzles of the human mind, my friend. I do not pretend to solve the puzzles of international politics. Let us only hope that Lindhurst did not tell the Communist agents too much about the contents of this plane. It is clear that a confirmation of Bose's death here would give them an advantage."

Blake was deep in conversation with the men from the helicopter as we walked towards them, probably deciding whether a bomb might bury the remains of the plane once and for all. I didn't think much about it, because I was busy thinking about the Wizard, with his beard and his locked closet, who'd died only because I'd picked out his theater on a hot afternoon.

I thought about him, and I thought about Lindhurst, if that was really him stretched out on the sand behind me. He'd travelled a long way to end up back here. A long way through seventeen years we couldn't even imagine, with a rusty cigarette case that had finally in some mysterious way of its own, made the circle complete.

"Come on, my friend," Simon Ark said. "It's time to be going back . . ."